JUST SAY YES

A Strictly Business Novel

ELIZABETH HAYLEY

WITHDRAWN

A SIGNET ECLIPSE BOOK

SIGNET ECLIPSE
Published by New American Library,
an imprint of Penguin Random House LLC
375 Hudson Street, New York, New York 10014

This book is an original publication of New American Library.

First Printing, December 2015

For more information about Penguin Random House, visit penguin.com.

ISBN 978-0-451-47553-4

Printed in the United States of America
10 9 8 7 6 5 4 3 2 1

PUBLISHER'S NOTE
This is a work of fiction. Names, characters, places, and incidents either are the
product of the author's imagination or are used fictitiously, and any resemblance to actual persons, living or dead, business establishments, events, or
locales is entirely coincidental.

Penguin
Random
House

For our agent, Sarah Younger.
Because you put up with us and somehow
make it seem like it's a pleasure to do so.

Chapter 1

Slow Simmer

Quinn popped a guacamole-covered chip into her mouth and looked up at the man seated across from her. "I love Mexican food, and I didn't even realize this place was here." There were plenty of Mexican restaurants in the area, but she didn't know of any that felt as authentic as the one she currently found herself in. The intimate space was dimly lit, with small wooden tables and colorful murals decorating two of the walls. The short, plump woman who had seated them had introduced herself in a thick accent as the owner. Quinn also noticed that some of the entrees came with a complimentary shot of tequila—which was a nice touch, though she had chosen to order a dish without one because she didn't think having any more alcohol would be the wisest decision. She'd been sitting there with Jeremy for only a little more than twenty minutes and had already drunk half her margarita—which the restaurant served in something that resembled a small mixing bowl with a glass stem. She was sure she'd feel buzzed after just one. And she didn't want to make a poor first impression, or worse yet, have absolutely no recollection of the night. She knew the girls would want the details when they met for lunch the next day. "Do you come here a lot?" she asked.

Jeremy took a sip of his beer before answering. "No. I've never eaten here. Why?" He furrowed his brow a bit, looking as though her question threw him, though Quinn wasn't sure why.

"You were quick to pick this restaurant, so I just figured you liked the place."

"Actually, I review restaurants, and this was the next one on my list. I've heard good things about it, so I figured we'd give it a try."

Quinn smiled, relieved that they'd found common ground so quickly. "Do you review for a local paper or a magazine? I'm actually a writer myself." When Jeremy had approached Quinn at a coffee shop near her office, they hadn't really shared many details about themselves. He was cute and seemed normal, so when he'd asked her out, she'd agreed.

His eyes lit up. "Oh, I don't get paid to do it. It's sort of a hobby." He removed his phone from his pocket and typed in his code before clicking on a few things and angling it toward Quinn so she could see the screen. "I review them on Twitter."

Quinn's eyes widened. "EatandTweet?" Quinn asked, referring to his Twitter handle.

"Yeah, pretty cool, huh? I give each one a rating and a hundred-and-forty-character review. This last one got three forks. See?" he said, pointing to the silverware emojis. Clearly, Jeremy had mistaken Quinn's shock for excitement. "I'm up to almost two hundred and seventy followers."

That seems like way too many. "I see that."

Jeremy laughed. *"To pee or not to pee?"* he said, quoting his last tweet with amusement as he opened up a picture he'd taken of the restaurant restroom. "Clever, right? That bathroom was disgusting." Jeremy inched his chair closer to the table, clearly excited to share his hobby with someone. "The embarrassing part is that my mom was the one who came up with the idea. I critique her cooking every night—"

That's not the only embarrassing part. "Wait—*every* night?" *Does he still live at home?*

"Well, other than the nights I have band practice."

"Oh," Quinn said, eager to discuss something else. "You're in a band? What do you play?" Though she didn't usually go for guys in bands, she couldn't deny the appeal of a musician. Trying to make it in the music industry would help her overlook the fact that he probably slept on a futon in his parents' basement.

Jeremy brushed a few errant strands of light brown hair away from his eyes. "Oh no. I'm not *in* a band. I'm the band director at a middle school in D.C. We have a pretty impressive woodwind section, given that I used to play the clarinet."

And with that, all hope of salvaging the date was lost. Quinn couldn't deny that he was good-looking. He had a strong jaw, broad shoulders, and lips that begged to be kissed. And for a moment she actually considered it if only for the sheer fact that it would pre-vent him from saying anything else that negated his handsome features.

Thankfully, Quinn had to hear about Jeremy's latest band competition for only a minute or so before the waitress arrived with their food. "Chicken mole," she said, placing the plate in front of Quinn. Then she gave the other to Jeremy. "And beef enchiladas. Can I get you anything else?"

Jeremy lifted up his Heineken and wiggled it back and forth to show it was nearly empty. "I'll take another Hiney when you get a minute."

Another Hiney?

Quinn saw the waitress trying to suppress a smirk. "Another beer coming right up. Anything for you, miss?"

Yeah, a shovel so I can bury what's left of my sex drive. Be-ginning to rethink her original vow to remain relatively sober, Quinn considered ordering another drink. The only thing as painful as having to experience this disaster was having to remember it. But ultimately she decided against a refill. Because there was one thing worse than remem-bering this date: agreeing to another one. And she didn't trust an alcohol-hazed mind to make sure that didn't hap-pen. No, she just needed to finish dinner and then get out of there as quickly as possible. "No, thanks," Quinn an-swered with a polite smile.

The two spent the next few minutes eating and engag-ing in forced conversation. Well, it was forced on Quinn's end at least. Jeremy, on the other hand, seemed to be having a good time. He asked her about her chicken—whether it was too dry, whether the sauce was the right amount of sweet and spicy. She could almost see the wheels turning in his brain as he composed pieces of his review in his head while they spoke. He even offered to get her something else if she didn't like her meal. Thankfully, her dinner was good, saving her the embarrassment of Jeremy sending it back. Though she had to admit the offer was sweet.

Jeremy asked her about her family, job, and hobbies. And Quinn politely did the same. That is, until they were interrupted by a deep, booming voice singing in Spanish. Quinn looked to her right to see the owner approaching them as she belted out "Feliz Cumpleaños" in an operatic solo. The rest of the diners focused their eyes on Quinn and Jeremy as the owner set a slice of cake in front of Quinn. She hated being the center of attention, especially when she wasn't expecting it. She wanted to crawl under the table and hide. But instead she widened her eyes at Jeremy before turning to the owner. "I'm sorry. It's not—"

"Of course it's necessary," Jeremy interrupted.

"I was going to say 'my birthday.'" Quinn had lowered her voice, though she wasn't sure why. There was no way the woman could hear their conversation over the sound of her own singing.

"I know. It was last week though, right? I looked it up on Facebook."

Goddamn social media. Realizing that the serenade would end only when the song lyrics did, Quinn collapsed her face into her hands. She could feel the warmth coming from her cheeks. She was sure they were nearly as red as her hair.

"If it makes you feel any better," Jeremy said sympathetically, "I'd heard that the owner is a phenomenal singer. Singing Spanish opera to the customers is kind of her . . . thing. I wanted a reason to hear her so I could include it in my tweet. You're doing me a favor really."

It didn't make Quinn feel any better. And she couldn't help but feel bad that she had no interest in Jeremy. Despite his gentle eyes and sweet nature, he just wasn't for her. And Quinn couldn't help but worry that no one else seemed to be for her either.

The rest of the girls were already seated around the table at Panera when Quinn arrived for lunch on Sunday. "We said one thirty, right?" Quinn asked, double-checking her watch. It was one twenty-eight. She wasn't late, but the group already had their meals in front of them.

"Yeah, we got here a few minutes early," Cass replied. "Guess we were all eager to hear the deets of your hot date."

Quinn set down her French onion soup and salad and took a seat across from Lauren and Simone. "Not sure that date would qualify as 'hot'—unless you're counting the green salsa. Of course, if you follow Jeremy on Twitter, you probably already knew about the salsa."

She anticipated the confused stares on the girls' faces.

"You heard me right. The guy tweets reviews of restaurants like he's Zagat. It's his 'hobby,'" Quinn said, adding air quotes for emphasis.

The girls all tried to rein in their laughter.

"I think it's creative," Lauren chimed in.

Quinn glared at her. "Surprisingly, so do two hundred and sixty-eight other people." She broke off a chunk of her bread and dipped it into her soup. "Hmm, I wonder how many *forks* he'd rate this fine meal."

"Stop," Simone said, dragging out the word as if she felt bad for Jeremy. "You said he was cute, right?"

Quinn swept her deep red hair around to rest on her left shoulder and sat back in her chair. "Yeah. Kind of like a three-legged dog. You can't help but think it's cute because you feel so sorry for it."

Quinn felt an elbow dig into her arm, courtesy of Cass. "Don't be mean. It doesn't suit you."

"He's twenty-eight and still lives with his parents, Cass. And he spent most of dinner telling me about how the middle school band he directs came in second in their latest competition because he thinks one of the boys from another school stole the reeds to the clarinets so they couldn't practice beforehand. We had *nothing* in common. I seriously contemplated telling a story that began *This one time at band camp* just so I had something to contribute to the conversation." Quinn huffed. "I'm not trying to be mean to him. I'm just . . . I don't know."

"I meant don't be mean to the three-legged dogs of the world. They have it rough," Cassidy deadpanned. "This guy sounds like a complete tool. And that was a missed opportunity if you didn't tell him you masturbated with a musical instrument. That movie's classic."

Quinn ignored Cass and released a heavy sigh. "Okay, enough about my nightmare of a dating life. What's going on with you girls?"

Cass perked up. "I just might have a story to rival yours, Quinn. I was talking to Alex the other day, and he—"

"Since when do you talk to Alex?" Simone questioned.

"What do you mean? I talk to him all the time. We're friends."

"God, you want on his dick so bad," Simone quipped as she plopped a chip in her mouth.

Cass at least had the forethought to *act* appalled. "I do not!" She looked around at the three unconvinced faces staring at her. "We are *friends*. He has enough family drama going on his life to warrant a Lifetime movie. I don't have any room in my life for that mess beyond a phone call here and there."

Quinn didn't have to sneak a glance at the other girls to know they weren't buying Cass' story either. But none of them called her on it. That's what good friends did: let you stew in your own denial for as long as you needed to fester there.

"Anyway," Cass continued. "He went on a date with some chick last weekend. It was a fucking disaster." She snickered as she took a sip of her lemonade.

"What happened?" Lauren asked. "I'm surprised Scott hasn't told me about it."

"Maybe they haven't talked yet. Who knows? Boys

are weird. I mean, if you can't tell your embarrassing life stories to your best friends, who *can* you tell?"

Quinn propped her elbow on the table and dropped her chin onto her hand. "Are we going to hear a story sometime soon?"

"I'm getting there. God, you're so touchy when you haven't gotten laid recently."

Quinn stuck her tongue out at Cass, which she ignored and continued on. "So Alex was superexcited about his date with this girl. Heather, I think her name was. He met her at the gym, and he said they totally hit it off. He asked her out and suggested they go to that nice new Italian restaurant that opened over on Broad Street. But she wasn't having it. She suggested they go to Blue Wave, that new age hippie joint where wheat germ is the ingredient of choice." Cass' lips quirked. "Maybe we can ask Jeremy if he's reviewed it yet."

"Go to hell," Quinn quipped.

Cass suppressed her smile. "He should've known the date was a bad idea then. But being the nice guy he is, he went. She even insisted she pick him up. In her *electric* car. She proceeded to talk the entire time about solving world hunger and tried to convince him to become a vegan. Poor Alex. He really knows how to pick 'em."

Quinn couldn't help but feel a pang in the center of her stomach. *I seem to really know how to pick 'em too.* "What do you mean?"

Cass swallowed a bite of sandwich before answering. "He always ends up with these nightmares." Cass shook her head. "I dunno. I think all the drama with his ex is really doing a number on him, so he convinced himself that he has a certain type. But that type is boring as hell. He needs to stop taking the safe road and look for someone who will challenge him. Someone with a little edge to her. Sure, the guy's strung tighter than piano wire and has got to loosen up, but he also needs someone who can keep up with his freaky intellect."

Cass kept speaking, but Quinn wasn't listening anymore. Alex's story was hitting a little close to home. *Is that what my problem is? Have I pigeonholed myself into a type I'm not even all that into?* Quinn thought back over the guys she'd dated the past couple years. They'd all had that boy-next-door charm. The problem was, Quinn didn't want a *boy*. She wanted a man. Someone who had a career that was going somewhere, who could afford his own apartment but still knew the importance of watching a ball game or grabbing a beer after work with her. She wanted someone she could grow *with*, rather than have to raise like a man-child. There were only two problems: Why the hell hadn't she figured all of this out before, and where the hell did she find a guy like that?

Chapter 2

The Pitch

Quinn had been replaying her lunch with the girls the previous day. And it had caused her to come to a startling discovery: her life was boring.

But I'm not boring. Am I?

Granted, she was bored at that particular moment as she waited for her meeting to start. When she'd accepted the job at *Estelle* magazine in D.C., Quinn had thought she was taking a giant leap into the big time. But what she'd really stepped into was a hostile work environment where she was basically a glorified lackey. Every day for the past five months she'd ridden the elevator to the twenty-sixth floor of the thirty-four-story building in the business district with the hope that they'd actually let her write something worthwhile that day. And every day she rode back down with her hope cowering in a corner like an agoraphobic at a One Direction concert.

The unfulfilling job, her nonexistent love life, and

yesterday's conversation with her best friends made her realize that she was a naive idiot stuck in the rut of playing it safe and made her want to claw out of her own skin. *Like a werewolf. Werewolves are dangerous. Well, except for the ones in* Twilight. Quinn shook her head, chastising her inner child for proving her own point. She really *was* lame. What twenty-seven-year-old career woman read *Twilight*? A boring, safe, immature one, that's who.

Quinn clutched her notebook to her chest as she bit her thumbnail when Rita Davenport, editor in chief of *Estelle*, stormed in. "So, what have you got for me?" she demanded. No "Hey, how ya doing?" No idle chitchat, no warm looks or pleasant body language. Rita was all firm lines and cantankerous words.

Everyone in the room snuck glances at one another. Quinn was surprised she was actually allowed in these meetings, which her coworkers had dubbed the Dance with the Devil because that's exactly what they were. The writers did their best to make mundane stories seem interesting to Rita, hoping she wouldn't flay them alive. Quinn rarely said a word since she was firmly cemented in no-man's-land, also known as retractions and clarifications. She had inherited the distinct pleasure of addressing the feedback from readers, and the occasional lawyer threat, about what their magazine had screwed up in the previous month's issue. She had also written a few small stories for their Web site, mostly local human-interest pieces that no one read but made the magazine seem like it gave a shit about people.

Estelle magazine's core demographic was women in

the twenty to forty-five age bracket. And judging by the things that made it into the monthly publication, most women in that age range were vain, sex-crazed corporate climbers who would drain the blood from virgins and inject it with a syringe found in a crack den if they thought it would take a wrinkle off their foreheads. Quinn couldn't relate, and usually she was proud of that fact. But after obsessing about her date and why she always ended up with dorky mama's boys, she wasn't so sure. Maybe she was going about life all wrong. Maybe one had to be a little ruthless, a tad careless, and somewhat spontaneous in order to be happy. Because if there was one thing Quinn was sure of, it was that she wasn't happy.

"Really? Are you all suddenly mute? Let's go. Give me *something*."

Claire, a cute blond woman who had worked for the magazine for going on five years—a near record—cleared her throat. "I was thinking about doing a piece on the new female district attorney who's doing really great things to clean up the streets of D.C."

Rita looked at her like Claire had suggested an article on athlete's foot. "Boring. Next."

Tyler was next to speak up. He was as awesome as he was gay, and out of everyone in the room, he was Quinn's favorite. "What about a how-to on the different ways to tie scarves?"

Rita turned down the corner of her upper lip in disgust. "This is for the September issue, Tyler. I doubt people are going to be into reading about scarves while they swelter in the oppressive D.C. heat. Can anyone make sense today?"

Lucy, a twentysomething with blue hair, was the next to speak. "How about a makeup comparison? We can ask a few of our interns to try out different products and rate them."

"We do that every summer. It's unoriginal and safe. I want the September issue to be . . . edgier. More dynamic. Think, people."

The word "edgier" made Quinn retreat back into her brain. She could be edgy if she wanted to be. As Rita continued to verbally condemn people's ideas with words like "childish," "dull," and "conventional," Quinn couldn't help but apply every one of them to her life. She suddenly felt suffocated by all the things she'd never experienced because they were wrong, or against the rules, or dangerous. There was a whole world outside the confines of the office they all sat in. Its vibrant walls and trendy furniture made them feel hip when they were really just geeky posers who were able to string words together better than the average person. Suddenly, Quinn had an overwhelming need to feel deserving of the fuchsia Barcelona chair she was in. She wanted to belong in an office that had bright orange and lime green walls. A prudent, respectable girl didn't belong here. A badass did. "I have an idea."

Everyone's eyes swung to her, probably as shocked as she was to hear her voice.

"Well?" Rita said impatiently.

"I, um, was thinking that, um . . ." Quinn took a deep breath and organized her thoughts. Rita would never agree to the pitch Quinn was about to make if she couldn't even get it out. "We should do a lifestyle column that focuses on doing things that people always wish they'd done but never *actually* had the guts to do."

Rita was silent for a beat as she seemed to turn the idea over in her head. "Like what?"

"Like, uh, like . . ." Quinn hadn't thought that far ahead. "Asking a stranger out on a date . . . breaking a law . . . things like that."

Everyone in the room was silent as they watched Rita think the pitch over. "I like it. You have until the end of July. Since everyone here seems to work at a snail's pace, it should give you plenty of time to discover yourself before we need to go to print."

"Wait—you want *me* to write it?"

"It was your idea, wasn't it?"

"Yes, but—" Quinn stopped herself. It had come out as just an idea of something that she'd like to read about: how someone else took her life in hand and really lived it. She hadn't considered being that person herself. But the more she thought about it, the more she wanted to be. Even though it scared the hell out of her. "Never mind. I'll get started right away."

Rita gave her a curt nod before interrogating the rest of the group for viable articles.

Which gave Quinn plenty of time to burrow back into her head and wonder what the hell she'd just gotten herself into.

Tim shoved his hands in his pockets as he got out of his truck and walked toward the white house with blue shutters that his brother had told him to look for. He was happy to be invited to Lauren's parents' house to celebrate the fact that Lauren had gotten her master's in psychology.

Withdrawing one of his hands as he approached the front door, he briefly wondered if he should just walk in, but decided against it before reaching out to ring the doorbell. Lauren's mom had worked for Tim's dad before he had died and Scott had taken over his medical practice. Therefore, he felt some level of formality was required.

A small slightly round woman answered the door, smiling broadly.

"Hi, Mrs. Hastings."

"Tim, I'm so glad you made it. And call me Pam," she added with a wave of her hand.

Tim nodded and entered the house when she pulled the door open wider. "Your home is beautiful."

"You Jacobs boys are so polite. I'm not sure how either of you puts up with Lauren," she replied with a laugh. "But thank you. Make yourself comfortable. The gang is all out on the back deck."

"Thank you," Tim said as he started for the back of the house. It wasn't difficult to locate his brother; Tim heard his voice before he even reached the deck doors.

"Lo, if you don't stop spraying that damn bug repellent all over the place, I'm going to have to take it away from you."

Lauren huffed out a laugh. "I'd like to see you try."

Tim stepped out onto the deck in time to see Scott make a move toward Lauren, who quickly lifted the bottle as though she were going to spray him in the face with it.

"I'm not playing with you, Scott. This is my party, and I'll spray Off! if I want to."

"You're causing a haze to settle over the deck," Scott complained.

"That means it's working."

"Are you still getting bitten?" Scott challenged.

"Yes."

"Then it's not working. Give it to me." Scott rushed her, but Lauren threw the bottle into the backyard before he wrapped his hands around her stomach. "Do you want to explain what the point of that was?"

Lauren laughed and turned in to Scott's chest. "I panicked."

"Can you two stop canoodling? I'm trying to keep dinner down," Cass jibed.

Scott kissed Lauren on the cheek before he looked up and his eyes caught Tim's. "Hey, bro." He disengaged from Lauren and made his way toward Tim, pulling him into a one-armed hug.

Lauren hugged Tim after Scott moved away. "Thanks for coming. Even though it's completely ridiculous to have a party for getting out of grad school."

"It's not ridiculous," Scott said, appalled. "You worked hard. You should get a party just like everyone else."

"*Who* is everyone else? No one else I graduated with is having some big shindig in their parents' backyard. You and my mother are insane for insisting we have this."

Scott raised a hand. "First of all, 'big shindig' and 'parents' backyard' are mutually exclusive terms. If you'd let me rent out Clay's like I'd wanted to, *then*—"

"Then it would be pretentious and obnoxious in addition to being unnecessary," Lauren interjected.

Scott glared at her for a second. "Is dealing with you always going to be this exhausting?"

Lauren smiled brightly, looking pleased with herself. "Yup."

Scott pulled her into an embrace. "Just making sure." He chuckled right before kissing her chastely.

"Yuck. Get a room," Simone complained through a smile.

Tim shook his head at their antics. "How was your graduation?"

"Long-winded and dull," she replied with a smile. "Have you eaten yet? There's a ton of food in the kitchen."

"I'm good for now."

"Okay. Well, make yourself at home." Lauren drifted back toward her friends.

"How's the restaurant been?" Scott asked.

"Going well. Business is starting to pick up."

"That's great. So being an executive chef is everything Wolfgang Puck made it out to be?"

Tim smiled at his brother in response before his eyes began to skim the crowd congregated on the deck. He tried to act disinterested, as though he were casually taking in the people before him.

But that wasn't the truth. And as he stretched his six-foot-two frame to get a better look around, he caught a glimpse of the familiar head of red hair that made his heart rate jack up every time he saw it. Quinn was sitting alone in the backyard by the pool.

"Who are you looking for?" Scott questioned, making Tim shrink back slightly.

"No one," Tim lied. "I'm going to grab a water. You want anything?"

Scott looked at him curiously for a second before shaking his head.

"Be right back." Though Tim hoped he wouldn't be. He walked over to the coolers that were lined up against the railing and dug around for a water before he descended the three steps that led to the yard and began walking toward Quinn.

Tim had seen her a dozen or so times since Scott had begun dating Lauren, and he'd looked forward to it every time. Not that he'd ever let anyone know that. Tim was almost eight years older than Quinn, and he had a history that was seven shades of fucked up. There was no way a girl like her needed to waste her time with a guy like him. But that didn't stop him from dreaming.

He couldn't help but feel a twinge of concern. Quinn's best friends were all enjoying the party, yet she was sitting alone in the backyard. He took in her posture as he approached, immediately knowing that something was off with her.

"Hey, stranger," he said as he plopped down in the chair beside her.

"Hey," Quinn said quietly.

He noticed the way her eyes drifted over him, taking him in from head to toe. It made him feel like fucking Superman. "So what's up? Why are you sitting over here?"

Quinn took a long drink from the beer bottle she was

holding. "That's an interesting question." The words were slow leaving her mouth.

Is she drunk? "That's why I asked it," Tim said with a grin.

"Cheeky."

Yup, she's wasted.

Quinn was sitting cross-legged in the chair, and she turned her entire body toward Tim when she spoke again. "Did you know that I'm safe and traditional and predictable and a whole lot of other boring things?"

Tim took a sip of his water. "I did not."

"Well, I'm glad that I was here to enlighten you," she said as she drained the rest of the beer.

"How many of those have you had?"

"I lost count at seven."

"Wow. Looking to dash that whole boring thing by getting your stomach pumped?"

"If that's what it takes," she murmured as she lifted the bottle back to her lips. Upon realizing that it was empty, she muttered a "figures," and set it clumsily on the ground under her chair.

"Who told you you were all of those things anyway?" Tim asked.

Her only response was a slight shrug as she looked out over the pool.

"Okay, I'll just ask all of them, then." Tim stood up and turned toward the deck, where her friends were still congregated. "Hey, everybody, I was just—" He was cut off by Quinn leaping onto his back.

"Shh. Don't be embarrassing."

Tim tried to ignore how good it felt to have Quinn pressed up against him. Her long, thin frame molded against him, her full breasts pushing onto the corded muscles in his back. He quickly gave his dick a silent warning to behave as he reached up and unhooked Quinn's hands from his shoulders. He kept hold of one hand as he turned around to face her. "Then tell me. Who said you were boring?"

"I just am."

"Bullshit."

Quinn's eyes widened slightly. "You said a bad word," she teased.

"I did. And I'm going to say a lot more of them if you don't tell me who was calling you names."

"Aww, you going to defend my honor?"

Tim didn't return her smile. "Absolutely."

Quinn tilted her head slightly, and he would've given anything to know what she was thinking. She blew out a breath, pulled away from him, and sank back into her chair, resting her arms on her thighs. "Do you ever wish you were someone different?"

Tim wasn't sure how to answer that question. He was sure she knew about his past—at least the highlights. He'd drunk enough water at bars while he was out with them to make it pretty obvious. Not to mention the fact that Lauren knew all about Tim's problems with addiction. The girls didn't seem like the type of friends who kept secrets from one another. "I've been someone different," he finally answered as he sat back down beside her.

Quinn looked over at him. "Oh. Yeah. Sorry. That was a stupid question."

"No, it wasn't. Now tell me why you asked it." Tim couldn't believe Quinn would want to be different. As far as he was concerned, she was perfect.

She sighed. "I don't know. I just . . . Sometimes I feel like this isn't how my life is supposed to shake out. That there's so much more out there waiting for me if I'd just grow a pair and go look for it."

Tim couldn't help but smile at Quinn's choice of words. She wasn't a saint by any means, but she didn't typically speak so candidly either. "What's stopping you?"

She looked confused.

"From looking for it," he clarified. "If you think life has more to offer, then why aren't you doing something about it?"

"I already told you. Because I'm safe, and traditional, and—"

"Don't give me that shit again," Tim interrupted. "Give me the truth."

"That is the truth. I'm cocooned so deeply into my own comfort zone, I can barely breathe, let alone get out."

"Just take it one step at a time."

"I kind of already did that, actually," she explained. Tim gave her a look that told her to keep going, so she did. "I pitched an idea for an article. A kind of exposé into the life of a sheltered woman looking to spread her wings, if you will."

"That sounds great."

"Yeah, except now I have to actually go through with it. I was only pitching the idea, but now my editor wants *me* to write the article. And I have no idea how I'm going to do that. I don't even know the kinds of things I should write about." Quinn sighed deeply. "How am I supposed to know what type of person I want to be? I can't even pick the right type of guy to date."

Tim felt his jaw tighten at the mention of Quinn and guys, but he ignored it because there wasn't anything that could be done about it. "What type *do* you date?"

"In a nutshell, mama's boys," she said with a hollow laugh. "It's fine. I just couldn't understand why I always date these guys who still live at home and think playing video games is a stimulating activity. Then I started reflecting on it and realized that it's because I play it safe and look for guys who will be the least likely to hurt me. I don't take risks, and I don't like leaving things to chance. It's just how I'm wired."

He wanted to tell her that was a good thing. There was a reason she was attracted to guys who were essentially the opposite of him: they were better. They hadn't spent years on the streets doing whatever it took to get their next fix. They didn't hurt the people who loved them. They didn't fuck up everything they had to chase a high that was never as good as promised. "There's nothing wrong with that, Quinn. Trust me. I've taken enough risks in my lifetime to satisfy the quota for a football team. And it hasn't made me a better person, or more fulfilled, or happier. It made me stupid and thoughtless."

"You don't think you're those things now? Happy and fulfilled?"

"I am them now, for the most part. But that's because I've stopped being a reckless jackass."

"Don't you think those experiences enabled you to be them though? That by making mistakes and seeing how bad things could get, you actually found out how you *did* want to live?"

She had him there. Tim was one hundred percent formed by the lessons he'd learned. He was a better person at thirty-five because he'd been such a bad person from ages fifteen to twenty-seven. Tim had hit rock bottom about four times, and each time that rock bottom had gotten deeper. It made him appreciate being firmly aboveground. "I'm kind of an extreme case though. I don't recommend my type of living to find out who you are."

Quinn offered him a slight smile. "I'm not saying I want to hang out in dark alleys and befriend gang-bangers. I just want to push the envelope a little. I don't want to look back on my twenties and be bogged down by all of the things I *didn't* do."

Tim sat quietly for a minute. "Okay, you want to unleash your inner rebel, then we'll do it."

"We?"

"Oh yeah. There's no *way* I'm missing out on this."

Chapter 3

Recipe

Sunday morning Quinn woke up more hungover than she'd ever been. Sure, she'd been known to have her fair share of drinks when she and the girls would go to a bar or a club at night, but she didn't make a habit of drinking during the day. There was something about drinking when it was still light out that made her head hurt. Maybe it was the fact that she'd sat outside in the heat for most of the party. Or that she hadn't had much to eat and had hydrated herself with nothing other than beer. But she had a sneaking suspicion that much of the reason she didn't feel well was because her head had been so clouded with its own thoughts lately. Typically, Quinn was up early, opting to make the most of her time. But as the morning sun streamed in through the windows, she covered her head with the blanket in an attempt to block out any light and willed herself to go back to sleep.

She could hear the quiet that had become a staple of

her home since her roommate, Kristen, had gotten en-gaged and for all intents and purposes moved in with her fiancé. But her phone dinging for the second time to alert her that she'd received a text made it clear to Quinn that she'd be getting up. *Probably the girls making sure I'm alive.* And she knew they wouldn't stop until they at least got some sort of a reply.

She rose slowly, as if the subtle movement might literally make her head explode, and headed for the hall bathroom to get some Advil and water. When she returned to her room, she moved toward her dresser, where she usually kept her phone charging overnight. But it wasn't there. In her drunken state, she must have forgotten to plug it in and instead left it in the clutch she'd brought to the party. Her phone dinged once more as she grabbed the purple Vera Bradley off her bed. She was sure the last ding was from one of them too. But when she slid her phone out and clicked the HOME button, there were two texts from a "Mr. Sexy."

> Hope it's not too early and I didn't wake you.
> But I thought you might be in dire need of a
> caffeinated beverage this morning.

Then there was the second text that had come through a few minutes later. Meet me at Espresso Your-self?

Who is this? Quinn replied.

She stared at her phone for a few moments until she saw the dots indicating that the other person was composing a reply before it came through. Lol. Who do you think Mr. Sexy is?

Though there was no one in the room with her, she felt her face heat with embarrassment. She didn't remember ever programming anyone's name into her phone as "Mr. Sexy." And that could mean only one thing: she'd done it yesterday, and now she had no recollection of it. Quinn thought back to what she could remember of the party. Tim? she wrote back.

The reply seemed to come almost immediately. See, I knew you'd remember. Now, what about that coffee? I'm headed into the restaurant in a bit to do some inventory and make up schedules. I could meet you at 10 if that works.

Sure. Coffee sounds good. And I didn't actually remember. Just used a little deductive reasoning (which is actually pretty impressive given my current state). The only two guys I recall talking to at the party whose numbers I didn't already have were you and Lauren's grandfather. I was pretty sure I was more likely to call you Mr. Sexy than a white-haired eighty-two-year-old. Quinn figured her lengthy explanation had been a sufficient reason for giving Tim such an embarrassing moniker.

Lmao. I should probably say thanks for the compliment. But before I get too excited about being better-looking than someone almost two and a half times my age, I should probably mention that you didn't plug my number in as Mr. Sexy. I did.

Quinn felt her stomach flip as a wave of nausea hit her. Something told her it was more from calling Tim sexy than from her hangover. Before she could think of something to write back, another text came through. *And don't forget to bring your list.*

Somehow, despite her vague recollection of yesterday's events, she knew exactly what Tim was referring to. He'd asked her to compile a list of five to ten things that were out of her comfort zone. And apparently he wasn't letting her off the hook.

By the time Quinn looked at the clock, she had only fifteen minutes to get ready before she had to leave. She'd have to skip a shower—which she desperately could have used since she was pretty sure she smelled like a brewery. Instead, she quickly washed her face, put on a little moisturizer, and ran a brush through her hair before throwing it up in a loose ponytail. Frantically, she searched her closet for something that was cute but didn't scream, *I took time to get ready.* She opted for coral linen shorts and an off-the-shoulder white tee. She hoped the look said flirty-casual, though she didn't know why she was so concerned with how her outfit would be perceived.

She barely made it to the coffee shop by a few minutes after ten. The bells jingled as she opened the door and shifted her large sunglasses from her eyes to the top of her head so she could scan the tables for Tim. Maybe she'd get lucky and be there before him so she'd have time to settle her thoughts. Was someone with such a checkered past really the right person to help her figure out how she wanted to live her life? She knew that didn't mean Tim was a bad *person*. He wasn't *now*. And truthfully, he probably never had been. But his bad-boy image couldn't be ignored. And if she were being honest with herself, the last thing she wanted to do was ignore it.

Quinn was reminded of that when she spotted Tim seated at a small, two-person table by the window. He was leaning back in the chair, his broad shoulders open and relaxed. His army-green V-neck tee was stretched deliciously over his chiseled chest. As she took a seat across from him, Quinn noticed how the copper tones in his blond hair nearly glowed in the sunlight.

Tim smiled brightly. "Here she is in the flesh. I'm glad to see you survived."

As he lifted his cup of coffee to his lips, Quinn's eyes raked over the tattoos that covered his strong arms. Deep blacks to subtle grays, bright oranges, shades of red, and some cooler tones as well. She could see two gold wings surrounded by a deep blue background peeking out of the top of his collar. His skin was like a canvas, and she couldn't help but wonder what else was under that T-shirt.

It suddenly occurred to her that she'd been so caught up in her visual molestation that she hadn't even said hello to him yet. She laughed awkwardly, unsure of exactly how long she'd been staring at him without saying anything. "Yeah," she finally responded. "I survived. Although barely. I haven't been that drunk since my uncle's wedding when I was sixteen."

"Now we're talking," Tim said, with clear enthusiasm in his voice. "Not that I encourage underage drinking, but it'll help with this whole . . . process if we know there's a rebel inside you somewhere that just needs to be unleashed. You know, instead of having to create one from scratch."

"Don't get too excited. It wasn't intentional. My cousin and I ordered piña coladas from the bar all night. My parents used to get me virgin ones when I was a kid when we went to dinner sometimes. Guess the bartender at the wedding assumed we were twenty-one. I didn't even realize they had alcohol in them until I drank five and fell asleep at the table."

Tim barked out a loud laugh. "Now that sounds more like the Quinn I know."

"It was so embarrassing." Quinn shook her head. "Mainly for my parents, though, because I was too hungover to go to the family brunch the next morning. I can't even wash my hair with coconut shampoo. The smell still makes me sick."

Tim ran a rough hand over the scruff on his face. "Well, I think you've clearly come a long way. You're hungover now, and you managed to come to a place with coffee and muffins. Consider it a do-over."

"Speaking of coffee," Quinn said with a smile, "I'll be back in a minute. Do you want a refill?"

"Actually, I do. I'll get it, though. What would you like?" Tim asked as he rose from his seat.

Quinn's mouth opened, her lips preparing to say *medium hot coffee, two creams, one sugar* as if by reflex. But thankfully her brain censored what would have been her standard choice of beverage, the one she'd had a thousand times. Here she was, having coffee with Tim Jacobs so they could devise a plan for how to accomplish all the things she'd been too afraid to do all her life. "How about a mocha latte?"

Tim returned to the table a few minutes later and placed one of the drinks in front of Quinn, who eyed the beverage suspiciously. "Whipped cream?" she said, spinning the cup in her hands. "That's different."

Tim chuckled. "If you're that scared of whipped cream, I think we have our work cut out for us."

"I usually only eat it on ice cream, but I like it."

Quinn laughed softly, and the sound made Tim smile. In fact, Tim found himself smiling almost nonstop when he was around Quinn. Maybe it was her bubbly personality—how naturally warm and charming she was to be around. Or maybe it was the fact that she was genuinely innocent without being naive. Whatever it was, Tim had never known anyone like Quinn before.

"What? What's so funny?"

Tim blew on his coffee and then took a drink before answering. "It's just that you said you liked it, but implied that if you didn't, you weren't even going to try it."

Quinn stared at him in silence for a moment before finally saying, "Well, I mean, I would have at least *tried* it."

"Good." Tim gave a firm nod. "Because you're about to try a lot of things you're not sure if you'll like. Speaking of which, let's hear 'em."

He could sense Quinn's nervousness as she removed

her phone from her bag. She let out a long huff, which blew a strand of hair from her face. Tim's eyes watched her slender fingers as she tucked it behind her ear. Then his gaze dropped lower, to the soft, lightly freckled skin on her cheeks and neck and then down to her exposed shoulder. For a brief second, he let himself imagine what it would be like to run his tongue along that same path. But he immediately halted all inappropriate thoughts. He was there to help her. As a friend.

"Okay, so how does this work? Do you just want me to read it to you?"

"Sure," Tim said.

"Well, I didn't have a whole lot of time to think about this list since you just gave me this assignment yesterday, and I was drunk up until a few hours ago. And the first two are ones I had to put because I mentioned them in the pitch meet—"

"Quinn."

She looked up from her phone. "Yeah?"

"Just read them. No qualifiers."

"Okay." She took a deep breath before continuing. "Commit a crime, ask a stranger on a date, pose nude for an art class, get a tattoo, sing—"

Tim nearly spit his coffee out. "Wait. Back up a second. "You're going to pose nude? You, Quinn Sawyer, are going to sit naked in front of a roomful of strangers and let them stare at you while they re-create your image on a canvas?"

Quinn looked confused. "I didn't say I was going to

actually *do* all these things. I thought we were just tossing around some ideas."

"No way. This is it, baby." Tim clapped his hands together once, hoping his excitement might rub off on her. "This is the list. There's no going back. Besides, I've always wanted to learn to paint. This seems like the perfect opportunity, don't you think?"

Quinn's eyes widened in what looked like horror.

"Relax. I'm kidding," Tim said. When Quinn settled, Tim added, "We might be using pastels."

"Tim, I'm trying to be serious here." She crumpled up a napkin and threw it across the table at him.

"Me too. And if it's on your list, you're doing it."

Quinn looked at her phone, and Tim could see her right thumb tapping.

"Uh-uh. No erasing. Give it here," he said, reaching across the table and playfully stealing Quinn's phone from her.

He studied it for a few seconds before reading the rest of the list aloud. "Sing karaoke . . . That's an easy one. Play hooky from work." He glanced up at Quinn, confused. "You've seriously never even called out of work and said you were sick when you weren't?"

Quinn shrugged. "I don't like lying."

"It's not really lying. You *are* sick. Sick of working." Her face told him she wasn't buying it. "Okay, okay," he conceded, returning his attention to her phone. "What does 'hit' mean? The one you started to erase."

Quinn crossed her arms and bit her lip as if she were physically forcing her mouth to keep quiet.

"Fine. Guessing will be more fun anyway." Tim's eyes narrowed as he thought. "Hit an old woman in the face?"

"Why would I want to do that?" Quinn asked in shock.

"*You* tell *me.* It's *your* list."

"It didn't say *hit an old woman in the face.*"

"Hmm." Tim lifted his eyes toward the ceiling in thought. "Hit it and quit it."

Quinn's response was a simple "No."

"Hit on a sexy tattooed chef."

"Stop," she said, though her smile told him she was actually enjoying his game.

"Then you'd better tell me, because they're just going to keep getting worse."

"Fine. It said hitchhike. But there's no way I'm doing that. It's dangerous. I could be raped or killed."

Tim felt his demeanor change immediately. His muscles tensed at the thought of someone . . . *any*one hurting Quinn. He would never let that happen. He took a deep breath and looked into Quinn's sweet blue eyes. "Everything we do, we do together. I would never let you get hurt, Quinn."

Quinn's posture seemed to soften slightly, but she still looked unsure.

"Stop thinking so much, Quinn." Tim put his arms on the table and leaned toward her. "Just say yes."

"Okay," she said quietly. "I say yes."

"Good." He took a slow sip of his coffee, eyeing Quinn mischievously. "So . . . that means it's cool if I take that art class, right?"

Quinn shook her head, a laugh escaping her, though it was clear she'd been trying to hold it in.

Tim couldn't help thinking how much he loved her smile. And he was happy that he'd been the one to put it there.

Chapter 4

Rough Draft

Quinn swung back and forth in the ergonomic chair her parents had bought for her when she'd landed the job at *Estelle*. She was supposed to be sifting through e-mails to see what the magazine had done to incur the public's wrath last month, but her brain was too preoccupied to concentrate on the trivial complaints in front of her. *Who cares if the cheeseburger one of our models was photographed with has more than eight hundred calories? She was only pretending to eat it anyway.*

No, Quinn's mind was resting solidly on the tattooed, reformed bad-boy brother of her best friend's boyfriend. She remembered back to their meeting the day before: how one of his tattoos had peeked out from beneath his V-neck T-shirt, making her want to pull his collar aside so she could see the intricacy of the design more fully. How willing he was to help her with her article/new-life plan. How he never gave the slightest intimation that he thought her idea was stupid or juvenile. How, after admiring him from afar for months, she now had the excuse to spend time with him.

Not that anything will come of it. Quinn could only imagine the types of girls Tim attracted. With his intense green eyes, strong, lean build that was riddled with tattoos, and his square jaw with a permanent hint of stubble across it—yeah, there was no way he'd ever go for someone like her. And she wasn't entirely sure she wanted him to. Because as hot as he was, there was something dangerous about him. Something that made her question if she could even survive a day in his world. And while the tiny rebel within that she was trying to unleash was up for giving it a go, the rational side of her—*the traditional, safe side*—was satisfied with just getting to know him better. *Besides, he's probably only helping me because he thinks I'm some defenseless little girl who'll get in trouble without someone looking out for me.* Shockingly, Quinn was fine with that, as long as it meant she got to stare at Tim more often.

"Is there a Quinn Sawyer here?" a voice asked, breaking Quinn from her thoughts.

"Uh, yeah, I—I'm Quinn." She slowly raised her hand so the stranger knew where her voice had come from.

"This is for you." The man handed her an envelope and then abruptly turned and left.

Quinn stared at the envelope like it had anthrax in it.

"You gonna open it or what?"

Tyler's voice caused Quinn to nearly jump out of her chair. "Jesus Christ! You scared the hell out of me."

"Yeah, yeah, whatever. Open the envelope."

"Can I have a little privacy please?" Quinn said with a feigned tone of self-importance.

"No."

"Fine," Quinn muttered as she opened the envelope, though she did turn her chair so that Tyler couldn't see its contents over her shoulder. Inside was a small sheet of lined paper.

Carpe diem, Quinn. Today is the first day of the rest of your life (is that how that corny saying goes?). Anyway, I decided that we needed to up the stakes for your first foray into Good Girl Gone Bad–dom. Make up an excuse to leave. IT MUST BE A LIE. Then get your ass downstairs and wait for further instructions.

The letter wasn't signed, but it didn't take a rocket scientist to know who it was from. Quinn felt a smile drift across her lips as her body surged with anticipation. She'd had no idea Tim would want to start their little adventure together so soon, but she was glad for it. Quinn had been waiting to do something like this for her entire life, and suddenly waiting even a single day longer felt like it would cause her irrevocable harm. She glanced up, and her eyes met Tyler's. *Crap, I forgot he was here.*

"Well?" he prompted.

"It's nothing. Just a reader who wanted their complaint delivered with a little extra pizzazz." She watched Tyler deflate.

"Damn. I thought something interesting was finally happening around here."

"Sorry to disappoint." Quinn dropped the letter on her desk like it wasn't one of the most exciting things she'd ever received and turned back to her computer, hoping Tyler quickly took the hint. Which he did.

Quinn waited until he returned to his cubicle and set to work before grabbing her purse and heading toward Rita's office. *Let the games begin.*

Quinn felt her confidence slip with each step. She reached the closed door and proceeded to stare at it for a moment. "Come on, Quinn," she whispered to herself. "Just get it over with." Finally she straightened her spine, lifted her head, brought her hand up to the door, and knocked firmly.

An audible groan sounded through the door. "What is it?"

Quinn took a deep breath and pushed open the door.

Rita was hunkered over her desk, her designer glasses dangling from one hand as she sorted through the mounds of papers on her desk.

"Uh, I'm sorry to disturb you, Rita, but I—"

"If you were really sorry, you wouldn't be disturbing me in the first place."

"Oh, yeah, I'm really sorry." *Shit.* "I just wanted to ask . . ." Quinn let out an incredibly bad attempt at a cough. *God, I really can't lie for shit.* "I'm not feeling so well. I need to use half of a sick day."

Rita finally looked up at Quinn, eyebrows raised, but she didn't say anything.

"I just wanted to let you know. I'll take some work home with me."

Rita continued to stare.

"And I can log on from home and answer some e-mails."

"Quinn?"

"Yes?"

"Can this conversation be over?"

Quinn audibly exhaled. "Yes. Thank you, Rita. I'll see you tomorrow."

Rita waved her glasses toward Quinn, a gesture more of dismissal than farewell. Quinn gently closed the door as she left, thinking that hadn't been so bad.

Tim was oddly nervous. He was usually incredibly calm, completely unflappable. But he couldn't deny the slight flutter in his stomach as he waited for Quinn on the street directly outside her office building. He wasn't sure going all "007" with the letter was the right way to play their first excursion together, but the idea was too fun not to see through once he'd thought of it. He wanted to make this as fulfilling an experience for Quinn as he could.

Finally, almost fifteen minutes after he'd seen the messenger exit the building, he saw Quinn walk out and scan the crowd in front of her. When her eyes fell on him, she immediately flashed him a bright smile. He couldn't help but return it.

She walked briskly toward him. "I was expecting a car waiting to sweep me away to a secret rendezvous point."

Tim laughed. "Damn. I knew I forgot something."

"Eh, it's okay." Then she winked at him, and he felt his pulse hammer at every vital point in his body. "So what are we doing?"

"Just follow me, young grasshopper. I will show you the way." Tim wrapped his arm around her shoulder. It was a friendly gesture—something he would do to a buddy without hesitation. But the *reason* he did it couldn't have been more different. He wanted to touch Quinn, to know what she felt like in his arms, even if it didn't mean what he wished it did. "So what'd you tell them to get out of there?"

"That I contracted that chikungunya virus like Lindsay Lohan and I'm highly contagious."

"Chicken *what*?" Tim couldn't help looking at her like she was crazy, because in that moment, he kind of thought she might be.

"Or more simply, I said I didn't feel well and was taking half a sick day." They both laughed and continued to their destination.

He led her to a small convenience store three blocks from her office. He'd arrived early, since the restaurant was closed Mondays and because he wanted to scope out the perfect location for checking off the first task on Quinn's list. It was a mom-and-pop store that mostly sold newspapers and coffee to the businesspeople who passed by on their way to work. There were no surveillance cameras inside, no detectors at the entrance.

Tim had to admit, actively noticing those things made him catch a glimmer of a dark place. A place he tried to avoid at all costs. It was a place he used to know well—during a time when a criminal mind-set was his *only* mind-set. It felt odd, looking into darkness on behalf of someone who radiated so much light it was damn near blinding. It made him wonder if going through with their plan was a good idea. Made him wonder if going down this road could make Quinn actually lose more of herself than it helped her find. Then he reminded himself that they were talking jaywalking and karaoke, not armed robbery and manslaughter, and he was able to shake the feelings off.

When they arrived at the store, Tim dropped his arm from her shoulder, trying not to focus on how he'd left it there for three blocks, and turned to face her. "Here's the plan. We're going to go inside and look around, just a quick sweep. You're going to slip something small into your pocket. Pack of gum or something. Then we'll act like we didn't find what we were looking for and walk out. Easy."

He watched Quinn draw in a shaky breath and close her eyes briefly. When she opened them, she looked determined. It was cute.

"Okay. Let's do it."

Tim nodded as he put his hand on the small of her back and guided Quinn into the store. Once inside, he went left when she moved to the right. Her head whipped toward him, eyes widening as if saying, "What the hell?" But he ignored her and kept his trajectory. If she was going to have this experience, then it needed to be hers. Especially for the first time. He wanted Quinn to make all the choices, to take owner-ship of whatever transformation that occurred.

Tim pretended to scan the aisles, sneaking subtle glances at the shop owners every twenty seconds or so. He knew Quinn wouldn't get caught. Of the two of them, it was him who would draw attention. Not the fresh-faced, blue-eyed beauty at the other end of the store. Well, at least not *negative* attention.

Not three minutes after they'd entered, Quinn manifested by his side. "They don't have it," she said simply.

Tim nodded and followed her out of the store. They walked half a block before Quinn stopped suddenly. Withdrawing a pack of gum from her pocket, she showed it to him. "I did it," she said, beaming.

"I see that," Tim replied, giving her a genuine smile that he hoped reflected his pride. *Wait. Should I really feel proud of teaching her to shoplift?*

"I know. I'm a total badass." Quinn popped a piece of gum into her mouth, chewing slowly.

The way Quinn's tongue slipped across her bottom lip made Tim think about what it would be like to bite it. "Okay, Miss Badass, now we can check stealing and playing hooky off your list." Tim started walking again, but Quinn didn't follow.

"I, um, I actually did need something from that store. I'm going to run back in real quick since I'm already here and all." She started walking quickly back toward the shop.

"You're going to go pay for it, aren't you?"

Quinn threw him one of her bright smiles over her shoulder, never slowing her pace.

Tim shook his head but couldn't stop his own smile from overtaking his face as he thought about how they would make a terrible Bonnie and Clyde.

Chapter 5

Churning

Quinn plopped herself down on the couch Wednesday evening, settling in to catch up on some television, but her mind wouldn't relax. She was still reeling from the high of breaking her first major law. *Kind of.* Even though Tim razzed her about it, she *had* left the store initially without paying for the gum, so in her mind, it counted. The entire experience had caused an excess of adrenaline to pump through her body, and the effect still hadn't gone away. She'd never been so productive, answering e-mails and writing her retractions with the flurry usually reserved for people on excessive amounts of caffeine.

When her cell phone rang beside her, she didn't even look at the screen before answering. "Hello?"

"Hi, honey."

Mom. Quinn took a silent breath and braced herself for the conversation that would follow. It wasn't that Quinn didn't love her parents. She did. But being the single focus of their pure, unadulterated love was a little suffocating. Peter and Julia Sawyer had been involved in *every* aspect of their daughter's life from the moment she came into the world. She'd gotten a brief reprieve from their incessant interference when she'd left for college, but even that was mostly just an *image* of autonomy. They'd all but forced her to attend Marymount University, a Catholic institution about fifteen minutes from her house. And while Quinn had enjoyed her time there, she'd wished she could have spread her wings a little farther from the nest.

Finally severing the proverbial cord—or maybe stretching it was a more adequate description—Quinn had managed to distance herself since she'd moved out on her own. But her recent introspection had caused her to reconsider how much she'd actually escaped their prison of adoration and love. They may not have a say in how Quinn lived her life, but they had raised her to look at things a certain way. Their morals and expectations permeated Quinn's entire life, making her into the person she was now desperate to change. She wasn't looking to rewrite the foundations they'd built—Quinn was a successful, responsible adult. But goddamn, everybody needs to be a little wild *sometimes*.

"Hi, Mom," Quinn responded as she sank back into her chair. "How are you?"

"Oh, we're good. I just wanted to call and check in. How have you been?"

Quinn couldn't help but feel guilty for how agitated her parents made her. They loved her. There was no crime in that. *Crime.* That thought made Quinn smile.

Her mind naturally drifted to Tim, causing her smile to grow wider. She'd loved hanging out with him, talking to him in the casual way only friends could. "I'm good, Mom. Just relaxing. Nothing's really new." There was no way in hell Quinn was going to tell her parents about her article. At least not until it was published in the magazine. She briefly wondered if she should add telling them to her list but quickly banished the idea. She didn't want coming clean to them set in stone.

Her mom asked her a few other simple questions: how the girls were, if she'd been to the new restaurant downtown, how things at the magazine were going. They chatted for about five minutes before her mom asked the question Quinn knew was coming. "No new men in your life?" her mom needled.

There it is. Quinn's love life—or lack thereof—was a prime topic of conversation in the Sawyer household. If Julia had her way, Quinn would have been happily married to a successful man by now. "Nope," Quinn responded casually.

"Okay, then." Her mom sounded almost relieved.

"Okay?"

"Yes, okay."

"What did you do?" Quinn asked evenly.

"What makes you think I did something?" Julia asked innocently. *Too* innocently.

"Mom."

Julia released a frustrated breath. "Fine. I invited Carolyn and Spencer Clark's son to dinner on Sunday, and I was hoping you'd come."

"Yeah, I'm not going to be able to make that," Quinn said simply.

Her mom gasped. "Why on earth not? I told him you'd be there."

"Maybe you should have asked me *before* you told him that."

"Well, I didn't. It'll be rude of you not to come."

"So is trying to set me up with a guy who's in the seminary."

"His mother said that wasn't working out so well. She doubts he'll actually make it to being ordained."

Quinn silently counted to ten before replying. "Mom, I know you're just trying to do what's best for me, but please trust me when I tell you: this isn't it. Now, please call and tell him dinner's been canceled or whatever you need to do to make sure he's not expecting me to be there on Sunday." Quinn tried to keep her voice light. She'd never been very good at sticking up for herself, especially to her parents. It wasn't because she was weak-willed or a pushover. She simply liked to make people happy. And this applied to her parents most of all, because they had given her so much. The thought of disappointing them made her feel sick to her stomach.

"All right." Julia's voice was quiet, clearly displeased but still accepting.

"Thanks, Mom. I'll talk to you soon. Love you."

"Love you too, sweetheart."

Quinn disconnected the call, wondering if they'd love the new Quinn just as much.

*   *   *

"Been here long?" Tim asked Roger as he slid into the booth across from him.

"Nah. Just ten minutes or so."

"Sorry. I got hung up trying to sort out some scheduling issues," Tim explained as he picked up his menu.

"No worries. How's the restaurant doing?" Roger asked.

"Awesome. Getting some good traffic. We've gotten great reviews from the local papers."

"All wonderful news. And the new apartment? You settling in?"

Tim had moved into a new apartment a few months back when he'd gotten the job at The Black Lantern, a trendy eatery that specialized in classic American staples with fresh ingredients and new age twists. He had wanted to be closer to work but still within a reasonable distance from his brother. Tim was increasingly happy for that decision, as he and Scott had been spending more time together over the recent months.

Tim set his menu down and folded his hands on the table, smiling indulgently at the man in front of him. Roger was a forty-seven-year-old whose years of drinking and heavy drug use made him look fifteen years older. Tim literally owed his life to the nosy bastard in front of him. Roger had agreed to sponsor Tim when Tim was nothing more than a pissed-off, wild, twenty-eight-year-old criminal living in a halfway house upon completion of his most recent stint in rehab. But Roger hadn't been deterred by Tim's bad attitude. He'd barreled into Tim's life and insinuated himself into every aspect of it. It was *exactly* what Tim had needed. And now, seven and a half years later, Roger was still there for him. His involvement went way beyond what the twelve-step program called for. Tim was damn lucky to have him.

Tim's mind flashed back to how dark that time in his life had been. After driving high as a fucking kite to hang out with Scott on Thanksgiving eve, Tim had gotten into a car accident. Killing himself, frankly, wouldn't have been a bad thing as far as Tim was concerned. He'd been on a path with that inevitable end since he was fifteen. But the fact that Scott had been in the car—the fact that he could have killed his younger brother—was enough to make him want to get his shit together. But even with that as motivation, Tim never would have been able to make it without Roger.

Tim's parents had disowned him after his third relapse. Their complete dismissal of him from their family erased whatever rock bottom Tim may have had. If the people who were genetically programmed to love him unconditionally didn't see him as worth fighting for, why should he fight for himself?

But Roger had fought for him. He'd become a surrogate father to Tim, despite being only twelve years older than him. Roger had given Tim hope that a better life was out there for him. Showed him that he was worth giving a shit about. Because Roger had made it clear from day one: he didn't go out of his way for fuck-ups. And if he didn't think Tim was a fuck-up, then shit, maybe he wasn't. "Yeah, you'll have to come check it out sometime," Tim answered.

Roger stowed his questions long enough for them to order their meals. During dinner, they talked about innocuous things: Roger's daughter, sports, Tim's eighty-year-old neighbor who flirted with him constantly.

Finally, after they had both pushed their plates away and settled back into the booths, Roger started up again. "So job's good, health's good, what about your social life? How's that?"

Tim reached for his water.

"That good, huh?" Roger raised an eyebrow.

"Nothing serious. You know me. I'm all about the good time." Tim smirked, hoping that would help Roger believe his words.

"Yeah, I bet being lonely as fuck is a real good time."

Well . . . shit. "Blunt as always," Tim murmured as he took another sip.

Roger crossed his arms and rested them on the table. That was always a sign that shit was about to get serious. "When are you going to stop punishing yourself?"

"What do you mean?" Tim asked, genuinely confused. He wasn't sure what he thought Roger was going to say, but that wasn't it.

"Tim, I know that you have a mountainful of guilt, regret, and bad self-image. And as great as it is that you don't repress those things by taking whatever drug is available, you still make yourself suffer for them. How long are you going to make yourself pay for things you don't owe?"

Tim hated when Roger started in on him like that. Tim had hurt everyone who had ever mattered, and even some people who hadn't. He might not use anymore, but in his mind, he was still a junkie. And junkies only brought good people down. They were a weight to bear, a constant reminder of the darker side of human nature. It was what had kept Tim distant from even his brother over the past seven years. Granted, that was a wall Tim was allowing to crumble, but Scott was his blood, and Tim simply loved him too much to maintain emotional distance. It was the one allowance he made for himself. But he wouldn't allow any more.

It was why he silently pined for Quinn instead of trying to make his feelings known. She was innocent . . . pure . . . good. Even the article she was writing, the things she was going to do for it, were all basically harmless. There was no way he would let his life taint hers. They could be friends. He could maintain the necessary distance to ensure that she wasn't affected by the plague he carried. Plain and simple, Quinn was a good person who was attempting to do a few bad things. But Tim had been a bad person for much of his life, and no amount of good deeds would wipe that slate clean. Roger could talk until his last breath—he'd never convince Tim of anything different. "I get what you're saying, Rog. I do. But it's all a moot point. The things I owe? They can never be repaid. *That's* the reality I live with. So while I appreciate the concern, my life ultimately comes down to the decisions I make. And I can only do my best, which is what I'm doing. So drop it, okay?"

Roger pursed his lips as if he were trying to force himself to keep the words inside. "Fine," he said, finally letting one loose, though Tim would have bet anything it wasn't one of the ones he *wanted* to say.

They both declined dessert, and after arguing over the bill for ten minutes, decided to split it between them. Walking out of the restaurant, Tim turned toward Roger and drew him into one of those manly half hugs. "Thanks."

"What for? I haven't done anything."

It was a standard Roger response, and Tim let it slide without correcting him. Because, ultimately, Roger had done *everything* for Tim. And Tim hoped he knew it, even if he refused credit. "I'll see you soon?"

"You know it. Take it easy. Call me if you need me."

Then the two men turned away from each other and went their separate ways. Roger's last words echoed in Tim's mind as he walked toward his truck. Tim wanted to call someone, but it wasn't Roger. So, while convincing himself that he simply wanted to talk to a friend, Tim dialed Quinn's number.

Chapter 6

Style

Quinn glanced around the dimly lit bar tentatively. About fifteen glossy wooden tables sat behind the barstools, and six cracked red pleather booths lined the windows in the front of the run-down establishment. A worn-out baby grand piano stood on top of the small wooden stage at the one end of the room. Memorabilia from the local music scene hung on walls, as did some oversized mirrors, which Quinn figured were strategically placed to make the cramped space feel somewhat larger. There was no doubt in Quinn's mind that, in its day, The 89th Key had been a hot spot where locals came to listen to music and blow off a little steam. But by the looks of things, "its day" had probably been about sixty years ago, and not much upkeep had been done to the dingy establishment since. As her eyes took in the bar's patrons, Quinn couldn't help but think that some of those same people were old enough to remember when the place didn't make you feel like you needed a shower after you left.

She took a sip of her soda and looked at her watch. Tim would be there soon, but it wasn't soon enough. When he'd called to say he'd gotten stuck at work covering the beginning of someone's shift, she'd been disappointed. But she hadn't felt the same sense of panic that she felt now. Thankfully, Scott and Lauren had agreed to go with her at the last minute, but their presence did nothing to quell her fears. Truth be told, she *should* have felt some sort of hesitation. That's how she knew singing karaoke in front of a crowd was something that was clearly out of her comfort zone. Sure, she'd been a little anxious before stealing the pack of gum the previous week. But there was something more . . . adventurous about that. It had felt like a challenge—a game she had to win. Quinn had a sinking suspicion that once she'd had a turn onstage, there'd be no winners in the place.

"Sooo, Quinn," Lauren said slowly as she sipped on her beer, "what exactly are we doing here?"

Quinn set her glass down gently on the table and settled back into her chair. She hadn't told Lauren much of anything when she'd called her earlier, despite the fact that they'd been best friends since elementary school. She took a deep breath as she prepared to explain herself. Quinn wasn't sure why she hadn't told the girls about her story assignment. But the more she thought about it, the more she realized it was probably because she didn't want to hear them deny what she knew was the truth.

But Quinn was relieved when, as she told Lauren

and Scott about her article and how Tim had become involved—which Quinn was grateful they didn't question her about—Lauren gave Quinn a warm smile. "I think it's an awesome idea. I can't wait to read your article." Lauren stared at her for a moment before confusion swept over her face. "But my original question still stands. Why are we *here*? I mean, there are plenty of other places for you to lose your karaoke virginity. What would possess you to pick a bar where you can contract gonorrhea from the bowls of pretzels they put on the table?"

Quinn dropped the pretzel she'd been holding before it had a chance to touch her lips. "Really, Laur? You had to go there?"

Lauren shrugged. "The truth hurts." She looked around until her eyes settled on two women at the end of the bar who looked like they hadn't changed their hairstyles since 1985. One of them leaned in to give the wifebeater-clad gentleman beside her a drunken, wet kiss. "Perhaps the more pressing question is how did you even know this place was here?"

"Well, since we're speaking honestly, the *truth* is that Tim picked this place." She didn't want to know how he knew it existed, but she had some idea. And a cursory glance at Scott told her he was thinking the same thing. Years ago, Tim had probably been well acquainted with seedy establishments such as this. "My guess is that he wanted to make sure I didn't run into any familiar faces. Not that it'll make much of a difference. The idea of singing in front of strangers is equally terrifying."

"You'll be fine," Lauren assured her. "These people

don't strike me as the judgmental type. If you want, I'll sing with you."

Scott chuckled through his gulp of beer.

Lauren shot Scott a challenging stare. "What? You don't think I will?"

"Never said that. I *know* you will. That's why I laughed."

Lauren rolled her eyes and let out a huff of what Quinn immediately recognized as feigned annoyance. The playful banter was as much a part of Scott and Lauren's relationship as the fantastic sex Lauren loved to brag about. "You'll see how good we are. Come on, Quinn."

"Um . . . I don't think it counts unless I sing on my own." Though Quinn did think it was important that she get the full karaoke experience—no matter how painful—the real reason she wanted to wait to sing was because she knew Tim hadn't arrived. He'd want to be there to silently cheer her on. And even more important, *she* wanted that. *Everything we do, we do together,* she thought to herself. "Plus, I want to watch a few people first, and they're just getting started. *You* can go up, though, if you want."

"Okay. I'll show you how easy it is. We used to go all the time when I was away at school."

Scott put an arm around Lauren's shoulder and squeezed her so close that she pressed against his side. "Go show 'em how it's done, Lo."

Lauren gave Scott a kiss on the cheek and headed up to talk to the girl who was in charge of the karaoke machine. Lauren didn't even bother flipping through the binder of song choices before leaning in to tell the girl her request. Quinn mentally noted the appropriateness of the current performer's choice to sing "Zombie" because her stained T-shirt and smeared eye makeup actually made her look like one. But Quinn kept her comment to herself.

As soon as *The Walking Dead* extra finished her last note, Lauren made her way onto the stage and positioned herself in front of the microphone, shifting it down a bit so it was a little lower. From the first beat, there was no mistaking Lauren's song selection. Quinn knew the song well. She and the girls had spent nearly the entire summer before seventh grade perfecting the choreography to the dance routine they'd made up. And to this day, whenever Quinn heard Cyndi Lauper's "Girls Just Want to Have Fun," she couldn't help but move to the rhythm as she remembered performing the dance in the late-summer heat for Lauren's parents and older brother, Cooper.

Lauren swayed subtly to the beat of the song's intro. But once she sang the first line, she immediately let loose, looking out into the crowd comfortably. Though she had never been a fantastic singer, Lauren's confidence made up for it. Quinn watched her as if studying a wild animal in its natural habitat. With each line, Lauren got into the song a bit more. And when Quinn thought about the lyrics, it became clear that the song held a greater meaning for Lauren than just the nostalgia it held for Quinn. The song was about making mistakes in life but still finding time to enjoy it.

As Lauren strutted across the stage, spinning and whipping her brown shoulder-length hair around just as their original dance routine required them to, she sang about the pressures that parents put on their children—about how sometimes we just need to do what *feels* right even if it isn't right at the time. After all, her mom was a nurse in Scott's practice, and he didn't exactly have a reputation that made him a parent's first choice for their daughter. But ultimately they loved each other. Scott was a good guy. His past was his past, and he'd been willing to change his mentality for a future with Lauren. Lauren continued her seductive routine, running her hands up and down her body and grabbing the mic from its stand. When she got to the line about her father asking what she was going to do with her life, Lauren captured Scott's attention completely as she slid down and back up an old wooden pillar on the side of the stage and sang, "Oh, Dr. Scott, you'll always be number one."

Quinn laughed at Lauren's ad-lib as her eyes bounced back and forth between Lauren and Scott. He fixed his emerald stare on her, his posture relaxed and a hint of desire in his eyes that he didn't seem to be making any effort to disguise. Quinn marveled at how he appreciated Lauren. And not just physically. Around Scott, Lauren was free to be whoever she actually *was*.

As the song ended, Lauren thanked the crowd and made her way back to the table, slipping in between the other customers' chairs with ease. Scott gave her a kiss on the cheek and slid his arm around her again. "You're certifiable, you know that?" he said with a smile.

"Of course I know that. I'm the one with the master's in psychology, so I believe I'm more qualified than you to make that diagnosis. Maybe I went a little over-board when I decided to lie on the piano, but in my defense, we choreographed that dance when we were in middle school. That part was where I rolled across a picnic table." She shrugged. "I had to improvise. Plus, I was trying to prove a point to Quinn."

Quinn shook her head in laughter. "What point is that exactly? That we probably looked like prepubes-cent strippers in front of your entire family?"

"Do I even want to know what this conversation is about?"

Quinn looked up to see Tim standing above her wear-ing a worn gray T-shirt. He'd probably come straight from work, not even stopping to change. "You just missed quite a performance by the one and only Lauren Hast-ings."

Lauren took a long sip of her drink, clearly parched from her recent exertion. "I was *trying*," she said, drag-ging out the word for emphasis, "to show Quinn how easy it is to get up there. Have a seat. You're just in time for her debut."

Tim took a seat next to Quinn, looking momentarily confused by Lauren and Scott's presence. But he didn't bring it up. "Perfect."

Quinn hesitated, feeling shy. It was one thing to *watch* someone else get up and act like a fool in front of an audience. But it was another thing entirely to *be* that fool. "Give me a minute. I don't even know what song to pick." It was just an excuse to procrastinate, and Quinn was okay with that.

"Then I'll pick one for you," Lauren said.

"Not a chance. You'll probably pick something super embarrassing. This'll already be hard enough. I wouldn't even trust you to pick out my socks."

"What do you mean? I have *great* taste in socks. Robert Kardashian's got nothing on me."

"Wait," Tim interjected. "Why do I feel like I have no idea what we're talking about anymore?"

Scott rolled his eyes and ran a hand through his messy blond hair. "That was Lauren's attempt at humor. Robert Kardashian has a sock line."

Tim cocked a brow at his brother. "Do I even want to ask how you know that?"

Scott shook his head and lowered his eyes in shame. "Probably not."

Tim seemed happy to change the subject back to why they were all there in the first place. "Come on," he said to Quinn, "the more you think about it, the more you'll psych yourself out. You just gotta get up there. You can't wait until the right moment because there will never be one." Quinn saw the encouragement in Tim's eyes as he spoke: a mixture of sweetness and reassurance. Tim rose and extended his hand to Quinn, helping her up but then releasing her once she stood. She missed the feel of his rough palm immediately, and Quinn couldn't help but wonder if he would have dropped her hand so soon if Lauren and Scott hadn't been there.

Quinn followed Tim over to the binder of songs and flipped through for a minute or so until she spotted the song she'd been looking for. If she were truthful, she'd always known what song she would choose. It was one that always brought out the best in her, made her feel upbeat and excited. She inhaled a long deep breath and slowly released it. Then she asked the girl to play Whitney Houston's "I Wanna Dance With Somebody." She knew it was an impossible song to do justice to, but if she was going to embarrass herself in front of an entire bar, she was damn well going to make it worth it.

"You got it, honey," the waitress replied.

Quinn turned toward the stage, mentally preparing herself for the fifteen or so sets of eyes that would be fixed on her in a few moments. But before she could take a step, Tim placed both his hands firmly on her shoulders, as if steadying her both physically and emotionally. "Look at me," he said softly. Quinn raised her eyes to meet his, and their deep green color soothed her. "You'll be fine. I promise."

Cautiously, Tim released his grip on her, and Quinn walked to the stage. She watched as Tim found his seat again, and her eyes stayed glued to his as if losing the connection would somehow cause her to lose her nerve too. She took a deep breath as the eighties beat started to play, and Tim gave her a slight nod of encouragement.

Softly at first and then a little louder, Quinn made it through the "huh"s and "woo"s and "hey"s. She even made it through the first verse. But it wasn't Lauren's performance that had helped to give Quinn the push she needed to get up there. It had been Tim's calming words and cool demeanor that had given her the strength to get started. Unfortunately it hadn't been enough to keep going. She stood at the microphone and let her eyes scan the crowd. Some unfamiliar faces stared back at her, but most people were too caught up in their own conversations to notice her presence at all.

Quinn froze. And the music continued. As if in a fog, Quinn searched for Tim in the crowd, so panicked that she couldn't even remember where he was seated. Finally she saw his face—a hint of a smile encouraging her to go on. *You got this,* he mouthed. But despite his strength and confidence, she just couldn't find it in herself to continue. Out of the corner of her eye, she saw the next verse and the chorus scroll by unsung as she stood stock-still.

The thirty seconds or so seemed like an eternity. She felt the apathetic eyes of so many strangers upon her. The beat of the music seemed to fade around her until she could barely hear it. That is, until without warning, Tim stood . . . and started to sing . . . the wrong words. "I did it, love. Hmm, hmm, hmm, hmm, hmmmm. Something in the town."

Thankfully, all of the focus that had been on Quinn only a few moments before had shifted to Tim as he made his way to the stage in time to see the words to the next verse. He didn't seem to care that he couldn't sing or that, even once he turned to face the monitor, he struggled to say the right lyrics.

Here was this ruggedly handsome, tall guy with his arms in the air as he clapped to the beat. The crowd ate him up. And Quinn couldn't blame them. As fearful as she'd been to sing in public, she couldn't *not* sing with Tim by her side. All of her trepidation seemed to dissipate as Tim's eyes met hers. His close proximity and his

easy smile calmed her nerves. And by the time the chorus was repeated a second time, not only was Quinn
singing along, but much of the audience was as well—
at least those who were sober enough to know what
was happening.

Tim stole a glance away from the screen to look at
Quinn. She looked . . . happy, relaxed even. This was
the Quinn he hoped to see more of. He'd seen a glimpse
of her when he'd entered the bar, stopping at the door
to watch her interact with Scott and Lauren. She'd sat,
shoulders back, a bright smile on her face as she spoke.
And now she was clapping along with him in front of
an audience as she sang about how she wanted to
dance with somebody who loved her.

Tim let his body take over during the chorus, unable to
resist pulling Quinn to him, swaying to the beat, and then
spinning her out toward the edge of the stage like they
were two little kids trying to dance at a wedding. They
continued like that—moving their feet, wiggling their
bodies. And when the song began to fade out, so did
Tim's voice. He got quieter with each line until Quinn
was the only one left at the microphone. After she'd sung
the last word, she looked over at Tim, who had taken a
few steps back to let Quinn have her moment in the spot-
light. A moment she had earned. It was as if he'd been
teaching her to ride a bike and he'd let go of it without her
noticing. And when she realized he wasn't holding on
anymore, she seemed surprised that she hadn't crashed.

*   *   *

Tim walked Quinn to her car shortly after Scott and Lauren left. Everyone but Tim had an early morning the next day.

"Sorry I didn't tell you I invited Scott and Lauren. They were kind of a last-minute addition when I realized you'd be late," Quinn said.

"It's fine. No need to apologize," Tim said as they strolled through the parking lot. Then he got quiet for a moment as he stole a sideways glance at Quinn out of the corner of his eye. "So you did it," he said quietly, the corners of his mouth turning up into the same proud grin Quinn sported.

"Yeah, well . . . with *your* help."

Tim shrugged as if he hadn't done anything special. And in truth, he hadn't. He loved watching Quinn gradually emerge from the shell she'd spent so much of her life inside. And he'd do whatever he could to help her. "I guess *we* did it, then."

"Yeah. We did." Then Quinn laughed softly. "I still can't believe you sang the song and you didn't even know any of the words."

"Hey, give me a *little* credit. I knew *some* of the words."

Quinn raised her eyebrows.

"Okay, maybe like one or two."

Quinn stopped at her gray Jeep Liberty and hit the button to unlock her doors. "I don't know how you're not embarrassed by stuff like this."

Tim's eyes locked on Quinn's as she leaned against her car to face him. "I've done some pretty stupid shit in my life. Shit I don't even like to think about, let alone talk about. So trust me when I say I know what embarrassing feels like." He could sense Quinn's features soften as if she regretted what she'd said. "But being here with you tonight, getting to see you accomplish something that was so important to you, something that was so difficult for you . . . there's nothing embarrassing about that. No matter how you look at it."

Quinn's pink lips tightened, and Tim mentally scolded himself for wondering what they'd feel like against his. "Right. I get that." She pushed off the car and put her fingers on the door handle. "I guess I'd better get going."

Though he didn't have anywhere he would have rather been, he replied, "Yeah, me too." As Quinn pulled away, he added a loud "Drive safe," hoping she would hear it, but knowing that the comment wasn't even necessary. Like she would drive any other way.

Chapter 7

Subplot

Quinn fanned her hand through her curly mane as she and her friends strolled through the shopping center Saturday afternoon and chattered about . . . well, Quinn wasn't exactly sure what they were talking about. She had things on her mind. Big, handsome things. Her brain replayed the karaoke night, how confident Tim was in his smooth, colorful skin. It wasn't that Quinn lacked confidence altogether. She had long ago perfected the art of holding her head high when she entered a room, flashing a white smile to be inviting to friends and strangers alike. Quinn had finesse. She could work a room and make conversation with pretty much anyone about pretty much anything. But karaoke had shown a chink in Quinn's well-constructed armor. Her self-assuredness arose from a pack mentality. She was strong because her friends were strong. She was outgoing because with her group of mad hatters, the outside world didn't matter. They were one another's safety net. But without them, Quinn faltered. Karaoke had left her hanging on to the trapeze for dear life without a net to catch her if she fell. And goddamn, how close she'd come to falling.

Until Tim had swooped in and gotten her swinging again. She envied his quiet confidence. From what Quinn could tell, Tim's strength was innate—as natural to the man as breathing. But this only made him more enigmatic to her. How had someone so strong, so sure of himself, spent years of his life as an addict? Quinn didn't know the gritty details, but she knew that his parents had disowned him, that he'd bounced from rehab to rehab, his relapse imminent each time. She had a difficult time reconciling *that* Tim with the one she had been spending time with. The one who was an executive chef at a hip new restaurant. She just didn't . . . get it.

"And then I glued my hands to my ass and strutted around the office nude."

I wonder what Tim's . . . Wait . . . What? "What the hell did you just say?" Quinn asked Cass.

"About time you started paying attention. If I'd have known I only had to mention my ass to get you to listen to me, I'd have said it ten minutes ago."

"Sorry. I have a lot on my mind," Quinn explained.

"Anything wrong?" Lauren asked, narrowing her eyes as if she were trying to read Quinn's mind. Though Quinn was sure Lauren had a guess as to what could be on her mind, Lauren still appraised her as she would a serial killer. Ever since she'd gotten her master's degree, Lauren thought she was a real Sigmund Freud.

"No. Just work bullshit. I'm fine."

"Those bastards still not letting you write anything?" Simone questioned, a hard edge to her voice that let Quinn know she'd shank a bitch for her.

Quinn huffed out a humorless laugh. "The opposite actually."

Cass and Simone exchanged confused glances, while Lauren kept her eyes trained on the brick pathway that snaked through the shopping center.

"We're confused," Simone said. The girls quickly zeroed in on Quinn. "So you are working on something?"

"Yup." Quinn rarely had information they wanted. She was going to soak up the attention for all it was worth.

A hand reached out and clamped down on her forearm, jerking her to a stop. "Excuse me, you hooker, but would you care to elaborate before we take turns beating the shit out of you?" Cass threatened.

Quinn smiled at the girls, placating them before speaking a taunting "No" and starting to walk again.

The two girls flocked around her, impeding any further movement. Quinn burst out laughing. "Okay, okay, yes, I am writing an article. It'll be in the September issue. It's a feature on . . . me, actually."

"On you?" Simone asked excitedly. "What about you?"

Quinn searched for the right words. "It's sort of like a self-discovery piece. I'm undertaking a list of tasks that are a little beyond what I'd normally do."

"What does that mean exactly? Oh shit, I was kidding when I called you a hooker, but it's true, isn't it? You're selling your cooch for cash," Cass teased.

Quinn stared at her for a minute. "You know, for someone with such a fair complexion, you have a dark and twisted soul."

Cass shrugged happily. "I know."

Quinn shook her head before continuing. "I'm not getting quite that extreme. Tim and I are starting out slow. I—"

"Hold on. Did you say Tim?" Cass asked.

Shit. "Uh, yeah."

"Since when are you hanging out with Tim?" Cass brought a finger up to her temple. It reminded Quinn of Professor Xavier from *X-Men*.

"Since Lauren's party. We got to talking about my assignment and he offered to help." Quinn shrugged like it was only logical that she'd be spending time with a reformed drug addict who was eight years her senior.

Cass gasped and grabbed Quinn's arm in an intentionally dramatic fashion. "Do your parents know?" Her eyes gleamed like she'd unearthed a tabloid-worthy scandal.

Quinn jerked her arm free as Cass' face broke out in a huge smile. "Why would I tell them? It isn't their business who I hang out with."

Simone barked out a laugh. "Since when?"

"I can just see Julia's and Peter's faces now. Oh my God, they may almost look at you with disappointment. The horror," Cass joked.

Quinn rolled her eyes. She was used to jabs from the girls about her overprotective, overinvolved parents. The girls knew how they clung to her like the prized possession they considered her to be.

"They'd have no reason to be disappointed. Tim's a great guy." Lauren's voice was firm and steady. Quinn knew Lauren really liked Tim. And she damn sure loved his brother. And even though Cass' assessment held a bit of credibility, Quinn knew Lauren wasn't going to stand by while the girls insinuated that Quinn's parents wouldn't think Tim was good enough for their daughter.

"You're right. He is."

Lauren's gaze flew to Quinn, but Quinn didn't hold it, afraid of what Lauren would see there.

"Wait. Why have you been so quiet this whole time?" Cass narrowed her eyes at Lauren. "You *knew* already, didn't you?"

Lauren let her smirk answer for her.

"I see how it is. Get a psychology degree and suddenly you're the one everyone trusts with the deep shit."

"So what have you guys been doing?" Simone asked, probably to end Cass' tirade.

"So far, I lied to get out of work, stole a pack of gum, and sang karaoke."

"What a rebel," Cass muttered.

"I said we were starting small," Quinn said indignantly. "We're working up to the big stuff."

"What kind of big stuff?" Lauren asked, concern clear in her voice. Even though Lauren had known about the article, they hadn't actually discussed the types of things Quinn had included on her list.

Quinn had the girls' full attention. It was the first time they had been this interested in the goings-on of her life. Not because they didn't give a shit about what Quinn did, but because Quinn hadn't *done* anything worth giving a shit about. And she damn sure wasn't ready to relinquish center stage just yet. "Guess you'll just have to buy the September edition of *Estelle* and find out for yourselves," she taunted as she pulled open the door of a clothing store and waltzed inside, leaving the girls speechless on the pavement.

"So you going to tell me what's *really* going on with you and Quinn?" Scott asked, spotting Tim as he bench-pressed.

Tim exhaled a deep breath as he gave the bar a final surge upward and cradled it back onto the rack. "What are you talking about?" Tim asked as he sat up.

"Come on. You're practically glowing, you pansy. It's gotta be her. I mean, who else could get you to make a complete ass of yourself in front of a roomful of strangers?"

Tim bit his tongue, not wanting to sour their afternoon by reminding Scott that Tim had embarrassed himself in front of strangers too many times to count. He also wondered how it was possible that Scott was able to read him so well, considering how little time they'd actually spent with each other growing up. "It's not a glow; it's called sweat. Maybe you'd know the difference if you exercised something other than your mouth." Tim stood and made his way over to the squat rack.

Scott leaned against the machine as Tim adjusted the weight. "Fine. You don't want to tell me? No problem."

Scott cut Tim a sideways glance, making sure he was watching before he turned on the little-brother pout.

"Knock that shit off. If there was something going on with Quinn, I'd fucking tell you." *I'd actually love to be able to tell you that.*

"You kiss your new girlfriend with that mouth?"

"No. I kiss *your* girlfriend with it."

Scott laughed at that. "You wish, asshole."

Tim settled himself under the barbell and then stood straight up, giving himself a second to acclimate to the weight before squatting under it. He didn't bother to correct his brother. While Lauren was a great girl, she wasn't the one Tim pictured his lips on. Nor was she the one he fantasized about exploring with his hands, feeling her creamy skin sprout goose bumps as he caressed every square inch of her. *Fuck.*

"So if it's not Quinn, what is it? Some other girl?"

"What are you giving me hell for? Can't I just be happy to spend time with you?"

Scott softened for a second, looking at his brother with discerning eyes before the smart-ass veneer slid back into place. "Not this fucking happy."

Tim racked the bar and stepped out of the way so Scott could do a set. "You may want to take some weight off. You're not looking as spry as usual," Tim taunted.

"Fuck off."

They were quiet as Scott completed his set. But as soon as he set the bar down, he started in again. "Fine, man. You wanna leave your little brother in the dark about your life, fine."

"Oh, Jesus Christ. Since pouting didn't work, you decided to give guilt a try?"

Lifting one shoulder in a half shrug, Scott smirked.

"Listen, the restaurant's doing well. I'm doing well. Why does there need to be more to it than that?"

All signs of joking gone, Scott's face sobered. "There doesn't. I'm happy for you. Glad everything is going well. I guess it was just . . . wishful thinking."

Scott started walking toward the free weights, but Tim stepped in front of him. "What does that mean? Wishful thinking?"

"Nothing," Scott answered, dragging a hand through his blond hair. "I just . . . I was just hoping that maybe you'd met someone is all."

"Why would you be hoping that?"

"In the seven years you've been clean, have you had a single girlfriend?" Scott's voice was hushed, but Tim heard him just fine.

Tim felt his jaw tighten at the question. That was none of Scott's business. Tim knew he was only asking because he gave a shit, but what the fuck? "I don't have time for girlfriends."

Scott stepped up to him, looking him dead in the eyes that looked like his own. "Bullshit."

Tim sagged back and let out a long breath. "I'm not saying I haven't gone out with girls in the past seven years. I'm not a fucking monk."

"That's not what I'm talking about and you know it. Sure, you've had your fair share of one-night stands and blitz romances. We both have. But there's a lot to be said for being in a real relationship. With a girl who's looking for more than just a good time."

"That's all I'm good for," Tim muttered as he turned and headed for the other end of the gym, not even sure of his exact destination. He just wanted to get away from Scott. Away from their conversation. But before he made it two steps, he felt a solid hand on his forearm. He allowed Scott to turn him around, even though Tim was stronger than his brother. At least physically.

"What the hell does that mean?"

Suddenly Tim's anger surged. If Scott wanted to get into it, then that's exactly what they'd do. "Come on, Scott. My life isn't a goddamn fairy tale. It's a jumbled mess of fuck-ups, relapses, cravings, jagged scars, and canyons of regret. No woman worth spending a lifetime with is going to want to deal with all of the shit that comes along with loving me. I'm more trouble than I'm worth."

"You don't really believe that." Scott looked as if Tim had punched him. "You haven't relapsed once in seven years, Tim. For Christ's sake, if anyone deserves some fucking happiness, it's you."

For all Tim knew, Scott meant his words. But the more likely scenario in his mind was that Scott was just talking bullshit to make Tim feel better. To keep him from sinking into a place so dark and depressing that he turned to drugs to claw his way out. What Scott didn't know, though, was that Tim lived in that place for at least part of every day. He didn't turn to drugs anymore because they added another wrinkle to the equation, one Tim couldn't handle anymore: isolation. At least without the dope, he still had his brother. That thought didn't stop him from lashing out, though. "Why? Why do I deserve that?" He was practically growling the words, but Tim couldn't bring himself to care. "And seven years is nothing. Do you know that not a single day goes by that I don't think about using? I'm not even sure an hour goes by, Scott. This"—Tim pounded on his chest with a fist—"is a fucking life sentence. Being in this body, stuck with this weak mind." He said the words with a vehement disgust that made Scott wince. "Why would I ever saddle someone else with that? Now, just fucking drop it."

And with that, Tim whirled around and took off toward the locker room, leaving Scott standing in the middle of the gym, as Tim struggled not to self-destruct. *I guess some things never change.*

Chapter 8

Blend

"Tim, I don't care if it's on the original list. I *can't* get a tattoo. It's too . . . permanent."

Tim shook his head and laughed. "Isn't that the idea? That's why you never would've done it. And besides, what's the alternative? You can't get some kind of henna tattoo or one of those kids' ones that come off with rubbing alcohol."

Quinn used the red light to slow down and catch her breath on the corner. She'd always considered herself a runner. But since she'd started jogging with Tim a week ago, after he'd casually invited her to join him, it had occurred to her that maybe she wasn't quite deserving of the title. At least not when she compared herself to Tim, whose long, muscular legs carried him swiftly through the streets at a pace more suited for a cheetah than a human being. Not that she was complaining. It was a small price to pay for getting to see Tim in mesh shorts and a tank top, sweat glistening on his biceps.

And now that the late-May weather was getting increasingly hotter and more humid, he'd taken his shirt off about four blocks back. As the two bounced up and down, waiting for the light to turn green, Quinn's eyes scanned Tim's body—she hoped discreetly—until her gaze settled on his pierced nipple, which she hadn't known he had until . . . right . . . now. *Jesus, the man gets sexier by the second.* She wondered if she'd been staring at his chest long enough for Tim to notice. But it was at eye level, so she couldn't help it. *Sure, that's why you can't take your eyes off his muscles and the small hairs that lead down to his . . .*

"What?" he asked, looking down.

Shit. "Um," Quinn thought quickly, "I was thinking I'd get a piercing. I've always wanted one." *No, you haven't.* "I just saw yours and thought maybe I could do that instead." *Stop. Talking.*

"Get your nipple pierced?" Tim took off when the light turned green, causing Quinn to have to sprint after him.

"Well," she huffed, "not my nipple." *What else do people pierce? I probably shouldn't ask that.* "Maybe my nose or something."

"Like a bull?"

"Nooo," she said, dragging out the word as she punched his arm playfully. "Like a little stud on one side or something."

They stopped at Quinn's building, and Tim remained silent for a moment, clearly trying to look pensive. "I guess that's acceptable," he finally said. "I'll meet you at 202 Ink at six. It's on M Street."

"Sounds good." Quinn unlocked the door that led to the lobby and pulled it open.

"Oh, and, Quinn," Tim called from the sidewalk, still jogging in place. "Better take a couple extra Tylenols before you go, 'cause this is gonna hurt like a bitch."

What the hell have I gotten myself into?

Quinn arrived a few minutes before six and was already looking in the case of jewelry when she heard the bells on the door jingle and turned around to see Tim stroll in.

He looked fresh out of the shower, his blond hair a little darker than usual because it was still damp. He wore a dark gray fitted T-shirt with the logo of a band that Quinn had never heard of. "I'm surprised you're here," Tim said eagerly. "And early. I thought I might have to drag you out of your apartment and carry you here."

Quinn felt a pleasurable shiver at the thought of Tim's hands on her, but she pushed the image aside. "Well, I figure, what's the worst that can happen? If I don't like it, I can just take it out, right?"

"This is true." Tim leaned over Quinn's shoulder, entering into her personal space. "So, which one are we looking at?"

She breathed in his scent—a spicy clean that was all his own—before answering. "Whichever one will hurt the least."

"Well, then you want to steer clear of the larger gauges," he said as though Quinn knew what he was talking about.

"The what?"

Tim laughed. "Sorry. The thick jewelry right there. The lower the number, the more it will hurt." Tim raised his eyebrows. "But truthfully, they'll *all* hurt. Your nose is all cartilage."

Quinn felt her face and neck warm. "Maybe I should just get a second hole in my ear."

"Oh no, I don't think so," Tim warned, putting his solid arm around Quinn's shoulder as he led her away from the case. "You're not getting off that easy. Come with me."

Before she could do anything to stop it, she was seated in an old leather chair that looked like it was more suited for a dentist's office than a tattoo parlor. Tim asked for the smallest diamond stud they had, and a scruffy man with low pants and a navy beanie cap returned a minute or so later to set up.

"I like your wallet chain," Quinn said to the man nervously. "I didn't think anyone still wore them. I haven't seen one since middle school. My eighth-grade boyfriend had one until they got banned because Gavin Whitfield tried to whip—"

"Lean back," he ordered suddenly.

Quinn hesitated. "Um, can I just have a minute? I'm not quite ready."

The man huffed, his stench reminding Quinn of her grandfather's after he'd smoke a pipe on his back patio: a mixture of smoke and sweat. "I'm gonna grab a cigarette before we get started anyway. Relax for a few minutes and I'll be right back."

Once he left, Tim took a seat in the swivel chair beside Quinn. "You sure you want to do this?" he asked, sincerity in his eyes. "We can always go another time if you want. It's important that you're comfortable."

Quinn knew Tim was trying to be sweet. But she didn't need that. She just needed a minute or so to compose herself. "I'll be okay," she assured him before glancing around the small room. Skulls, photographs of half-naked women, and a few signs with some curses hung on the walls. Then she spotted the tray with the piercing supplies and felt the color drain from her face. The needle was thick. Like, really thick. And in a few minutes, that really thick needle would be going through her face. Then she turned to Tim, and the two stared silently at each other for several minutes, Quinn inhaling deep breaths as Tim rubbed the outside of her biceps soothingly.

"Ready?" the man asked, and then closed the door behind him.

She swallowed hard.

"Actually," Tim said, "there's been a change of plans. I'm gonna get one first."

Quinn looked at Tim curiously. *What the hell is he doing?*

Tim shrugged. "This way you'll see how easy it is. Plus, we promised we'd do everything *together*. I'm just holding up my end of the deal."

Quinn was so thankful for the respite, she allowed herself to pretend that his explanation made sense. "What are you gonna get pierced?"

"Whatever you want," Tim said simply. "You pick."

"Seriously?"

"Seriously."

Quinn thought for a moment. This was a major decision. She was choosing where to put a hole in this man's body. She looked Tim up and down, feeling free to study him without reservation until her mind finally settled on a part of him she'd often caught herself fantasizing about. Well . . . *one* of the parts anyway. "How about your tongue?"

The left corner of Tim's mouth quirked up into a half smile as if Quinn's selection amused him. "You heard the lady," he said without taking his eyes off of her. "Just a silver barbell will be fine."

A few minutes later, Tim was seated where Quinn had just been. His tongue was out, and the man held it in place with a metal clamp before sliding a needle through, followed by the jewelry.

Quinn's face scrunched up in empathetic pain. But there was nothing to empathize with. Tim barely flinched.

"See? Simple," he said, somehow still able to speak. "You're up."

Quinn sat down and felt her muscles clench immediately. She gripped the armrest tightly and shut her eyes. It was bad enough she'd have to *feel* whatever was about to take place. She didn't want to have to *see* it too. But what Quinn wasn't expecting to feel was Tim's palm slide underneath hers as he peeled her hand off the cracked leather gently and interlaced his fingers with hers. The contact with his skin made her own tingle at his touch.

She didn't need to hear him or see him. Feeling him was enough to ease her nerves. She took a breath and relaxed right before the needle stabbed through her nose. "Ahh . . . fuckety, fuck-fuck . . . shit." But those were all the expletives Quinn could expel before it was over. At least the pain was short-lived.

"You kiss your mother with that mouth?" Tim joked.

He was still laughing as the man held up a mirror for Quinn to see her new image. And she liked what she saw: the rebel inside her that had probably always been waiting to be unleashed. "I'll kiss whoever I damn well please," she replied with a playful grin.

Tim walked out of the tattoo parlor and held the door open behind him for Quinn.

"Thanks," she said. "It's beautiful out tonight."

"Yeah. It is," he agreed. Tim slyly snuck a glance at Quinn's new piercing. It definitely added a hint of rebel to the all-American Quinn. Tim felt some of his mirth fade away. His argument with Scott was still fresh in his mind. He'd meant the things he'd said. Tim was trouble with a capital T. And as he glanced at Quinn's new body jewelry, he couldn't help but think that he was corrupting the fresh-faced beauty. He'd been able to talk himself down from those thoughts when she'd stolen the pack of gum because, well, it was a pack of gum. But that had morphed into her getting stabbed in the face, putting a permanent hole where it wasn't meant to be.

Quinn stopped on the sidewalk and looked up at him. She looked . . . happy. The tumultuous storm within him quieted slightly. If he had played any role in making Quinn feel better about herself, then that was enough for him to stop mentally assaulting himself. He had a sudden need to keep her that way. To keep that proud, buoyant look on her face. "What are you up to for the rest of the night?" He looked down at his watch. *Only seven o'clock.*

Quinn shrugged. "Nothing, I guess. The girls all had stuff going on, and I had this. I don't know that I can handle much more excitement anyway," she joked.

"What? It's Friday night. You going to sit at home and knit or something?"

"Why, yes. Would you like me to make you something?"

Yes, you can make me worthy of you. "I could use a scarf, old maid."

Quinn laughed. "Now you're just being insulting." She tucked a strand of hair behind her ear.

Tim's fingers itched to touch her. "Come out with me." Tim had said the words before really thinking about them, but not a single fiber of him wanted to retract the offer. "I'm meeting up with a few of my buddies to play pool. Nothing major." The truth was, it *was* major. He'd never brought a girl to hang out with his friends. Tim felt like that implied a certain amount of substance to a relationship: meeting each other's friends. But he knew Quinn's friends, even if their own relationship was stalled at friendship. The truth was, she meant something to him. She meant a lot.

Quinn scrunched up her face. "I don't want to intrude on guys' night."

"We're not a bunch of chicks gossiping about boyfriends and offering sex advice. We're just hanging out."

Quinn looked at him curiously.

"What?" Tim asked.

"I'm trying to figure out if I should be insulted by that or not."

They both laughed. "Present company was clearly excluded from that statement."

"Clearly," Quinn said.

"Come on." Tim bumped their shoulders together. "You know you wanna come. Think of it as a bonus to your list. Chill with a bunch of thugs at a pool hall." Tim's voice had been light, but the truth of his words hit a nerve somewhere deep in his body. The reality was, a girl like Quinn was much too good to be hanging around with his roughneck crowd. But that didn't make him regret the invite. He wasn't ready for their time together to end, even if it was selfish of him.

"You're not a thug." Her voice was adamant. It was endearing, even if it was misinformed.

"Okay, reformed thugs, then." He smiled as he spoke, but Quinn's demeanor didn't change. She just stared at him for a few seconds, as if she were looking for something. The look made him feel naked. Exposed.

Finally she spoke, her voice soft but strong. "Okay, I'm in."

"Good," he replied. "I'll drive us there, and we can come back for your car later. I'm not meeting them 'til nine. You want to grab dinner first?"

"Are you sure you feel like eating?" she asked, pointing to her mouth.

Tim shrugged. "Gotta get used to it eventually. Might as well start now."

"Sounds like a plan, Stan," she said as she slid her arm through his and let him lead her to his car.

"I got a bacon cheeseburger and fries and you're just getting salad?" Quinn asked after handing her menu to the waitress. "I thought you were a tough guy," she added with a sly grin.

Tim raised his eyebrows. "I'm adventurous, not psychotic."

"That second part's up for debate. You just got your tongue pierced like you were deciding what laundry detergent to buy." Suddenly Quinn propped herself up onto her elbows and leaned across the table. "Let me see it anyway."

"You sure?"

"Positive."

Tim stuck his tongue out slowly.

He could tell Quinn was trying to disguise her initial squeamishness as she put her hand over her own mouth. "Looks . . . swollen."

Tim laughed. "Definitely feels swollen. But tongues heal quickly, so I'm sure it won't be long before I can use it for things again."

Tim didn't miss Quinn's sudden inhale and the way her cheeks flushed. It was nice to be reminded that Quinn wasn't as innocent as she often seemed. Even her mind ended up in the gutter from time to time. He couldn't help but enjoy watching her squirm for a minute before he added, "I should be able to eat a real meal in a few days, I'm sure."

"Right," she said simply as she leaned back in the booth to allow the waitress to set their drinks in front of them.

As Tim watched her take a sip of her drink, his mind instantly wondered how those lips would feel on his, or wrapped around him. He quickly realized he was staring and shook his head slightly.

"You okay over there?" Quinn questioned coyly, as if she knew where his mind had been.

"Never better," Tim replied as he took a gulp of his water, wincing as the icy-coldness hit his tongue.

"Whatever you say."

Soon after, the waitress brought their food and they ate quietly. Once they were both finished, Tim ordered a chocolate shake for them to split. He figured putting his mouth anywhere Quinn's had been could only help the throb in his tongue. Plus he'd have the added bonus of watching Quinn suck hard on a straw.

By the time they'd left the restaurant and headed to the pool hall, they were already forty minutes late to meet the guys. Quinn looked at her watch as they entered the dimly lit establishment.

"It's no big deal. We're not punching a time clock or anything," Tim joked.

"Yo, buddy. Where the fuck you been?"

Quinn turned to glare at Tim, to which he smiled and shrugged.

Tim led them over to the loudmouth, slapping his hand and pulling him into a one-armed embrace. "Dante, this is Quinn. Quinn, Dante."

"Nice to meet you," Quinn said as she shook Dante's outstretched hand, smiling widely.

"Whoa, do my eyes deceive me? Did you actually bring a girl to hang out with us?" his buddy Rudy asked.

Tim groaned. "Can it, Rudy." The rest of the group closed in on them, and Tim continued with the introductions. "Guys, this is Quinn. She's a *friend* of mine." Tim hoped that emphasizing the word "friend" would keep the guys from embarrassing the shit out of him. "That's Rudy, Dom, and Aidan."

"Friend, huh?" Rudy asked as he stepped forward to shake Quinn's hand. "So that means you're single?"

Tim slapped the back of his head, allowing that to serve as an answer.

Quinn giggled. "Good to meet you guys."

"You too, Quinn. Ignore these assholes. Their mamas didn't teach them manners," Aidan said as he held Quinn's hand and brushed a light kiss across her knuckles.

"And who taught you manners? The Knights of the Round Table? Like she wants you kissing her hand," Dante scolded.

Quinn laughed again, seemingly comfortable with the group of marauders Tim had just introduced her to. They were good guys, but, like Tim, they each had checkered pasts. They'd all become acquainted on the streets, each simultaneously chasing and running from his own demons. Even though Tim had met most of them at separate times, they'd fallen in with one another, forming a little gang of men who had solid characters buried underneath the rubble of addiction. They'd stuck together through prison stints, rehabs, relapses, vagrancy, and finally, sobriety. Rudy often joked that they were their own five-step program, better than any AA meeting. They were accountable to one another, each knowing the tells of every other person in the group. They could spot a high member in their ranks from a mile away. And the penalty for such a fuck-up was an ass beating and a ride to rehab.

But even Tim had to admit they weren't the most approachable group. Covered in ink, all of them muscled because all addicts substituted one jones for another. The gym had become their drug of choice when they'd vowed to get clean and stay that way. Though in reality, the appeal of the gym was that it was a place they could all go and hang out without the added pressure of alcohol being served. It was years before they started venturing into places like the pool hall, where the smell of liquor beckoned some of them like the vengeful bitch she was.

"You guys are a trip," Quinn said. "So do you have only one table going?"

"No. We have two. You play?" Dom eyed her skeptically. Out of all of them, Dom was the most serious. Tim couldn't remember the last time the man had cracked a genuine smile.

"A little," Quinn said as she went over to the pool sticks and selected one.

The men crowded around the tables they'd reserved for the evening and watched her chalk up the tip of the stick.

"Mind if I break?"

The guys murmured *go ahead*s and *sure*s. They continued to stare as she lined up her shot, struck the cue ball dead center, and sank three balls.

"Two were stripes, so that's what I'll take. Who am I playing?"

The stunned group looked at one another until Dom spoke up. "You brought her. You lose to her." He handed Tim a pool stick.

Tim grabbed it and then walked over to Quinn. "You play pool?"

"Maybe. You look surprised," she said with a smile.

"Don't try that innocent act on me. I know you too well to fall for that."

"Can't blame a girl for trying." Then she winked at him, and he nearly passed the hell out. He hadn't met this Quinn before, though he'd suspected she existed. This was a Quinn who was confident in her own skin and in her abilities. And it was sexy as hell. He wasn't sure why it had taken four burly strangers to bring this side of her out, but he sure as hell wasn't complaining.

Though the urge to complain did surface after she ran the goddamn table on him.

Chapter 9

The Lead

Quinn sat in her cubicle Monday morning alternating her stares between her computer screen and her cell phone. She was completely disinterested in the former, completely obsessed with the latter. Her fingers slid from her mouse to the keypad, then back to her mouse. *I'm not going to text. I'm not going to text.* She repeated the mantra even though she really didn't know what the issue was. She could text him. They were friends. *What's the big deal?*

But Quinn knew what the big deal was: the thoughts that were running through her mind were *anything* but friendly. Having his help in her quest to find herself was one thing. Kind of like a good Samaritan looking after a pathetic stray puppy. But all of the things they'd been doing in addition to that—the running, the frequent texting, and the hanging out with his friends—were enough to make her mental.

So she wasn't going to text because that would only

make her feel more like a nerdy teenager pining after her hot teacher. And she refused to sink to that level. She'd learned that lesson in high school. But that barely counted because Mr. Driscoll had been a *student* teacher, so her incessant doodling of Quinn Driscoll all over her binder wasn't all that inappropriate.

Frustrated, Quinn opened her desk drawer and tossed her phone inside. She ran her hands through her hair, blew out a deep breath, and willed herself to concentrate on her computer. She had finished reading the second complaint e-mail when she heard her phone chirp. She was almost embarrassed for herself at how quickly she wrenched the drawer open.

Hey, what are you up to?

Such a simple message, but one that infused happiness into every cell of Quinn's body. *Shit, I have it bad.*

Just working. So, in essence, nothing important :)

She waited as Tim typed his response, a grin overtaking her face in anticipation of his next words. Pathetic didn't even begin to describe her.

Me neither. How's the nose?

Quinn lightly brushed her finger over the stud. Pretty good actually. I love it. How's your tongue feel? Despite feeling her cheeks flush with desire, Quinn couldn't contain her eye roll as she processed the words she'd just sent through cyberspace. God, how she wished she could find out the answer to that herself.

Feels . . . interesting. I'm still getting used to it.

Quinn racked her brain for a response when she noticed that he was typing again.
So I was thinking, he sent.
She smirked as she replied. Sounds dangerous.

Very funny, smartass. I was thinking that we should probably hitchhike Sunday because people are nicer on Sundays.

Quinn narrowed her eyes at the phone. They are?

Of course.

Quinn waited for more of an explanation, but one never came. Though his next text did shed a little light on his decision.

Besides, I can't get off Saturday because I took off this past one. But I'm always off Sundays and don't have to be in until Monday afternoon for inventory.

Do you really think hitchhiking is a good idea? Quinn bit her lip nervously. Of all the things on her list, that was the only one that had real potential for getting them both kidnapped, tortured, and executed in the woods somewhere.

No. But that's why it's on your list, isn't it?

His response made her smile.

Do you trust me?

And that one made her warm all over. She didn't have to think before replying. Yes.

Then trust that I won't let anything bad happen to you. I promise.

A part of Quinn wanted to ask if he would let *good* things happen to her. Or more truthfully, if he would *do* good things to her. The thought made her squirm in her seat. But, I know, was all she could bring herself to type.

Good. So I'll see you Wednesday for our jog?

Ugh. You know . . . running wasn't on my list. We should probably table it until after my article is complete.

Nice try, Quinn. See you Wednesday.

She set her phone back in her drawer, acting more disgusted by the thought of running with Tim than she actually was.

*   *   *

"What if we get raped?" Quinn was traipsing after Tim as he walked down the highway about five miles outside of Falls Church. They'd, or rather Tim, had decided that it would be a good idea to park their car in a shopping center next to a busy highway that ran the length of Virginia. That way they would be unlikely to encounter anyone they knew who might have them committed once it became clear what they were doing.

"Rapists usually like men *or* women. Not both," Tim replied as he shifted the book bag he was carrying on his shoulder. He had told Quinn to pack a change of clothes, since part of the plan was for them to go wherever their chauffeur was heading. When she'd arrived, Tim had shoved her stuff into his large Under Armour bag and hit the streets.

"Great. They'll just kill me so they can have you all to themselves."

Tim looked over his shoulder and shot her a half-withering, half-amused look.

"Seriously, Tim. All of the nice people are at church right now. We're left with the sinners."

"What do you think we are, sweetheart?" Then he shot her a wink that nearly leveled her. "Now, stick your thumb out. We have a better chance of someone pulling over for you than for me."

"I'm not sure that's a good thing," she muttered as she raised her hand in the universal symbol for "Pick me up. I swear I'm not a criminal."

They walked for an hour, not talking but not minding the silence either. The businesses were becoming more sparse as they walked, and Quinn was suddenly confronted by another unwelcome thought. In addition to one that left them decapitated in someone's basement. "Is it legal to hitchhike?"

"What?" Tim slowed down so he could walk beside her.

"Is it legal to hitchhike?"

Tim thought for a second. "Probably not."

"So we could get arrested for this?" Quinn's voice was nearly a screech.

"It's a real possibility." Tim laughed when he turned to look at Quinn. "Relax. I think we'll be okay. We aren't trying to do anything harmful. We're just looking for a ride. I'm sure we'll be fine if a cop stops us."

"Damn, and here I was hoping to get our prostitution ring off the ground."

"You know, you're getting much snarkier the more I hang out with you. I'm beginning to think I'm a bad influence."

Quinn slid her hand into the crook of Tim's elbow. "You know what they say about dancing with the devil," she joked.

Quinn watched Tim's face fall slightly, and she immediately wished she could take back her words, though she wasn't sure what she'd said wrong. He didn't drop her arm though, so she guessed that meant he wasn't mad at her.

They were back to walking in silence, but it was charged and tense. Quinn actually found herself wishing a mass murderer would pull over just to distract them from whatever she'd done to ruin their easy companionship. And then, as if in answer to her silent prayer, an old blue VW Bug pulled onto the shoulder in front of them.

"Stay toward the back of the car. I'll talk to them," Tim said firmly.

Quinn sighed and slowed to a stop at the rear of the beat-up Bug. She couldn't quite make out what was being said, the highway traffic creating too much noise. But she turned her head sharply at the sound of Tim banging his hand against the car's passenger door before it pulled back into traffic. "What happened?" she asked when she was beside him again.

"He was a little . . . strange."

Quinn chuckled. "Well, isn't that the pot calling the kettle black? We're the dopes wandering down the highway looking for a ride."

Tim's face split into a wide grin, and just like that, the tension that had been between them vanished. "Yeah, but we're not wearing clown suits."

"Shut up!" Quinn stopped walking. "He was not wearing a clown suit."

"If you say so." Tim laughed.

"Wow. How very John Wayne Gacy."

"My thoughts exactly. I figured everyone driving has the right to be selective, so maybe we should exercise that right too."

"Good call," Quinn agreed. "I hate clowns."

"I never get that. So many people say they're afraid of clowns. Why?"

"Stephen King's *It*," Quinn replied, as if that was all the explanation that was needed. "Besides, you clearly aren't too fond of them either. You turned Hobo the Hitchhiker-Killing Clown down all on your own."

"Yeah, but that was more because he had a box of condoms and a bottle of Jack Daniel's sitting on the passenger seat."

Quinn stared at him. "I know I've been joking about it, but now I'm convinced. We're going to die today."

Tim wrapped an arm around her shoulders, which warmed immediately at his gentle touch. "At least we'll go together," he said teasingly.

Quinn didn't verbalize that she didn't feel as bad about that prospect as she should.

Two hours and countless walked miles later, Quinn and Tim were offered and finally accepted a ride from an older woman who looked like she'd spent most of her life performing hard labor. She had a throaty rasp that made Quinn think she probably smoked two packs of Newports a day. She introduced herself as Clarabell, and Quinn had to repress the urge to ask her if she had grown up on a farm.

As luck would have it, Clarabell was also a bit of a Bible-thumper who lectured them on the hazards of hitchhiking as she quoted Gospel verses. Quinn was go-ing to remind her that she'd picked up hitchhikers, which was equally dangerous, but she decided not to look a gift horse in the mouth. Clarabell was heading to a swine auction in Sceaty, Virginia, which was damn close to North Carolina. It was at least a three-hour drive away from home, and they weren't all that close to their destination yet. Quinn hoped a train passed through Sceaty, since that was how they planned to get home.

Almost as if he'd sensed her worry, Tim turned around in the passenger seat of the rugged Dodge Ram and gave Quinn a small but comforting smile. They would be okay. She was with Tim, and he'd make sure she got home in the same condition she'd left. Though she wasn't sure if that was really what she wanted.

Chapter 10

Marinate

Clarabell dropped them off at a small motel just off the highway. She thanked them for listening to all of her stories—especially the one about her cousin getting married in a barn, which she'd told several times along the way, putting a different twist on it each time. "It was nice to have company on the drive for a change."

Tim and Quinn wished Clarabell good luck at the auction before saying their good-byes and heading for the motel office. "See, told you we wouldn't get murdered," Tim said confidently.

"Too bad we can't say the same for the pigs she's about to buy."

They both laughed loudly, and Tim held the door for Quinn to enter. A woman greeted them warmly as they stepped inside. "What can I do for ya?" She spoke in a strong Southern accent, and her gray hair was as big and round as she was.

"We just need a room for the night," Tim said, reaching into his pocket to grab his wallet.

"Sure. So what brings you to Sceaty?" she asked as she reached behind her to grab two keys off the hook.

"Just passing through. You have a beautiful town," Tim replied. And it wasn't a lie. The place was as rural as he'd expected, but from what he'd seen, the landscape was pretty, with bright green grass that seemed to go on for miles due to the flat terrain. They'd passed a few quaint shops on the way to the motel, and Tim guessed they were still owned by the same families who had originally opened them. He could see the appeal of a town like Sceaty, with its slow-paced living.

"Why, thank you," the woman replied. "Hope you enjoy your stay. It's room six. To your left when you walk outside."

Tim handed the woman some money and thanked her before taking the keys. But just when he was about to turn around, he spoke again. "Sorry. I totally forgot to mention this, but is this a room with two beds?"

"Just a king bed. It's the only one we've got left. Lots of folks are in town for the auction."

Tim hesitated, turning to Quinn, whose expression gave no indication of her thoughts. "If that's all you have, it'll be fine, I guess. You have a cot or something, right?"

The woman stared blankly before answering. "We have a *floor*, honey."

"Right," Tim replied with a polite nod before turning toward the door.

*   *   *

"You hungry?" Tim asked, tossing the bag onto the small burgundy desk chair near the door.

"Yeah, I am, actually," Quinn replied. "I guess we haven't eaten anything since this morning, huh?"

"Nope. I'm starving. All that talk of swine made me want some bacon or something."

"I actually may never eat that again," Quinn admitted. "I did see a pizza place up the road though. Not sure how it'll be, but it's probably one of the safer bets. How bad can you screw up a pizza, right?"

Tim shook his head and let out a soft laugh. "You and your safe bets."

Quinn gave an innocent shrug. "Shut up," she said playfully. "I'm making progress." She pointed over her shoulder toward the bathroom. "Do you mind if I hop in the shower first? Clarabell's backseat had some sort of a red stain on it, which I tried to pretend was fruit punch."

Tim furrowed his eyebrows in disgust. "By all means." He gestured to the bathroom. "Don't let me stop you." Then he added, "Actually, why don't you relax and take your time. It's been a long day. Do you want me to just go pick it up and we can eat it here?"

"That works. You sure you don't mind?"

Mind? Is she kidding? First of all, Tim felt it best to escape the room while a naked Quinn showered just a shabby wooden door away from him. And second, Tim would never mind being alone with Quinn. Because even though he reminded himself hourly that there could never be more between them, that didn't stop him from wanting it. Wanting a private evening with Quinn—one away from piercers, amateur singers, and friends—that he could store in his mind for when he needed a reason to smile. "Nope. Not at all. Take your shower and I'll be right back."

Tim returned about a half hour later to find the bathroom door shut and the water running. He set the pizza on the bed and removed the napkins and paper plates he'd gotten from the restaurant. For a place in rural Virginia, the pizza actually smelled pretty good. "I forgot to ask you what kind of pizza you liked," Tim called when he heard the shower shut off.

Quinn's voice echoed through the door. "All the normal stuff . . . plain, pepperoni, mushroom."

"Oh, good. I got those, plus sausage, Hawaiian . . . Sorry, forgot about the pig thing." Tim smirked as he lifted the lids, trying to remember the rest. "Peppers and onions, ground bee—"

"How many pizzas did you *get*?"

Tim looked up to see Quinn standing at the bathroom door, steam escaping from behind her as she bent over, drying her damp hair with a towel. "Um . . . only two. But I had them split the toppings into quarters. I wanted to make sure I got something you liked."

Quinn lifted her head to look at him, her loose white tank top revealing a dusting of freckles on her smooth shoulders.

God, she's beautiful.

"That's cute," she said as her pink lips slipped into a sweet smile.

Tim wasn't sure he'd ever been called "cute" in his entire life. But he liked the way it sounded. Especially coming from Quinn. And as she strolled toward him in those turquoise cotton shorts, Tim felt a stirring in his pants. *Get some fucking control. If you can't even look at her for ten seconds without getting hard, how the hell do you expect to sleep in the same room as her?*

Quinn plopped down on the bed, legs crossed in front of her like she was in preschool. "I hate to disappoint you, but I'm pretty sure I can't eat a whole pizza," she said, looking at the two open boxes.

Tim laughed. "That's okay. I'm pretty sure I *can*. So there won't be much going to waste." He thought for a minute. "Or any really. They have a fridge. So we can eat the rest for breakfast."

Quinn's eyes lit up. "You like cold pizza too?" she asked. "The girls always make fun of me because I prefer it to hot pizza. I eat tons of things they think are weird. Popcorn in milk like you'd eat cereal, French toast with ham and melted cheese in between it, bacon and jelly on toast."

"Yeah, Quinn?" Tim's eyebrows shot up. "I hate to break it to you, but those things sound totally disgusting . . . in my professional opinion. Remind me to never let you cook me breakfast." Tim immediately realized the implications of what he'd said. There would be only one reason why they would have breakfast at one of their apartments.

"Shut up," Quinn said with a playful punch to Tim's arm. "Don't knock it till you try it."

They spent the next few minutes eating silently. Tim

had moved to rest his back against the pillows on the headboard as he finished his fourth slice. He took a sip of his soda and let his gaze move toward the middle of the bed where Quinn was. She sat comfortably as she reached into the box for a second slice of extra cheese. A little sauce rested below the corner of her mouth. "You have a little something," Tim said, gesturing to his own lips.

Quinn's face got visibly flushed as she wiped her mouth with her napkin, somehow still managing to miss the sauce.

Tim smiled. "It's still—" He didn't bother to finish his thought. He just reached over and wiped away the sauce slowly with a clean corner of his own napkin.

"Thanks," Quinn said softly. She dropped her eyes to the bed for a moment before raising them again to meet Tim's.

He wasn't sure what he saw in her stare, but when her mouth dropped open, he recognized the emotion immediately: fear. "What? What's wrong?"

Without warning, Quinn bolted off the bed, crashing her back into the opposite wall and pointing. "Get it! Get it! It just jumped. Do spiders *jump*?"

"Some do," Tim said on a laugh. "Where is it?"

"It's near the corner of the pizza box closest to you. It jumped off the wall right over your head. I don't know how you're so calm right now."

"Most spiders are harmless," he said, picking up the bug with a napkin and then getting up to flush it down the toilet. When he emerged from the bathroom, Quinn was still against the wall. "It's gone. You can relax."

*   *   *

Quinn's heart beat rapidly as she watched Tim return to his seat on the bed. "I'm guessing you're afraid of spiders?" he asked, though it obviously wasn't really a question.

"Yeah, just a little," Quinn answered, poking fun at herself. "Though I swear I'm not usually *that* crazy. I don't think I've ever seen a spider move that fast before."

"I don't think I've ever seen a *human* move that fast before."

Quinn was self-conscious of what Tim probably thought was an overreaction to a tiny insect. But it was impossible for any amount of embarrassment to last more than a few seconds around Tim. Things felt so comfortable with him. So . . . easy. She liked that he always made her feel taken care of—like he was watching out for her . . . protecting her. Slowly, she peeled herself away from the wall and walked toward the bed, searching for a place to sit like she was trying to avoid broken glass. "Now you know one of *my* fears. So tell me," she said, finally finding a place to sit that felt relatively safe. "What's the big, bad Tim Jacobs afraid of?"

He shrugged. "Not much, really."

Quinn tilted her head incredulously. "Oh, come on. Our entire relationship was basically founded on my insecurities and fears, and you can't tell me one thing you're scared of?"

She thought she could see the statement register in Tim's mind as his face grew more serious. "I have only one real fear. And it's not the usual, like bugs or heights or anything."

"Well, then what?" Quinn noticed herself involuntarily inch closer to Tim until they were only about a half a foot away from each other on the edge of the bed.

"It's not a fear I've ever told anyone about before. At least not directly."

"Is it something strange?" She was excited at the prospect of Tim being slightly odder than she was—even if it were only in one aspect of their lives. "I saw this episode of *Maury* where this person was scared of cotton balls. It was something about their sound. I didn't even know cotton made a noise."

"No, nothing like that," Tim said simply. "Just more personal, I guess."

Quinn's lighthearted smile faded, now mirroring Tim's sober expression. She hadn't meant for her question to have this effect on him. She'd meant it to be harmless—a topic of conversation to pass the time. "I'm sorry. I didn't mean to—" She placed a hand on Tim's forearm. "You don't have to tell me."

Tim raised his eyes from where they'd clearly been directed at Quinn's fingers draped on his skin. "No. I want to," he said quietly, a rough edge to his voice as he spoke. "I've never wanted to tell anyone until now."

Not knowing what to say to that, Quinn stayed silent.

Tim inhaled deeply as if he needed the extra oxygen to give him the strength to speak. But despite how difficult it seemed for him, he maintained eye contact with Quinn. "I'm scared I'll never be the man I'm trying so hard to be." It sounded so natural, as if he'd rehearsed the sentence a thousand times. "That these past seven years were all for nothing because no amount of right can undo the wrong I've done." Tim shook his head. "Sorry. You probably don't want to hear all this heavy shit."

Quinn looked down to where Tim had placed his hand over hers before bringing her gaze back up to meet his again. "No, I do. Tell me."

Even before Tim began to speak again, Quinn saw a wave of relief flood through him. His rigid face began to soften, and she felt his muscles relax. She'd never seen Tim like this: so vulnerable. It was such a stark contrast to his hardened exterior.

"I began trying drugs for the same reason most teenagers do. I just wanted to see what it was like. But drinking and smoking a joint here and there just made me want to experiment with other substances. Once I got involved with the harder stuff, it was impossible to stop." Tim shot his gaze to the floor, clearly ashamed of what he was about to say. "Especially when I didn't want to. Not for a while anyway. Getting high was an escape from some . . . difficult things that were going on at home."

"What kinds of things?" Quinn didn't want to push for more than what Tim wanted to share, but she also wanted to make it clear that she was interested in his life, that she wanted to know everything he was willing to tell her.

Tim looked down at the floor. "My mom had affairs. When Scott and I were kids, she used to take us to the house of some guy she was having a relationship with so we could play with his kids, keeping us all occupied while they snuck off. One night over dinner, my dad asked what I did that day, so I told him the truth—not realizing its implications at the time." Tim paused, his jaw flexing. "She never forgave me for that. Said *I* ruined her marriage. Not that my dad divorced her or anything, but things were never the same between them. A day didn't go by when she didn't make some comment about what a terrible son I was. So, since she already thought I was a fuck-up, it made it easier to start hanging around with other fuck-ups. At least they didn't judge me for being myself." Tim shook his head. "That probably doesn't make a lot of sense."

"It does actually." Quinn's heart broke for him. Though she knew about his history with drugs, she hadn't known any of the specifics until he'd opened up to her about them. And even though Quinn's past wasn't nearly as difficult as Tim's, she found herself able to relate to the pressure he'd felt from his parents. "Not that my past is anywhere near as difficult as yours, but I was always afraid of that kind of judgment from my parents too. They have high expectations and have done so much for me. I'm always scared to let them down. Afraid to see disappointment on their faces that I would have caused. So I spent most of my life doing things with their happiness in mind. And it was sometimes at the expense of my own." Quinn thought about how strangely their lives paralleled each other's. That if either one had taken a different path at one time or another, they wouldn't be sitting there in some small-town motel together talking about things they'd never shared with anyone. And she was thankful for that. "That's kind of why we're here right now, I guess. Because we both made wrong choices that felt right at the time."

Tim shook his head slowly. "I'm not sure I even know how to explain the way I am now." He let out a soft laugh. "That's probably because I've never told anyone I was actually close to."

Quinn knew he'd probably had to share his past in rehab, but the last thing she wanted to do was make him uncomfortable now. She wanted to tell him he didn't have to talk about it—that he shouldn't reveal anything he'd rather not discuss. But she didn't. The truth was, she loved knowing Tim felt close to her, that the feelings she had for him were reciprocated.

His eyes met hers as he inhaled slowly, clearly trying to prepare himself for what he was about to say. "You already know why my addiction began. But I think it's important you understand why it ended." He sighed. "Seven years ago—the night before Thanksgiving— Scott called to see if I wanted to go to a movie with him. He was still in med school then and was home for break. I hadn't seen him in a while, so I told him I'd pick him up from our parents' house later. That summer had been my fourth time in rehab, and I was still clean in November. At least I was until my buddy Jeff called." Tim's eyes seemed to glaze over at the memory. "Since neither of us was welcome at our family's house, he had nowhere to go for Thanksgiving eve either and asked if I wanted to hang out. I knew it was a bad idea, but I did it anyway."

Quinn could see the regret written on Tim's face,

and she wished she could erase it, wipe clean all the memories that made him so sad.

"I went out with Jeff earlier in the afternoon," he continued, "and that was the end of my sobriety. It doesn't even matter what we did or how much." Tim closed his eyes and squeezed the inside corners with his thumb and index finger. "I couldn't tell Scott I was too high to pick him up. He would have been so disappointed in me. It was always about me and how things made *me* feel. Never about anyone else. I realize that now. Every decision I'd made was out of pure selfishness." Tim glanced up at Quinn, and his eyes seemed to search hers for something, though she wasn't sure what. "I picked Scott up at my parents' house, and fifty minutes later he was in the hospital with a concussion and a broken collarbone. There's no excuse for what I did. Scott was the only person who always had faith that I could turn my life around. Even our dad believed that I'd fucked up my future permanently. But not Scott. That night I almost killed the only person who believed in me." Tim swallowed hard and let out a long exhalation, as if he were physically letting go of something that had been weighing him down. They both stayed silent for a few moments before Tim spoke again. "I lost a lot of time by being such a fucking mess."

Quinn didn't want to make light of what Tim had just shared with her, but she needed him to see just how similar they really were. "And I lost a lot by being too together. But that's what this is: our chance to atone for the time we wasted." Quinn shrugged her shoulders, letting the veracity of her words wash over them.

"You said your fear was that you'll never be the man you're trying so hard to be," Quinn said as she felt their weighted conversation beginning to come to a close. "Not sure what it's worth"—she shrugged—"but I think you're already that man."

Tim didn't respond to Quinn's comment with words, but he didn't have to. His small smile was enough to let her know that what she thought of him meant something to Tim. And from a man who didn't seem to care about what the world thought of him, that smile meant a hell of a lot.

The two cleaned up their dinner, putting the leftovers in the fridge before Tim went to take a shower. Quinn used the time to channel surf, finally settling on *The 40-Year-Old Virgin*. Though she'd seen it a million times, she lost herself in the movie, appreciating the comedy after such a serious discussion. She felt her eyes starting to droop, but she became instantly alert at the sound of Tim's voice. "I love this movie," he said, plopping his large body down next to her on the bed.

Out of the corner of her eye, she could see a glimpse of him. *Great. He's shirtless.* The fact that she'd become accustomed to seeing his naked chest when they ran together did nothing to diminish its effect now. Lying next to a barely clothed Tim Jacobs and *keeping* him that way would be a struggle. Every part of her wanted to see what was underneath—no, *feel* what was underneath those black mesh shorts of his.

He stretched out, his long legs in front of him and his hands behind his head. "Is it okay if I watch TV up here?" he asked, a certain amount of caution evident in his voice. "I'd like to avoid putting my face near that carpet for as long as humanly possible."

"Yeah, I don't mind," Quinn answered, sounding a bit too excited at the prospect of sharing a bed with Tim for a little while longer.

"Thanks," he said, a goofy grin on his face as he focused on the TV. "You think this is real?" Tim asked suddenly, pointing at the screen. "I mean, not this story exactly. But do you think there are people out there who stay virgins for so long?"

Quinn didn't need to think about her answer. "Yeah, I can see how that would happen pretty easily actually. Especially for a girl. You go through high school thinking if you lose it to some random guy you'll be the talk of the school. So you wait until college. Then you decide you might as well wait until it's someone special so it'll mean something. You date somebody for a while and it doesn't work out, and before you know it you've graduated. Then you're like twenty-two and still haven't had sex. You start to get nervous about it, so you just don't do it. Then the cycle continues."

Tim was silent for a minute before replying. "Uh . . . I'm sorry," he stammered. "I didn't know . . ." He looked to Quinn as if he were expecting her to finish his sentence.

"Oh my God!" Quinn yelped. "You think I'm a virgin, don't you?" She was sitting up now, facing him.

Tim hesitated. "Well, I mean, I didn't think it. I never

really thought about it one way or the other until now. But you gave that long explanation . . . and it made a lot of sense, and . . . I don't know what I thought."

"It's not *my* explanation. Someone I work with did a story on this exact idea a few years ago. I've had sex, Tim." For some reason, it seemed important that he know this fact about her. "*Lots* of it, actually."

"*Lots* of it?" Tim raised an eyebrow so high Quinn thought it might actually meet his hairline.

Hearing Tim repeat her words made her realize their implication. "Well, not *lots* like with a lot of people. Just lots with two people. Who I was dating," she quickly added. "I mean, not dating at the same time. I don't cheat." She could hear how fast she was talking. "And I'm not into threesomes, if that's what you were thinking."

"That's definitely *not* what I was thinking."

Quinn brought her hands up to cover her face. "I should probably just stop talking."

"Probably," Tim agreed.

The two laughed until Quinn was able to calm down enough to relax again. "You mind if I turn out the light?" she asked. "The TV won't bother me, but I'm exhausted, and we have an early train ride back."

"If you want, we could rent a car instead," Tim said, smiling. "I'll pour some ketchup on the backseat and you can pretend I'm Clarabell. You know, old times' sake."

Quinn thought for a moment. "I'm not exactly sure I need to relive that again."

"Neither am I, actually." Tim laughed. "Get some rest, Quinn."

*   *   *

Shit. Tim had no idea when he'd fallen asleep, but the fact that he'd just woken up confirmed that it had happened at some point. It wasn't so much that he found himself asleep *next* to Quinn that scared him. It was the fact that their limbs had tangled around each other at some point during the night. And Quinn's ass was now firmly pressed against Tim's erection. He liked the feeling way too much. And not just sexually. He enjoyed the smell of Quinn's hair as it brushed against his face, the steady rhythm of her heart as it beat inside her chest, and how right it felt to wake up with Quinn asleep in his arms.

But it was so *wrong* too. So he gingerly slid his arms out from around her, removed his leg from its place between hers, and pulled himself away slowly.

He felt Quinn stir at the movement. But until she spoke, he didn't know he had woken her. "Stay" was all she said.

And it was all he needed to hear.

They woke up the next morning like they had in the middle of the night: each person's body twisted around the other's. Since Quinn had taken the day off, they'd slept in, eaten the leftover pizza, and driven home in their rented Ford Focus.

Tim had expected Quinn to mention her late-night request for him to remain in bed with her, or their entwined bodies when they awoke, but to his surprise, she didn't bring it up. She just reclined in her seat comfortably, looking out the window as the world rushed past them. He wondered if she was concealing any awkwardness she felt by feigning contentment. But Tim didn't think so. It was as if the physical light of day had shed light on something they had both been trying so hard to keep hidden in the dark: that they were different sides of the same coin, neither as valuable alone as they were together. But just because they knew it didn't mean they were going to do anything about it.

Chapter 11

Sidebar

Quinn willed her eyes to remain open as she attempted to focus on the computer screen in front of her. As she'd recently discovered, actually *writing* for a magazine required more work than just responding to readers' frivolous complaints. Of course, she hadn't been assigned anything major—other than the article Tim was helping her with. Just a quick piece on summer's latest fashion trends and beauty recommendations for transitioning effortlessly from the beach to a night out in less than fifteen minutes. She was thankful for the opportunity, nonetheless. It required a few shopping trips with the girls, a day of sun and salt water, and so much testing of various beauty products that she felt like she was more suited to be in a wire cage in a lab somewhere than in her apartment bathroom.

But Quinn loved every second of it. And as she reread her recommendations for various body wipes, dry shampoos, and lotions, all she could think was that though your face and hair might look fresh, until you showered, there was no getting sand out of—

Before she could finish her thought, her phone dinged on her desk with a text from Tim. What are your feelings on wings?

What the hell was he talking about? Wings? she wrote back. Like on a bird?

She saw him begin typing immediately, and a few seconds later his text came through. Well, yeah, I guess at one point they were on a bird. But the type I'm referring to are on a plate and covered in hot sauce. Do you like those?

Ohhhh . . . that makes more sense lol. Yes, I like them. She hit SEND but then wrote another text. Wait, why are we talking about wings? You're not gonna add an eating contest to my list or something, are you?

Not a contest, Tim wrote back. I was thinking more like two friends grabbing a bite to eat at Johnny B.'s. Have you been there? They have wings for 25 cents on Thursdays.

Nope. Never been. I know where it is though.
Is 7 ok? I just have to finish up a few things at work first.

See you at 7.

His reply was simple. No hidden meaning or cryptic implication. Still, Quinn couldn't help but think about how datelike the get-together felt. Sure, they went running together and had grabbed coffee a few times, but this felt different. More intentional. More formal. *Wings aren't formal! What the hell is wrong with me?*

As Quinn approached the bar, Tim grabbed the door for her. "Sorry," she said, not knowing how long he had been waiting outside for her.

"Why do women always do that?"

Quinn turned to glance over her shoulder at him. "Do what?"

"Say they're sorry." Quinn's eyebrows rose in curiosity, so Tim continued. "What are you even apologizing *for*?"

"I'm late."

"You weren't late. I was just early. And I don't mind waiting. You shouldn't be sorry for that."

Quinn pulled on her lower lip with her teeth.

Tim cocked his head to the side and gave her that look that told her he knew exactly what she was thinking. "You want to say it again, don't you?" he asked, giving her a wide grin.

She shrugged her shoulders and flashed a shy smile in return. "Kinda."

Fifteen minutes later they had two baskets of wings, two iced teas, and a large order of fries sitting on the table between them. Tim wiped his face with his napkin before speaking. "So how's the story going?"

"Uh . . . it's going."

"Well, *that* sounds promising." Tim laughed. "What does that mean exactly?"

Quinn took a sip of her drink and stirred it needlessly with the straw. "I haven't actually started thinking about what I plan to write. I kind of figured I'd wait until closer to the deadline."

"So it's working."

Quinn was sure her expression conveyed how confused she was.

"Our experiment," he explained. "It's working. The old Quinn would never think to wait until the last minute to begin something she could accomplish early."

The old *Quinn.* Was there really something noticeably different about her? Something that made her the *new* Quinn? In truth, she felt like she *had* been approaching life a little bit differently lately. Now her first instinct wasn't to shy away from the unfamiliar like she usually did, or let herself feel so pressured by things she couldn't control. She liked the change in herself. But it surprised her that the small change was obvious to others. Of course, maybe it was only obvious to *Tim.* They'd been spending so much time together, and he'd always seemed so tuned in to her. "Well, I mean, I have some ideas," she said, finally responding to his observation. "Just nothing concrete yet. I think it's better to wait until we get through the list before I really start analyzing the entire experience. You know?"

Tim nodded. "Speaking of the list . . ."

"That sounds ominous."

"Ominous, no. Intimidating, maybe." He scanned the bar. "I thought we could check one of the items off tonight."

"I'm hoping you're talking about asking a stranger out, because I draw the line at letting my bare skin touch one of these booths while people sketch me."

Quinn laughed to hide the small pang of disappointment she felt that Tim had mentioned crossing something off the list. She'd originally felt excited at the thought of having dinner with him. But that excitement had dissipated a bit.

"Yeah." Tim rubbed the scruff on his face with his hand. "I thought we'd save the nudity for another time."

Quinn felt the lump slide down her throat as she tried to swallow it.

"You up for the challenge?"

Quinn thought for a second as her eyes surveyed the crowd. She couldn't deny that many of the men there were good-looking. They were put together well, most of them in suit pants and a dress shirt. She imagined that they'd probably just left their high-rise offices to come to the bar for a few drinks with clients or coworkers. Most probably didn't have a family, let alone the time for one. Which in a way made it that much less threatening. If she could hitchhike with a stranger, she could certainly ask one out. "Who do you think I should pick?"

Tim raised an eyebrow and sat back in the booth. "I'm not sure I have much experience choosing men." He smirked. "Maybe *you* should take this one."

"Okay. I'll be back in a few minutes," she said, rising to smooth her lilac pencil skirt and white top.

Tim barely recognized the woman who moved gracefully through the crowd toward the bar. Well, *barely* might be an exaggeration. He'd recognize her long red hair from anywhere. And he'd pictured the perfect curves of her ass more times than he'd like to admit. What he *didn't* recognize was how comfortable she seemed tackling something that should have been, at the very least, slightly daunting to her. But the way she strolled casually up to the bar, shoulders back and arms loose at her sides, hinted at a sense of confidence he hadn't seen in her before. She was really something.

He watched her lean in to say something to the bartender and then turn toward the man next to her. Tim couldn't see the man's face from where he sat, but he didn't miss Quinn's bright smile as she seemed to thank him for the drink before bringing it to her lips. The two talked for a few minutes, and Tim did his best not to look like some creepy stalker as he watched them. He didn't like what he saw—the man's hand on Quinn's forearm for a moment or the way she moved in close, probably to repeat something she'd just said. But Tim had bought a ticket for the show, so to speak. So as much as he didn't want to watch, he didn't look away.

After about ten minutes, Quinn returned to the table, even more confident than when she had left. She slid into the booth and was silent for longer than he thought she should have been.

"Well?" Tim asked, though he was as interested to hear what had happened as he'd been to learn about covalent bonds in his sophomore chemistry class.

"Wellll . . ." Quinn answered, drawing out the word, "his name is Will, and we're going out Tuesday night."

"Tuesday? Who goes out on a Tuesday?" Tim's tone sounded harsher than he'd meant for it to sound. But he couldn't help it.

"Will and I do, apparently. And aren't you supposed to be happy? One more thing to do and the list is complete."

"Sorry," Tim said. When he'd asked her to meet him for dinner, Tim had wanted to do just that—have dinner with her. But her immediate mention of the list had drawn attention to the fact that they were together without any real reason to be. So Tim had felt the need to create one. And he was regretting that in a big way. "So where are you two going?"

"I don't even know the name of the place, actually. Some new Mediterranean place one of his clients invested in."

"Clients?"

"Yeah, he's in investor relations or something. I'm not even sure what that means."

"It means he's rich," Tim said quickly.

"Oh. Yeah, probably. I don't know." Quinn tucked her hair behind her ear. "I'm not really into corporate types. We'll see what happens, I guess."

Tim had no interest in seeing what happened. It's not like he was ever going to date Quinn himself, but that didn't mean he wanted her dating someone she didn't even like. "You know if you don't want to go out with him, it's okay. I mean, technically speaking, you met the requirement of asking a stranger out. It didn't say you actually had to *go* out with one."

"I don't want to be rude. *I* just asked *him* out, re-member? Besides, he seemed nice. And he was pretty funny. You never know. Maybe I'll like him."

Tim shrugged. "Yeah, maybe."

Quinn took a sip of her drink and spun the glass between her hands. "Can I ask you something? I've wondered it for a while actually, but it never seems like the right time to bring it up."

Tim felt his expression twist into curiosity. He didn't know what Quinn was about to ask, but whatever it was, he knew he'd answer honestly. "Anything."

"You're in recovery," she said simply, "but you go out to bars, you're around alcohol at parties. Most ex-addicts don't do that, do they?"

Tim shook his head. "No, they don't."

"So how can *you*? Don't you worry you'll relapse?" When Tim didn't respond right away, Quinn contin-ued. "Sorry, you don't have to answer that."

"Quinn, after everything we've talked about . . . there really isn't anything I wouldn't tell you." But no one had ever asked him that before. Other than Scott, of course. He rubbed his thumb over an indent in the wooden table as he spoke. "I could say I like the rebel-liousness of it . . . being around something I know I shouldn't be. But I'm not sure that's the truth. I think in my case it's easier this way. Alcohol's a trigger for me. It is for most people in recovery. That's why they stay away from it altogether." He drew in a long breath be-fore continuing. "I guess I just like knowing I have the willpower to leave it alone. Probably not the *smartest* way to go about it. But then again, I've never really been one to take the orthodox approach to anything."

"I think it actually makes a lot of sense. Like each time you resist a temptation, it gives you the strength to know you can resist it *again*."

It amazed Tim how well Quinn understood him. Sometimes better than he seemed to understand himself. "I never really thought of it like that before. That maybe it gets easier each time." He put his right hand over his heart. "You know the tattoo I have on the left side of my chest? The one that looks like the inside of my skin's ripping open and you can see my heart and muscles and everything?"

"Yeah. But I have to admit that one kind of grosses me out. I almost failed biology in high school because I refused to dissect anything."

Tim smiled, thinking of how alike they were. "Well, I got that tattoo after I'd been clean for a year." He could tell Quinn was as confused as he'd figured she'd be. "It comes from my favorite line of a Rudyard Kipling poem."

Quinn's eyebrows rose in obvious curiosity.

He didn't expect her to know the poem. Not many people did. But it had held a special meaning to him since the first time he'd read it as a freshman in high school. *"If you can force your heart and nerve and sinew to serve your turn long after they are gone, / And so hold on when there is nothing in you / Except the Will which says to them: 'Hold on!'"*

Quinn smiled. "I've never heard it before."

"The whole poem portrays the balance you should have in life. That's why I love it. But I especially like that particular line. It's what stops me from giving up on anything."

"That's really cool. And your tattoo grosses me out a little less now."

Tim shook his head as they both laughed together. "Then my work here is done."

Chapter 12

Lukewarm

Cass pushed up onto her elbows and wiggled her toes in the sand. "So tell us about this Willll," she said, drawing out his name for effect.

Quinn wasn't sure why she'd even brought Will up to the girls. She'd known that a thorough interrogation would commence immediately. But something inside her liked the idea of her friends getting excited about the date. Mainly because she was hoping some of that excitement would rub off on her. Though he was attractive and, from what she could tell, relatively interesting, Quinn couldn't seem to pump herself up for her night out with Will. "There isn't much to tell. At least not yet. I only talked to him for a few minutes."

"Well, you at least saw what he looked like. Give us the deets," Lauren prompted.

"Um, he's maybe just over six feet, dark hair. Just long enough to be a little wavy. He has glasses."

Quinn knew that would get Simone's attention. Glasses

had become her latest obsession. She had a few different pairs herself and insisted that they gave even mundane-looking men enough character to make them sexy. "Oooh, are they the trendy ones that give guys that obscenely hot look? I'm already picturing James Franco meets Clark Kent."

Quinn thought for a moment, trying to picture Will in her mind. "I mean, *I* think he's hot. Not sure if he's James Franco. He kind of has that smart, classic look to him. You can tell he has style. It'll definitely be a departure from the norm for me."

Lauren reapplied sunscreen to her face. "What about his body?"

Quinn glanced around at the girls. "Do you know how superficial we all sound right now?"

The girls stayed quiet for a moment, having a silent conversation. Finally Lauren spoke on everyone's behalf. "Yeah. I think we're good with it."

Quinn rolled her eyes, but she enjoyed chatting about a gorgeous guy as much as the next girl. "Well, I didn't get a chance to see how built he was or anything. He was in suit pants and a dress shirt. It's not like I asked him to undress at the bar. And besides, Tim was waiting for me at the table, so I wasn't overly concerned with Will's musculature." She scanned the beach until she found what she was looking for. "If I had to guess, he probably has a similar build to that guy over there." She pointed. "The one in the orange board shorts."

The girls craned their heads to see, then nodded their approval and gave their okays.

"Wait," Lauren said suddenly. "Tim was right there when you asked this guy out?"

"Yeah. Well, like ten feet away. I asked Will out at the bar, and Tim was at our table. Why?"

"But Will must have seen him when you went back to the table."

"I have no idea. What does it matter?" Quinn lifted her sunglasses onto her head as if that would make Lauren's questions easier to understand.

"Just thought it would look weird. That you were there with a guy when you asked out another."

Quinn hadn't thought of that. She wondered what Will thought about her hitting on him and then leaving to go sit down with some other guy. For all he knew, she was dating Tim too.

"Although, I guess Will must have known you and Tim aren't together," Lauren said, clearly rethinking her original stance on the issue. "I mean, could you imagine Tim Jacobs standing by while a woman he liked asked someone else out? Will probably just assumed Tim was your brother or something."

Quinn felt her face drop slightly at Lauren's words, but she did her best to mask it. "Yeah, probably."

Concern swept over the girls' faces. Clearly, Quinn was a poor actress. "What is it?" Simone asked. "I thought you'd be more excited. You're going out with a gorgeous guy in three days."

"Yeah," Cass said, "I thought after that last date disaster, you'd be dying to go out with someone who seems relatively normal."

Quinn perked up. "That's actually it. I guess I'm just nervous about this date being a waste of my time too. I mean, why go out with someone you don't like?"

"How do you know you don't like him? You said yourself you only talked to him for a few minutes."

Cass had a good point. She didn't or *shouldn't* know if she didn't like Will. She certainly liked the *idea* of dating someone like him—someone who wasn't exactly her type. He definitely wasn't the boy next door. He had a good job, probably more money than he knew what to do with, and just as many women vying for his attention. He seemed charming and intelligent. Quinn certainly wasn't used to men like him, and though she thought a change of pace might be exactly what she needed, she wasn't sure *Will* was exactly what she needed.

Dinner on Tuesday was at the aptly named Mediterranean Kitchen in Downtown D.C., which Quinn was thankful for because it meant she could decline an awkward car ride with Will and just meet him at the restaurant after work instead. There was something about getting into a car with someone you'd conversed with only sparingly that screamed "Danger, Will Robinson! Danger!"

Though, as Quinn climbed out of her car and handed her keys to the valet, she guessed she'd done even less reconnaissance on Clarabell. But that had been different. Tim had been with her then. And as had become customary recently, the moment Tim entered her thoughts, he infiltrated them completely. He'd been . . . "Avoiding" wasn't the right word, but he'd definitely been absent from Quinn's social calendar since the previous Thursday. She'd texted Saturday to see how he was but had received a short Swamped at work. I'll talk to you later. She hadn't heard from him again until a few hours before her date, when he'd sent her another brief message: Good luck tonight ;). It made Quinn feel like Seabiscuit gearing up for the big race.

She walked into the restaurant and let her eyes wander around the space. It was rustic, with elegantly simple wooden tables and steel chairs. One wall was covered in wood with a faux barn door as an accent piece. A granite bar sat on the opposite side of the room, with decorative wooden light fixtures. The owners had clearly spent a small fortune creating the homey environment that screamed rural Italy. Quinn was momentarily worried that she wouldn't recognize Will when she saw him, but that fear was assuaged when she noticed him at the bar. He spotted her as she wove through the closely situated tables, a bright smile lighting up his handsome face.

He stood when she reached him, murmuring a "Great to see you" as he embraced her casually.

Quinn returned the brief hug before replying, "You too. Have you been here long?"

"No, not too long. They don't take reservations, so I wanted to get here a little early to get a table. *Then* they tell me that they won't seat me until the rest of my party arrives." He rolled his eyes good-naturedly, a smile playing on his lips.

"Sorry" was on the tip of Quinn's tongue, but before

she uttered it, she remembered what Tim had told her. "Well, here I am," she said instead.

"Here you are indeed," Will said quietly, his eyes gazing softly into hers.

If life operated in accordance with romantic comedies, that look would have been a *moment* between the two of them. Quinn's mind would have flashed with visions of her future with Will: their cozy Cape Cod home filled with the laughter of their two-point-five children as they playfully chased the family's doting Labrador retriever around the two-acre plot their house was nestled upon. There would be Sunday brunches at the country club and yearly trips to Martha's Vineyard. Life would be just swell. Except Quinn didn't think any of those things. No, all she thought was how she wished it were a familiar pair of green eyes looking at her instead.

And that's when Quinn knew the date was over. She didn't leave, but her emotional bags were packed and waiting for her by the door. Because while Quinn hadn't had a moment at the bar with Will, she'd had quite a reckoning with herself. Even though she'd known she had feelings for Tim pretty much since she met him, she hadn't realized they were so strong that she'd completely check out on an eligible bachelor who was both attentive and interesting. Well, at least she *assumed* he was interesting. Despite her best efforts, she caught only about every third word he said all evening. And she didn't even feel particularly bad about it. *God, I really* have *changed.*

Quinn wanted Tim, not the investment whatever in front of her who probably made more a year than she'd make her entire career. It was why Quinn hadn't been excited about the date in the first place. Why she hadn't so much as thought about dating since she'd started this project with Tim. She had a fleeting thought about how Tim had ruined her for all other men, but that felt a tad too dramatic, even for Quinn. In the moment, though, it was the truth. She had no interest in Will, only superficial attraction, and no desire to see him again. It was the best night of her whole goddamn life.

It took Tim approximately ten minutes to realize he was pacing. Granted he was covering substantial ground, traversing every square foot of his apartment, but it still was what it was: fucking pacing. He hadn't been this restless since the first symptoms of withdrawal more than seven years ago. And he knew why: because he was fucking pathetic.

The feelings coursing through him were new, and Tim hated every last one of them. He didn't *pine* for women. He didn't rack his brain for excuses he could give if he staged a "coincidental" run-in. He didn't *need* people like he needed his next goddamn breath.

And that's the thought that finally stopped his feet from moving. Of course Tim realized that he did rely on people to be there for him: Scott, Roger, the boys. But did he *need* them? The answer shocked him. No, he didn't. He wanted them in his life for sure, but he'd come far enough in his struggles to know that he'd be okay without them. He'd get by. But Quinn? His fucking chest constricted just thinking about not having her around. She made him happy, made him better, made him somebody.

But what she didn't make him was worthy. It wasn't the first time he'd forced himself to swallow that bitter pill, and it wouldn't be the last.

Tim had accepted that truth. He'd had to in order to remain sober. He wasn't special; he wasn't extraordinary. And he'd learned to be okay with that. But Quinn *was* those things. He couldn't let her settle for anything less than spectacular. So if that meant that he had to set her up with preppy investors, then that's what he'd do. Even if it fucking killed him.

Finally forcing himself to sit on the couch and stare at the TV, Tim started to relax. Or at least settle himself down from the frenzy. This could be his role in Quinn's life: to point her in the right direction, toward a guy who would be good for her. It would be something he could be proud of, a single good deed that might possibly right some of his wrongs. Yeah, he could do that. A gentle calm washed over him as he accepted his fate.

Until his phone dinged with an incoming text. Thank God that's over. Hope your night was better than mine.

Tim was trying to keep his mind from focusing on the fact that it was nearly impossible to have dinner and get laid by eight forty-five when his phone sounded with another message.

And stop being a crotchety old man and call me sometime :)

With a resigned sigh tinged with a flurry of relief, Tim typed in the number that he'd, at some point, needlessly come to know by heart. And when he heard the greeting from the familiar voice, he settled into the couch. "Tell me all about it."

Chapter 13

Deglaze

Quinn hadn't heard Tim's voice in days, and until the deep, gravelly sound vibrated her eardrum, she hadn't realized how much she'd missed it.

"Will's nice enough. And funny." *At least when I was paying attention.*

"So why don't you like him?"

He's not you. The words almost rolled off Quinn's tongue as easily as they'd popped into her head, but luckily she had the restraint to keep them in her mind where they belonged. If Tim was interested in how her date had gone, then he probably wasn't interested in *her.* "I don't know. You know when you just have an instant connection with someone? Like you look at them and you don't care if they're the only person you ever see for the rest of your life?"

Tim cleared his throat. "I think so."

"Well, I don't have that with *Will.*" She heard herself emphasize his name unintentionally, and she waited to see if Tim would ask her who she did have that with. In an instant, she pictured their conversation playing out like a scene from one of those TV shows where all the characters' problems were neatly wrapped up in one half-hour episode. *Cue the corny music while Tim and I profess our undying love for each other.*

"That's a shame," Tim said after what seemed like way too long for such a generic response.

Quinn was thankful they were on the phone so she didn't have to hide the disappointment that was surely written on her face. "Yeah, it is."

Despite the fact that, after their conversation, Quinn initially felt some tension between them—though she had a feeling much of it was sexual—things with Tim progressed much as they always had for the next week or so: running, a bite to eat here or there, random texts, and the occasional phone call. And she was thankful for the comfort it provided. If she couldn't have Tim the way she wanted, she was happy to keep him as a friend. It was . . . normal.

But what wasn't normal was the fact that Tim hadn't mentioned the last task on the list. She wasn't sure if he was actively avoiding discussing posing nude or if he just hadn't thought to bring it up. In either case, letting such a terrifying experience loom over her indefinitely had the same effect as standing at the edge of an airplane door ten thousand feet in the air wondering if her parachute was going to open. Eventually she'd just have to jump or somebody was going to push her. And she knew that Tim would be there to push her eventually.

"So listen," Quinn said in between breaths as they jogged past an outdoor café. "I went on Craigslist the other day and found someone who's looking for nude models for an art class he teaches on Wednesdays."

Tim's gaze shot toward her. "I'm impressed. I figured that one would take far more convincing. But Craigslist? Really?"

Quinn rolled her eyes and laughed. "It's legit. I went by his studio the other day and talked to him about it. He was finishing up a class when I got there."

"We'll see," he said, extending the last word as if he wasn't a hundred percent sold. "It's a good thing I have off on Wednesdays so I can be sure this doesn't involve fishing line, roofies, and you locked in some old dude's basement."

"It *is* a good thing you have off on Wednesdays," Quinn replied, trying like hell to contain the sly grin she felt surfacing, "because you'll be locked in the basement *with* me. I signed you up too." Before Tim could speak, Quinn sprinted ahead of him, turning around in time to catch his jaw nearly hitting the sidewalk as he slowed to almost a complete stop. "Come on. You'd better pick up the pace a little if you're going to call *other* people old."

Tim spent the next few days mentally preparing himself for his debut, so to speak. It's not that he was shy. Far from it. It's just that when he'd imagined Quinn posing nude for an audience, Tim thought he'd be part of that audience, not part of the show. His feelings alternated between excitement and complete anxiety. On the one hand, he'd get to see Quinn without any clothes on—something he'd thought about more times than he'd like to admit. But unlike in his fantasies, this experience would be entirely different. How was he supposed to sit there only a few feet from Quinn's naked body and *not* get turned on?

This would take an incredible amount of self-control. And though his past had given him plenty of practice with that virtue, something told him that his vices would ultimately win this battle. His only hope was that she would be so concerned with her own nudity that she wouldn't notice his. *Yeah fucking right.*

Wednesday afternoon came quicker than Tim did when he jerked off for the third time that day. He'd tried not getting hard when he pictured Quinn naked— an impossible feat. There weren't enough cold showers in the world to keep his cock from jumping at even the slightest thought of Quinn's soft skin and . . . *Fuck!* He figured he'd go with the *There's Something About Mary* method and hope for the best. Maybe "cleaning the pipes" a few times would lessen the chance of him sporting wood like a horny teenager.

But as he stepped out of his apartment to leave for the art studio, the only thing he could take comfort in was the fact that he was certain he didn't have any of his own semen in his hair. He'd checked four times.

As Tim wandered through the large industrial space, taking note of the vivid watercolors and black-and-gray sketches, he had to admit it was a real art studio. *Damn.*

"Back here," someone yelled in a thick Irish accent. Tim had no idea how the guy even knew he had entered. There were no bells on the door or anything. A dark-haired man emerged from behind a large drop cloth that was hanging on a clothesline to dry. He couldn't have been older than thirty.

Tim laughed to himself. If one of them was the old man, it was definitely Tim.

"I'm Niall," the man said, extending his hand. "You must be our male model for tonight."

"I must be," Tim said. "What gave it away?"

"Your tattoos and apprehension," he joked. "Quinn told me a little about you."

"Yeah, uh . . . I've never . . . *We've* never done anything like this before." Tim glanced around, trying to see past the easels Niall was preparing with drawing paper and pencils. "Is Quinn here?"

"Down the hall to the left," he said, nodding his head toward the back hallway. "There's a robe hanging for you in the bathroom where you can get undressed."

Tim hesitated a moment. "Okay. Thanks."

"Don't worry, buddy. With that beautiful redhead back there, I don't think you have to worry about too many people looking at *you*." Then Niall winked and moved toward the front of the studio, leaving Tim to go back to the room where that beautiful redhead waited in nothing but a robe. And the prospect that everyone would be looking at Quinn's naked body and not his own did nothing to ease his nerves. *Fuck.* The thought of all of that exposed skin so close to him, near enough that he could run his hands all over her body, feel the goose bumps that would spread over her, made his cock start to harden as he entered the bathroom to put on his robe. Images of other things they could do nude, with or without an audience, were enough to force him to firmly grasp the base of his shaft and hope that he could get himself under control before he actually saw Quinn. He exited the bathroom, grateful for the seclusion the hallway provided as he stood before the closed door that separated him from Quinn. A few deep breaths later and he had managed to quell his rising hard-on. *I can do this.*

As Quinn sat on the sofa in the small office of Niall's studio, she was surprised at how relaxed she felt. She no longer worried about people staring at her. She had accepted that fact weeks ago. It was the also-naked nonstranger who would be in the room with her that caused goose bumps to cover her skin at the thought.

At the time, it had seemed like a better idea to have Tim pose with her. She wouldn't be as "on display" as she would have felt if he were in the audience. Until today, it hadn't really sunken in that she'd have to see *Tim* with no clothes on. But there was no turning back.

Especially since Tim had just entered, the light hairs on his colorful chest peeking out from under his robe. They exchanged awkward I'm-about-to-see-you-naked hellos and were silent for a few moments before Tim spoke again. "This'll be easy."

Quinn lifted her eyebrows. "Are you telling me or yourself?"

Tim laughed gently. "Uh, probably a little of both."

Quinn exhaled a deep breath. "At least it's not just me." Though she had been relatively calm, seeing Tim with only one loose layer of clothing on brought a surge of adrenaline through her entire body. "I'm starting to freak out a little."

"Well, you could've fooled me. You hide your feelings well."

"Yeah," Quinn said softly, thinking Tim had no idea just how right he was.

A while later, Niall knocked and said the artists were ready for them. They stood, Quinn smoothing her robe and adjusting the belt.

The corner of Tim's lip quirked up playfully. "You know that thing's coming off in a few minutes anyway, right?"

"Oh yeah," she said, shaking her head. The nerves she hadn't felt earlier at the prospect of people seeing her naked now hit with full force as she walked down the hall.

Niall escorted Tim and Quinn past the students, ushering them toward a chair and small black couch at the front of the room. When Niall had discussed the details with her, he'd said that he would like four poses between the two of them: standing, sitting, semi-reclining, and prone. He'd said it was up to her and Tim to decide who would be responsible for what. However, though she'd notified Tim of the requirements, the two had never actually discussed the specifics of who would do which pose. And now they stood, about to disrobe in front of close to ten people, with no idea what to do next.

"Um, I can stand," Tim whispered in Quinn's ear, probably knowing that that position would be the most exposed. "Which one would you like to do first?"

Quinn looked at the firm black couch behind her. "I'll sit down, I guess."

When neither of them moved to undress, Niall prompted them from the side of the room. "Whenever the two of you are ready."

"Right," Tim said, as he brought his hands toward the belt of his white robe.

Quinn was momentarily frozen as her eyes fixated on his long fingers pulling at the knot until the robe hung slightly open. Then he carefully shrugged it off his shoulders and tossed it on the coatrack nearby.

Niall nodded toward Quinn, urging her to do the same. *It's now or never*, she thought to herself. Though the latter definitely seemed like the better option.

"You sure you're okay to do this?" Tim asked as he moved to face her.

Quinn nodded, but she stayed stock-still. Though she was certain she *wanted* to do this, she wasn't certain that she *could*. As if he could read her mind, Tim reached for her belt, tugging on it gently as he pulled the knot loose. Neither one took their eyes off the other's as Tim opened her robe enough to slide the fabric down her shoulders, dragging his thumbs down her skin softly. This time he let the garment fall to the floor, leaving his firm hands lightly grasping Quinn's biceps. He gave her a nod—one that felt full of pride and encouragement—and moved toward her side, gesturing to the sofa for her to have a seat.

Quinn followed his silent direction, suddenly no longer fearful or embarrassed. The two of them had jumped out of the metaphorical plane and were falling through the sky in tandem. Tim moved to stand to the side, a few feet in front of the couch. And this time, Quinn couldn't help but let her gaze wander as it followed the movement of his body—his strong legs and the taut muscles of his ass carrying him a few feet away from her.

She wiggled briefly on the cushions until she found a comfortable position and then let herself relax against the back and armrest. Crossing her legs, she brought her hand up to her chin and let her index finger drape over her bottom lip as she studied Tim's solid form.

Tim turned his head and looked over his shoulder just enough to catch Quinn's gaze as she brought it up to meet his.

"Perfect," Niall said. "Don't move a muscle."

And they didn't. There they stayed for several minutes, their bodies locked in place and their eyes boring into each other's. In that moment, Quinn felt it: the physical attraction, the connection, the intimacy that had always been present between them. All of it was undeniable now.

At least to her.

Chapter 14

Blanch

Things with Tim were weird because of how *not* weird they were. The guy had seen her naked, for Christ's sake, and Tim was playing it off with a nonchalance that would've rivaled a priest hearing confession. And quite frankly, Quinn had had enough.

Being sketched had meant something to her. Having Tim present during it had meant even more, and she was done pretending that it hadn't. Quinn wasn't much of a take-the-bull-by-the-horns kind of girl, but since her heavily tattooed, reformed bad-boy accomplice clearly wasn't going to bring up the proverbial elephant in the room, she'd have to. *What's the worst that can happen?*

Quinn immediately wished she could retract that thought, but the damage was done. Doubt began to creep in as she really considered what the worst would be: him being horrified at the thought of dating her, him laughing at the absurdity, him deciding that they shouldn't hang out anymore.

The mere thought of losing Tim was enough to make tears form in Quinn's eyes. Was it wise to risk losing the best thing in her life? Quinn let her hand rest on the keys she'd just put in her ignition as she contemplated an answer. And finally, she had one. An incontestable one.

Yes, it's worth it.

She quickly grabbed her cell phone and typed out a text to Tim. You busy tomorrow night? I wanted to talk to you about something.

His reply, as usual, was almost immediate: Oh boy. Sounds like I'm in trouble. But sure. You wanna come to my place? I'll cook us dinner. How's 6:30?

Quinn paused briefly before starting her car, wondering if it was smart to have their discussion in a place he could so easily throw her out of, but she quickly determined that it ultimately didn't matter. Sounds perfect.

Cutting vegetables normally soothed Tim. There was nothing like chopping the shit out of something to settle his nerves. But it wasn't working. He was hacking at the carrots and lettuce like they had gravely offended him, and he didn't feel a damn bit of relief at exacting his revenge. He dumped the veggies into a mixing bowl and started cutting the apples to add to the salad.

What the hell was I thinking inviting her to my apartment? It wasn't that Quinn had never been to his place, but she sure as hell hadn't been there since he'd seen her naked. Since he'd become able to meld his fantasies with the reality of Quinn's flawless body. How the fuck was he going to keep himself from throwing their dinner off his dining room table and feasting on Quinn instead? His dick perked up as he thought about the soft curves of her breasts and her smooth skin, and he quickly glanced at the clock on his oven, wondering if he had time for a cold shower before she arrived. It was six twenty-three. *Definitely not enough time.* And the rap on the door only served to confirm it.

Tim took a deep breath before walking over to the door and pulling it open. He barely contained his groan of frustration. How was he supposed to resist her if she insisted on wearing cute little yellow summer dresses? Her hair was an unruly mass of curls, framing her sun-kissed face. *I'm totally screwed.*

It took Tim a few seconds to realize that he was silently staring at her. She narrowed her eyes slightly, suddenly looking wary. "You okay?"

He shook his head and stepped back from the doorway so she could enter. "Yeah, yeah, sorry. I was, uh, just thinking that I may have forgotten an ingredient for dinner."

"Oh." Tim saw her smile falter as her eyes drifted briefly toward the floor, but he didn't have time to analyze it. "You need me to run out and grab something?"

"No, no, it's fine. I can work around it." *Stop saying things twice, asshole.* Tim closed the door and walked back to the kitchen, Quinn close behind him. He resumed his post at the counter, continuing to prep for dinner.

"What are we having?" Quinn asked as she stood closely beside him, turning her body so that she pressed gently against his arm.

Tim's eyes rolled around in his head at the feeling of her firm breasts pushed against him. *I'm going to lose my fucking mind tonight.* "Lasagna. That okay?"

She pulled back, and he instantly missed her. "Sounds good. I love lasagna."

"Good," he replied. "I picked up some sparkling water. Want some?"

"Absolutely."

Tim wiped his hands on a dish towel and walked over to the cabinet to retrieve two glasses. He handed Quinn one after pouring her some water. He watched her bring the glass to her rosy lips, then part them slightly as she allowed the liquid to slide over them. When she swallowed, his knees nearly buckled. His eyes darted up to hers, and he realized that she'd caught him watching her. It was sexy as hell yet scary as fuck. Clearing his throat, he asked, "Good?"

"Delicious."

Her response was seductively low, and Tim had to turn away from her in order to keep himself from grabbing her by the back of the neck and pulling her to him. "So, you wanted to talk to me?" *Please be about something innocuous. Like laundry or puppies.*

Quinn stayed standing behind him, not touching but still close. He heard her put her glass down on the counter. "Yeah, I did. Will called me."

So much for laundry and puppies. Tim felt himself tense and tried to force himself to relax. "Oh yeah?"

"He wants to go out again."

Tim was in serious danger of snapping the handle of the knife he was holding. It was one thing to know he couldn't have Quinn, but it was quite another to know he'd basically pushed her toward someone else. And she expected him to, what? *Encourage* her to date guys she wasn't interested in, when it drove him crazy to even see her talk to someone else? It didn't matter to him that Quinn would have no way of knowing how he felt. He knew he wasn't being particularly rational. What he was was angry. Angry at her for asking him to rip his own heart out. It didn't matter that Will was probably better for her. It didn't matter that Tim refused to throw his own hat in the ring for her. He'd be damned if he'd sit around and help some other asshole get the only thing he'd ever truly let himself want. Tim felt himself unraveling and he couldn't stop it. The prospect of another man getting close to her, touching her, being touched *by* her made him feel murderous. Tim closed his eyes and begged his body to get back under control. He couldn't let Quinn see the emotions that were warring within him. She'd run from him screaming, and he wouldn't blame her for an instant. So he managed to talk himself down enough to reply. "I thought you didn't like him."

"I don't. So I'm thinking maybe I should broaden my horizons. I mean, isn't that what this whole thing is all about? Stepping out of my comfort zone, being assertive, going after what I want . . . what feels right."

Her words cut through the haze he found himself in, though she sounded far away, like his ears weren't able to clearly interpret her words while his brain was gearing up to implode.

And now he was even more angry at her, but for a

very different reason. "You're going to become one of those girls who bounces from guy to guy until they find what they're looking for? Sounds like a great plan." Tim couldn't have kept the sarcasm from his voice if he'd tried, which he didn't. His words were cold and mean, but that was how he was feeling, and he had no idea how to mask it.

But if his remarks fazed Quinn, she didn't show it. "I didn't say anything about going after more than one guy. Quite the opposite, actually. I've had my eye on one in particular."

She let those words hang there, gave them time to seep into Tim and fill him. Finally, she spoke again. "So what do you think?"

"About what?" Tim's voice was rough, raspy.

"About going after the guy I want. You think I should?" She stepped toward him, her body lightly touching his.

Her voice was soft, almost pleading. He closed his eyes, but he still saw her question for what it was. *She's opening the door for you. Now you just need to decide if you can walk through it.* Tim had faced a lot of crossroads in his life, and he wasn't going to bullshit himself by saying that his choice with Quinn was the hardest or the most important, but goddamn, it felt that way. The choices he'd made in the past had all been largely because of other people: He'd started using drugs to not feel the pain of letting down his mother; he'd gotten clean so that he could have a healthy relationship with his brother; he'd gotten his life together so the people he cared about wouldn't be embarrassed by him. But the choice he faced in that kitchen was all about him.

Did he want to be happy even though it might not last, or did he want to be lonely but at least find some solace in the fact that Quinn would probably be better off without him? She was giving the decision to him. And he found it grossly unfair. He ground his teeth together before finally forcing his mouth to open. "Yes."

She pressed into him a little more. "Why?"

He set the knife down and turned toward her. "I think you know why."

"I need to hear it." Her blue eyes were wide and hopeful as they searched his.

"Because I want you too. Because I feel good about myself when you're around. Because I'm a selfish bastard who's not good enough for you, but I can't walk away from you either. And the thought of someone else putting his hands on *my* girl is enough to make me want to break everything in this apartment."

Tim knew his face was probably wild and intense, and he couldn't for the life of him figure out how Quinn could be looking at him with a smirk.

But that was exactly what she did. "Your girl, huh?" She let her hands drift over his chest and wrap around his neck.

Tim let his own hands find her hips and slide around her back, drawing her more tightly to him. "Is that the only part you heard?"

"No, but it's definitely the part I'd like to focus on right now." And then she lifted up onto her tiptoes as she applied pressure to his neck, pulling him to her. "That okay with you?" she said against his lips.

But she didn't give him time to answer. Her kiss was

soft, sweet, and soothing. For about three seconds. Then all of the heat and passion that they had both allowed to simmer just below the surface burst forth, and the kiss became downright carnal. And as their hands began to roam wildly over each other and they clutched at each other in an attempt to get closer, Quinn asked, "What about dinner?"

"Fuck dinner," Tim murmured as he sucked on the soft skin of her neck.

Quinn giggled breathily. "A man of few words. I like it."

"I like you," he countered.

"I like you too." She started to walk backward out of the kitchen. "You coming?" Quinn sauntered out of his kitchen and toward Tim's bedroom, and any remaining pretenses that he could walk away from her evaporated. He was a rogue planet who needed her gravity to keep him in orbit. And as he followed her into his room, he wanted nothing more.

Chapter 15

Boil

Quinn had been feeling pretty damn full of herself in the kitchen. But once she got into the bedroom and kicked off her sandals, she faltered for a second, chewing on her bottom lip as she looked at his large masculine bed: dark wood with a dark slate comforter. It was so *not* comforting. *I'm about to have sex with Tim. On a bed that screams Christian Grey, if for no other reason than because it's gray.* Quinn was spiraling into a nonsensical state of self-deficiency. Tim was nearly eight years older than she was—a seasoned pro compared to her. What if she didn't live up to his other experiences? What if he wasn't into it? What if . . . ?

"Whatever you're thinking about right now, stop it. Unless it's that you don't want to do this, in which case we'll go back out there and have dinner." Tim came up behind her and brought his hands up to her shoulders, sweeping her hair over one in the process so he could place gentle kisses on the back of her neck.

Quinn immediately relaxed into his touch. This was Tim. He'd opened a whole new world for her without ever once making her feel inadequate. She'd been a fool to think he ever would. "I definitely do *not* want dinner."

"Then tell me what you do want." His lips ghosted over her skin as he spoke.

"I—I want . . ." *God, how am I supposed to think when he's kissing me like that?* She forced her mind to work through the sexual fog he was blanketing her in. "I want to be with you. In every way two people can be together. But I think—no, I know that I want you to lead. Show me what you like. Show me how good it can be." It wasn't that Quinn hadn't had good sex before. She had, by her standards. But she was also convinced that sex with Tim would blow any previous encounter right out of the fucking water. She wasn't interested in timid first times. She wanted epic right off the bat. And Quinn knew Tim would deliver.

"Every way, huh? That almost sounds like a challenge."

"It is. You think you're up for it?"

At that, Tim ground his erection against her ass. An erotic moan left her as he said, "Oh, I'm up for it." He let her feel his hard-on through the denim of his jeans for only a moment longer before he pulled away, walked around her, and flopped down onto his side on the bed. "Strip for me, Quinn."

Quinn felt her face heat as she looked down at herself.

"Hey." Tim's voice was soft as it drew her attention

back to him. "I have been reliving your nude modeling for the past week. But see, that's a memory I have to share with all those other people. Not this time. This time is just for me."

His words emboldened her. It was just for him—it had been just for him then too, if she were being honest with herself. His were the only eyes she had cared about in that entire room. But in his apartment, with just the two of them, it was different. She couldn't claim that it was for the article, or about finding herself. In Tim's room, with only the soft pallor of the descending sun illuminating them, she was fucking found. So she reached under her arm and drew down the zipper that was hiding there, letting the dress fall to her feet. Her white satin bra fell next. And finally, with her eyes trained on Tim the entire time, she lowered her matching thong. Quinn stood before him, summoning a confidence she knew had been hiding in her somewhere, and watched as his eyes raked over her body. His gaze was all lust and need. And something else . . . reverence maybe? Like he had every intention of worshipping her body as though it were a temple. The thought made her stand up even straighter.

Tim rubbed his cock through his pants as he took in the sight of her. But just before she felt the slightest tinge of self-consciousness, he stood and walked back toward her. His hands came and cupped her jaw. "You're perfect," he whispered right before he pulled her lips to his. The kiss was intense as they spilled all of their wants into it.

Quinn basked in the feeling of Tim's tongue against

hers, his piercing turning her on even more than she already was. *He got that for me. And now I get to be the one who enjoys it.* Her hands skated down his chest to his stomach, where she yanked his shirt up and slid her hands beneath it. Her fingers adored his runner's body, the ridges of his hardened abdominals. He broke away from her lips long enough to pull the shirt over his head, and she took full advantage, moving up to feel his slender but muscular chest. Finally, when she felt like she was being a cocktease to herself, her hands landed on his belt, quickly unfastening it and pushing it out of the way so she could pop the button on his jeans and drag the zipper down.

He thrust his tongue harder, more passionately into her mouth as she pushed the pants and boxers off his narrow hips, letting gravity take care of the rest. She looked down at the cock she'd dreamed about since she'd first met him. It was long, not so thick that she thought it would hurt, but just enough that she knew she'd feel every ridge as it slid into her.

"Touch me, Quinn." His command was firm, yet the harshness of his breathing made it almost a plea.

And since she wanted nothing more, she enveloped the silky steel with her hand and caressed it from root to tip, trying to memorize it as if it were braille and could tell her all of life's secrets. Tim let out a harsh groan, and Quinn reveled in the fact that she was the cause of it.

"I've wanted you since the first time I ever laid eyes on you." Tim's tongue skated over every bit of skin he could reach as he spoke. "You touching me . . . it's making me lose what little control I had to start with. I want our first time to be slow, special, but I don't know if I can do that."

"We've taken it slow for long enough. You say you want me. Show me."

And with that, Tim's hands flew to her thighs and lifted her into the air. Though surprised, she immediately wrapped her legs around him, letting his cock nestle against the area she needed him the most.

He kept her suspended for a few seconds, allowing her to grind against him like the wanton woman it felt so good to be. Then he sank a knee onto the bed and held her tightly as they crashed the rest of the way down onto it. He kissed her deeply, dirtily, as he allowed his straining cock to slide against her clit, his precome mixing with her own wetness. The attention he lavished upon that throbbing part of her anatomy was mind-blowing. And he gave no inclination that he intended to stop anytime soon.

Quinn moaned loudly into his mouth. She clutched at his back with her fingernails as her body started to tense in preparation for her impending orgasm.

"Mmm," he breathed against her neck. "Mark me, Quinn. I want to wear the proof of what I did to you for days. I want to look at my back and know that I made you come so hard, you had to hold on for dear life."

And that was it. There was no way she could hold off an orgasm with him talking like that. So she gave herself over to it. Let him feel the rippling nerves of her body as they radiated pleasure while she clawed at his back.

"I can't wait to be inside of you. To feel you milk me as I make you come again."

"What the hell are you waiting for?" Quinn asked breathlessly as she came down from her release. Well, as much as she could come down, considering he was still gyrating against her.

"Fuck if I know." And with that, he leaned over her slightly so he could reach the bedside table. He searched for a few beats before finally withdrawing from the drawer with a condom. He ripped the foil package open and rolled the condom onto himself.

Then he ran his hands down Quinn's bent legs until he reached her apex. He pushed a finger inside her, causing her to arch off the bed in bliss. But he didn't finger her long, instead bringing the digit up to his mouth and licking her arousal off of it. "You're so wet for me, Quinn. So ready."

Quinn could barely manage a nod by that point. Though if he didn't get inside of her soon, she knew she'd be able to scrounge up enough courage to flip their positions and take what she so desperately needed.

But he didn't make her wait any longer. He positioned his cock at her entrance, and after a brief meeting of their eyes, pushed into her to the hilt, making her moan out in euphoria.

Tim fell forward, his hands landing on either side of her head as he thrust into her. "I can't . . . Fuck, Quinn, I can't go slow. It's too good. You feel too goddamn good."

She slid a hand behind his neck and pulled him

toward her. "I already told you—I don't want slow." Then she pulled him into a hard kiss. He seemed to get the message, because he let go, pistoning his hips against her, driving his swollen cock deeper than she thought possible. It was everything she'd hoped it would be and more. She began to feel the tingling sensation of an imminent orgasm again, and she beckoned it, craving the release like it would take away every care she had in the world. Hell, maybe it would.

Tim's rhythm became erratic as Quinn surmised he was also nearing the finish line. She looked up at him. And though most of her attention was focused elsewhere, she couldn't help but notice how beautiful he was. Even though she was sure he'd prefer a term like "ruggedly handsome," there was no mistaking it. Tim Jacobs *was* beautiful. Inside and out.

As if he could hear her thoughts, his eyes drifted from where he entered her up to meet her gaze. And in that moment, Quinn knew the truth: Tim was a complete game changer. Things would never, ever be the same. She would forever be chasing that moment, and he would be the only one who would ever be able to give it to her.

That was the realization that took her over the edge the second time. And she did just as he asked, tightening around his cock as he pumped into her, chasing his own release. He stilled as he caught it, bellowing out an elongated "Fuuuuck." Then he collapsed onto his elbows, still keeping the majority of his weight off of her, but pressing her into the mattress just enough for her to feel the warmth of him. He buried his face in her neck as they tried to catch their breaths. Once their chests were rising and falling in a more normal pattern, Tim pushed up a little and looked down at her breasts. "Damn, I didn't even get to play with these," he lamented as he pressed a chaste kiss to one.

Quinn smiled. "There's always tomorrow."

Tim smiled back, but there was a wariness to it. In that look, she was able to see the boy he'd once been. "Does that mean you're staying?"

She wrapped her arms around his neck. "Unless you want me to leave."

He huffed out a small laugh. "I hate when you leave." And, as if it was too much to admit and maintain eye contact, he lowered his lips to hers and captured them in a sweet kiss that lingered longer than such a gentle one normally would. Not that either of them was complaining. "I'll be right back," he murmured before getting up and heading out of the room, she assumed to go to the bathroom. He was back a couple minutes later, crawling into bed beside her, tucking his arm underneath her so she could rest her head on his chest. "It's still pretty early. You want me to finish dinner?"

"Hmm. That would mean we'd have to get out of bed, wouldn't it?"

He pulled her closer to him. "Unfortunately, yes."

She let out a dramatic sigh. "I'm just not sure I can agree to anything that involves you putting clothes on."

"I said we'd have to get out of bed. I said nothing about putting clothes back on. In fact, I may never let you wear clothes again."

"That would cause quite a stir at the office."

They both laughed, and then Tim gave a light slap to the side of her ass cheek. "Come on, get up and let me feed you. You're going to need your energy for what I have planned."

"Oh really? And just what would that be?"

Tim simply shrugged as he pulled Quinn up from the bed. "I show better than I tell."

Quinn had no doubt his words were the utter truth.

Tim woke up the next morning with a familiar warm, slender body entangled with his. He momentarily thought he'd died and gone to heaven. He even repressed the urge to pinch himself, mostly because he was afraid he'd wake Quinn. And as she snuggled tightly into his side, resting her head on his shoulder, the last thing he wanted was for her to wake up. It was one of those moments he wished he could freeze and live in for a while. He'd had so few perfect moments in his life; he wanted to savor it.

So he stayed put, allowing his mind to relive the previous night. He had been worried that sex would make their relationship awkward, but as they'd sat at his dining room table eating salad and lasagna, they'd conversed as they always had. Well, maybe with a little additional flirting. And afterward, once Tim had made good on his promise for a round of show-and-tell, they'd curled up together like they'd been sleeping that way for years. *Maybe I am dead.*

As he lay beside Quinn, he developed big plans for breakfast, and he needed to get started before she'd have to leave so she could get ready for work. So eventually Tim decided that he should get up.

He kept the banging around to a minimum as he flew around his kitchen. He'd hoped to surprise Quinn in bed, but just as he was transferring the bacon to a plate, he saw her.

Je-sus Christ. If I'm not dead, she'll kill me soon enough. Quinn was in the doorway of the kitchen, one hip resting against the wall, wearing nothing but the sheet from his bed. He knew he was staring at her—like creepy, obsessed, stalker staring—but he couldn't help it. There were simply no words.

"Whatcha making, chef?"

Making? What is she . . . Oh, the food! "Breakfast."

Quinn's face contorted slightly as she tried, and failed, to suppress a smile. "Well, I can see that. Anything specific?"

Tim blinked hard and refocused himself. *This is Quinn. A woman you have spent countless hours with during the past month. Stop acting like a middle schooler who just landed his first girlfriend.* "You'll see," he replied casually as he resumed cooking.

"Need any help?"

"Nope. I'm good."

"Definitely wasn't debating that."

The seductive lilt in her voice made him turn. "Get over here."

She rushed toward him, their arms twining around each other as they pulled each other into a passionate kiss. And it likely would have become more if Tim hadn't smelled his French toast burning. "You're making me ruin breakfast," he murmured against her lips.

"Who cares? This is already the best meal I've ever had." But she released him anyway. Quinn took a quick look around at the food occupying the counters as he removed the toast from the griddle. She let out a delighted laugh. "Stop. You did *not* remember me telling you about all of this."

But he had remembered. He remembered everything that had to do with Quinn. All around them were the weird foods she'd told him she loved during their hitchhiking adventure. The bacon and jelly on toast, the popcorn and milk, the French toast with cheese and ham—though he'd had to skip the ham because he didn't have any. He shrugged. "It's not a big deal."

Quinn tugged on his arm, prompting him to turn around. The look she gave him was one he'd never forget: it was so heartfelt, sincere, and adoring, it nearly made him gasp. "It is a big deal." She moved closer to him, slipping her arms around his waist. "You're literally the best boyfriend ever, you know that? Lauren brags about Scott, but I clearly got the better Jacobs brother." Her words had an air of joking to them, but her look said she meant them.

Tim returned her hug, pulling her tightly to him. He was going to ignore the comment about being better than Scott, because reviewing the long list of reasons for why her words weren't true wasn't important in that moment. Or maybe he just didn't want to set her straight about it. Either way, he decided, for the first time in a long time, he wasn't going to think the worst of himself. He was going to bask in the fact that this gorgeous girl thought he was the best. "Boyfriend, huh?"

Quinn bit her lower lip. "You caught that?" She looked uncertain.

"Yup." He kissed her softly.

"I just figured that since you called me your girl . . ." Quinn didn't finish her thought. She looked flustered. It was adorable. "I guess I should've waited until we talked about it. We still can . . . over breakfast. If you want. I mean, I shouldn't have assumed anything. I guess it's just wishful thinking. Or something. I . . . God, can you just kiss me again so I stop talking?"

Tim laughed as he pressed his mouth to hers again. "I want to be your boyfriend, Quinn."

"You do?" Her blue eyes widened as a huge smile broke out across her stunning face.

"I do." And with those words, Tim decided he was going to try to let it all go. To stop thinking in negatives. He'd let *I can't*s and *I don't deserve*s run his life for a long time. And while there was really no denying that he didn't deserve Quinn, he was going to try to let himself have her anyway. At least for as long as she wanted to be his.

Chapter 16

Writer's Block

Quinn twirled her phone in her hand as she worked on her article. The damn thing was becoming nearly impossible. How the hell was she supposed to convey the past month and a half of her life in words when the experience defied them? It was the first time in her twenty-seven years that Quinn felt words weren't enough. She suddenly understood why Shakespeare had found it necessary to invent so many—the English language was suddenly sorely lacking.

Her phone vibrated in her hand, and she smiled before even glancing at the screen. It had been two days since she'd spent the night with Tim, and they had been in almost constant contact since. Since Tim was always scheduled to work Thursday through Saturday nights unless he put in for time off well in advance, she hadn't seen him since their night together. And odds were she wouldn't see him tonight either, though she was giving serious thought to waiting until he got off work and showing up at his apartment.

I'm peeling potatoes at work, and it's making me think of you.

Quinn chuckled quietly as she read his text, trying to figure out what the hell he was talking about. I'm trying really hard to see the compliment in that.

Oh, it's a compliment. Believe me.

Explain it to me, she typed back.

I'm sitting here, thinking about how I want nothing more than to be peeling layers of clothing off of you to reveal your soft skin underneath.

Quinn blushed even though doing so was ridiculous. Tim had seen every inch of the soft skin he was referring to Wednesday night, and then again yesterday morning before she'd hurried off to change before going to work. But reading his dirty words while she was at her desk was equal parts embarrassing and arousing. More arousing, if she were being honest with herself. She forced her fingers to formulate a response. I think I'm speechless.

HA! I'll record the day on my calendar.

Way to ruin the mood, wise guy. Quinn couldn't contain her smile. She loved this flirty banter, the ease with which she and Tim communicated.

Let me make it up to you.

How? Quinn bit her lower lip, hoping like hell sex was in some way involved in his plans.

I should be able to leave tonight around 1. Let me pick you up afterward and take you home to my place.

Quinn wanted to high-five herself. Why don't I just meet you at your apartment around 1:30?

I'm not sure exactly what time I'll get out of there, and I'd rather you weren't out alone at that time of night. Especially since you won't be able to get into my apartment. Can I pick you up? Please?

Quinn wondered if her inner feminist should be offended that Tim didn't think her capable of taking care of herself enough to make it to his apartment unscathed, but she was too busy fawning over his concern for her. She'd thought about asking him to stay at her apartment but had reconsidered when she'd realized he would need to stop at home first to get a change of clothes. And putting off getting Tim naked wasn't on her agenda. Sure. Just text me when you're leaving work and I'll be ready.

Great. See you later. Can't wait.

Quinn wasn't sure she'd be able to wait either.

It had been a long night of barking out orders and helping put out fires. Literally. Tim loved his job. He was good at it, it paid reasonably well, and it was fun. But with a certain gorgeous woman waiting for him, he had wanted the night over before it even started. So when the dinner menu closed at eleven, Tim went into drill-sergeant mode, ordering his team to clean up dinner service, restock the walk-in, and do any prep work that needed to be completed for the next day as quickly as possible.

A couple of his guys stayed on until the bar closed at two in case anyone wanted to order appetizers or simple sandwiches, but everything else had to be wrapped up and put away for the next service. Finally, at twelve forty-six, everything was cleaned and organized, and Tim could get the hell out of there. He yelled his goodbyes as he exited the restaurant and climbed into his truck. Then he shot Quinn a quick text to let her know he was on his way.

He had barely had time to put his truck in park before Quinn was walking out of her apartment building. He quickly jumped out to greet her properly. "Hey, you," he murmured as he pressed a soft kiss to her lips.

"Hey, yourself. You smell—"

"Gross. Don't try to sugarcoat it," he said on a laugh as he grabbed her bag before resting his forehead against hers. "I missed you."

"Mmm, I missed you too." Quinn kissed him quickly before pulling away and taking the last two steps toward the passenger-side door Tim had opened for her. "Now take me home so we can get reacquainted."

Tim let out a low chuckle. "I like your style," he said as he closed her door. He climbed into the driver's seat, reached for Quinn's hand, and entwined their fingers.

He felt Quinn's gaze on him, so he chanced a brief look in her direction. "What?"

Quinn looked . . . smug. "Nothing. I just didn't know you were such a romantic."

Tim's brow furrowed. "I'm not."

Quinn lifted their hands. "Oh really?"

"Holding my girlfriend's hand is romantic?"

"Well, no, not just that. But getting out to open my door, telling me you missed me, cooking my favorite foods for breakfast. That stuff is romantic."

"Huh." Tim was puzzled. It wasn't that he didn't want to be romantic; he'd just never pegged himself as the type.

"It's not a slight or anything." Quinn laughed. "It's a compliment, I swear. Haven't any of your other girlfriends ever called you romantic?"

Here's where things get awkward. "I've never really had a girlfriend."

His peripheral vision caught Quinn's head turning slowly toward him like she was auditioning for *The Exorcist.* "What? Never?"

Tim shook his head. "Most respectable girls would rather not date a drug addict. Shocking, isn't it?"

"But you've been off drugs for a long time."

"I'm not saying I haven't been with women." He noticed Quinn sink back into her seat slightly. *Okay, maybe I didn't need to say that part.* "I just haven't really *dated* any." *Fuck, she's going to think I'm a manwhore.*

"What about when you were a teenager?"

Tim turned onto his street and into his building's parking lot. He pulled into his spot and cut the engine before looking at Quinn. "I started doing drugs when I was fifteen. That and rehab took up most of my time."

Quinn sat speculatively. Suddenly, her eyes lit up. "That means you never got to experience the awkwardness that is the teenage dating scene." Excitement was nearly emanating off of her.

Tim couldn't figure out what she was so happy about. "No, I guess not. Though I can't say I'm sorry I missed it."

"Oh, you're not going to miss it, my friend. We're totally going out on a teenage date."

"We are, are we?" Tim was definitely amused. Excited Quinn was completely adorable.

"We are. When can we go?"

"Well, I have to work tomorrow. I need to be in by three. I was hoping to not get out of bed until two at the earliest." A sly smile overtook his face as he spoke.

Quinn tossed her hair over her shoulder. "Okay, so tomorrow is out," she said, returning his smile. "What about Sunday?"

"I'm yours all day."

"Awesome." Quinn turned and hopped out.

Tim followed her. "Wait. Aren't you going to tell me what we're going to do on this date?"

"Nope," she said, not slowing her pace.

"But isn't it customary for the guy to plan it?"

"Don't argue with me. It's probably the only time I'll get to be the more experienced one."

They walked to his door, and Quinn waited for Tim to unlock it. But before he did, he leaned in to her, his mouth tantalizingly close to her ear. "I have a few other things I'd like to experience," he whispered.

Quinn released a low hum of arousal. "Do they involve us naked?"

"Every last one."

"Then you'd better open the door so we can get started."

"Gladly," he murmured before sucking her earlobe into his mouth. He quickly released her so he could open his door and stepped back so Quinn could enter first. But he didn't let her get too far inside before he pushed the door shut, grabbed and spun her around, and pinned her against the wall. Tim claimed her mouth as she let out low moans of satisfaction. The kiss lasted for a few more minutes before he finally forced himself to pull away. "Damn, I need a shower."

"What do you know?" Quinn said as she stepped around him and started walking down the hall. "I could use one too." She pulled her purple racerback over her head and let it fall to the floor like a bread crumb for him to follow. It took Tim a second to notice that she wasn't wearing a bra. *Could she be any more fucking perfect?* She paused at the door to his bathroom, her arm draped across her bare breasts. "You coming?"

"You keep asking me that. The only response I have is 'God, I fucking hope so,'" Tim muttered as he stalked toward her.

Quinn giggled as she stepped into the bathroom and out of sight. But he heard her voice clearly. "Better bring a condom, then."

Nope, she couldn't possibly get any more perfect.

Their shower sex had been passionate and frantic. Hands were everywhere: groping asses, running through hair, dragging across wet skin. And after their touching had brought each of them nearly to the brink, Tim pushed inside of her and thrust from behind with everything he had.

Her groans of "harder," "faster," "more," caused him to piston his hips like a man possessed.

When he felt his sac draw up and the familiar zing begin to shoot up his spine, he reached around and rubbed his fingers over her sensitive clit. The gasp she let out signaled that he'd found his mark, and he kept working her with his fingers as his cock swelled inside her with his impending release.

He felt her body tighten as he brought her closer to the edge.

"Oh, fuck. Tim," she mewled in ecstasy.

"Come for me, baby."

She went rigid in his arms as her orgasm raced through her body. Her moans echoed off the bathroom walls as he thrust erratically into her, finally erupting with a guttural sound of his own.

Once their orgasms had receded and their breathing began to return to normal, Quinn turned in his arms. "Shower sex may be my favorite."

Tim smiled. "Don't go making your mind up just yet. I have some more tricks up my sleeve."

She looked up at him, her blue eyes gazing adoringly into his green ones. "I'll delay judgment then." And then she lifted onto her tiptoes and kissed him. The kind of soul-searing kiss that made his heart want to explode out of his chest.

Tim cupped her jaw to deepen the kiss, his thumb brushing over her cheek. They stayed that way until the water started to get cold, then quickly finished cleaning up, toweled off, and made their way to the bedroom. Tim wished he had a round two in him, but he was fucking exhausted. And Quinn seemed to be in the same boat, as she nestled into his side, her head on his chest, and immediately fell asleep. Just before he dozed off himself, Tim thought he might just be the luckiest son of a bitch in the world.

"Why the hell do they put water everywhere? It's like they want you to fail." Tim was exasperated as he fished his ball out of the water for the second consecutive time as he tried to navigate hole number two.

"They're sadists," Quinn joked as she watched Tim drop the ball onto the green carpet and shake the water off his hands. Despite Tim's gripe, she was so glad she'd chosen miniature golf as their teenage date.

Tim's eyes couldn't hide his excitement when they'd first pulled up. "I haven't been miniature golfing since I was little," he had said.

"They have an arcade too," Quinn added.

"You'd better not be toying with me, woman."

Ten minutes later, they had chosen their clubs, picked their balls, and grabbed a scorecard. Quinn had tried to tell him that keeping score wasn't necessary, but Tim had insisted. A point he was probably regretting since he seemed determined to hit every water feature on the course.

"Pick up your ball. We need to move on to the next one," Quinn gently commanded as she grew increasingly wary of the line building behind them.

"I didn't get it in yet."

"You only get six strokes," she reminded him.

"I only took four."

"Hitting the water counts as two."

Tim swiped his ball off the ground as he jokingly stalked toward the third hole. "I hate this game. Worst awkward date ever."

Quinn shook her head as she laughed at his antics. Her mom had made her feel guilty about not coming over for dinner that night since she hadn't been over recently, but watching Tim pretend to have a bad time was totally worth it. Quinn could see the truth: the lopsided smile, the crinkling of the skin by his eyes, the smooth gait. Tim was having a blast, and they'd only just begun.

"I think the reason I'm doing so poorly is because I'm lacking the proper motivation."

Quinn tried to repress a smirk. "Oh, is *that* what the problem is? I knew it had to be something completely logical."

Tim wagged a finger at her. "You think I'm kidding, but you'll soon see. Let's place a wager."

"Okay. What?"

Tim stood stock-still and thought for a moment, completely oblivious to the *actual* teenagers waiting behind him.

"You guys may as well play through. This might take a while," Quinn called to them.

The kids all muttered their thanks as they passed. It took Tim a moment to realize the teens were even there, but when he finally did, he glared accusingly at Quinn. "We're doing it wrong."

"What?" Quinn's face reflected her confusion.

Tim pointed at the group in front of them. "We were supposed to be in a herd. Like a group date."

Quinn rolled her eyes. "You're completely ridiculous," she said, though the idea appealed to her, and she suddenly wished she'd thought of it. She'd been so wrapped up in Tim and her article, she hadn't even talked to the girls to tell them about her new relationship status. It would've been fun for them to all go out together. However, she had to admit, she also liked having Tim all to herself. "I don't think you're quite ready for outsiders to see your golf skills. It's best that it's just us."

Tim laughed and walked to her, enveloping her in his strong arms. "You're probably right." He leaned in closer. "Besides, I like having these experiences with you. Just you."

Quinn rubbed her hands down his ribs. "See? Romantic."

"I am good, aren't I?"

"At some things," she replied, casting a fleeting glance at the course.

"Now, that's just cruel," he added as he gave her a quick peck before stepping back. "So, our bet. If I win, which I will, you have to watch all of the Rocky movies with me when we get back to my place. In order."

Quinn forced a shudder. "You wouldn't."

Tim waggled his eyebrows. "I would. What's the matter? Not so confident in your abilities anymore?"

"Do I have to remind you of your unfortunate experience playing pool against me? What makes you think this will be any different?"

"Because this time I have a bet to win."

Quinn scoffed. "Dream on. Fine, I'll accept your terms. But if *I* win, you have to watch the Lifetime Movie Network with me for the rest of the night."

"You drive a hard bargain. But I accept." Tim offered his hand, which Quinn shook. Then he walked over and placed his ball down, taking time to line up his shot. He swung too hard, causing his ball to ricochet off a stone obstacle and bounce wildly through the course.

Quinn cackled as Tim gave chase. "I'm glad I brought you here when it was still light out. Otherwise you'd never find your ball."

"I'm just working the kinks out," Tim said when he returned to line up his shot again.

Unable to resist, Quinn walked up to him, crowding his back. "Hopefully you left a few kinks for later."

"Are you attempting to distract me?"

"Ha, like I need to. You'd need an act of God to win this game."

"We'll see," Tim replied as he concentrated on the task at hand. Tim's gaze traveled from the ball to the hole, from the hole to the ball. Then he made contact, causing the ball to ping gently off the far wall, glide under the windmill, and sink into the hole. He smirked victoriously at her as he strode off to retrieve his ball.

"Did you hustle me?"

"I have no idea what you're talking about. Your shot."

It took Quinn three strokes to put the ball in the hole, which gave her the same score as Tim since his ball had left the course. She still had a decent lead overall, but there was a prickle of worry in the back of her mind. The threat of having to watch the Stallone flicks had her sweating a little.

The fourth hole only confirmed her fear, as Tim banked his ball off the wedge, causing it to come to rest right beside the hole.

"You totally scammed me," she accused.

"I did not." Tim had the nerve to look affronted. "I just had to knock a little of the rust off."

"You're a miniature golf shark."

"A what? That's not a thing."

"It is a thing." Quinn glared at the cheating bastard. "It's like a card shark, but with mini golf."

"Did I ever tell you how cute you are when you're nervous?"

Quinn shrugged off the arm Tim had draped over her shoulder. "I'm not nervous. I got this."

"Then get it." Tim motioned for her to take her turn.

Quinn came out of the fourth hole with four strokes to Tim's two. *This isn't good.*

And things didn't get any better. Quinn quickly lost her lead, leaving her to rely on skill she clearly didn't possess. Tim, on the other hand, was like some sort of golfing savant. They approached the last hole with Quinn needing to score four strokes lower than Tim to win. It didn't happen. Tim putted the ball perfectly, knocking it cleanly through the stupid, swirling helicopter and scoring a hole in one.

He threw up his arms in victory, yelling, "Yo, Adrian. I did it!"

Smug jerk. "You hustled me. How could you do that to your girlfriend?"

"You deserved it," Tim quipped, making Quinn laugh at how unapologetic he was.

"Seriously, is this what you do in your spare time? How are you so freakishly good at golf?"

Tim shrugged. "I used to hustle little kids for drug money when I was in high school."

Quinn was sure her face looked horrified. And a little sad. She hated to think of Tim so hard up for drugs.

Tim looked at her solemnly before breaking out into a raucous laugh. "You seriously believed that? I think I'm offended."

Quinn playfully slapped his arm. "You asshole. I felt sorry for you."

Tim doubled over he was laughing so hard. Once he finally got himself under control, he explained. "My dad had one of those putting machines. Scott and I used to play with it all the time, making our own obstacles and stuff. I got pretty good."

"Thank God. That's a much better story." Quinn nuzzled into him. "This was fun, even if you are a cheater. Ooh, our next date should be something college kids would do. We can bring you up to proper dating speed."

"I'd like that," he said as he pressed a gentle kiss to her forehead.

"Okay, you're on deck for planning the next one. I'm spent."

"I sure hope not." Tim winked at her as he stepped back.

"You're bad," Quinn chastised with a grin.

"I know. But for some reason, you like me anyway."

They both took a turn at the final hole, which offered a free game for a hole in one. Thankfully, Tim missed that time. As they returned their clubs, Quinn looked at him with her best puppy-dog expression. "You're not really going to make me watch all the Rocky movies, are you?"

"Aww, poor baby. Yes. I am."

Quinn pushed him playfully. "You're so mean."

"You love it," Tim retorted.

Quinn had to admit . . . she kind of did.

Chapter 17

Exclusive

"So listen," Tim said, as he inhaled the scent of Quinn's freshly shampooed hair: a mixture of citrus and almond. "I'm thinking for our college date, I'd like you to take me to a concert."

"Is that right? You'd like *me* to take *you*?" Quinn asked, applying a bit of blush to her cheeks.

"Well, I mean we can *meet* there if it's easier. I just thought it would be kind of pointless to take two cars. Not to mention wasteful. Don't you care about preserving the earth for future generations?" Tim felt the smile he'd been trying to suppress surface.

Quinn threw an elbow into his ribs playfully and laughed. "You're such an ass."

"Hey," Tim said, bringing his hands up in feigned innocence, "don't blame me when our grandchildren don't have parks to play in." He heard the implication of "*our* grandchildren" after he'd said it, and he hoped Quinn didn't read into it. He could have just meant that they'd *each* have grandchildren and there would be no parks in which those respective grandchildren could play. He hadn't necessarily meant their grandchildren *together*. Although the idea didn't seem all that difficult to imagine now that he was picturing it.

Quinn cocked a brow at him in the mirror, and Tim readied himself to explain. "Suddenly going green, are we?"

He shrugged. "Better late than never."

"Well, then, you should probably start by getting rid of that F150. That thing gets like six miles to the gallon."

He'd gotten the truck six years ago, and she still ran great. "Okay, so maybe I was less concerned with environmental conservation and more concerned with getting you in the backseat of a car that actually *has* a backseat." Tim slid a hand around Quinn's neck and swept her hair to the side so he could plant light kisses just below her ear. "You know, since we missed that particular rite of passage during our teenage date."

She put down the makeup she was holding and leaned in to him. "Well, how can I say no to that? That's kind of been a fantasy of mine ever since I saw Kate Winslet's hand slide across that fogged-up window in *Titanic*." Tim felt Quinn shiver as he continued to kiss her neck. "I mean, we already kind of reenacted the scene where she poses nude on the couch. We might as well go two for two, right?"

"Never seen it. Though now I kind of want to," he said, running his tongue down to Quinn's collarbone as his thumb traced the edge of where her towel met the skin just above her breasts.

"You're going to make me very late for work if you keep that up."

Tim smiled against her warm flesh. "I'm going to make you a lot of things."

"So you never even told me who the band is," Quinn said as Tim opened the door to the bar for her.

"They're just a college band. Kind of a mixture of punk rock and metal, if that makes sense. You probably haven't heard of them."

"What?" Quinn asked, putting a hand to her chest in exaggerated disbelief. "You don't think I'm hip enough to know about some indie band?"

"Well, now I *know* you're not," Tim said, laughing as he gripped Quinn's hand tightly.

"Shut up," Quinn joked loudly over the crowd. It was just before ten, and the place was packed with early twentysomethings high on adrenaline and alcohol. "Try me. Remember—I *do* work at a magazine with college interns."

"I wouldn't have even heard of them myself except that this guy Lennie, who's a waiter at the restaurant, goes to Georgetown, and he's been bugging me for months to check them out. He's the lead singer. They're called Waiting for Someday." Tim looked over his shoulder as he led Quinn closer to the stage where the band was setting up. "Have you heard of them?"

Quinn smirked. "Nope. I like the name though."

A half hour later Quinn stood at a small round table, tapping her foot in time with the music. She looked around at the crowd, watching people's bodies moving robotically to the beat. Most of them had large holes in their ears, stretched by metal rings, and a few of them weren't wearing shirts. She could almost picture a younger Tim out there among them, banging into his buddies as they laughed the night away. The image made her happy and sad at the same time.

The music was actually very good, even if it was more alternative than Quinn's usual tastes. Lennie had a great voice, though Quinn couldn't ignore that the whole scene made her feel like she was ten years older than most of the other attendees rather than a mere four or five. Twenty-seven-year-old Quinn preferred songs she could sing and dance to and bars where she could hear herself talk, or at least think.

She remembered back to her days in college, hanging out in places like this and listening to bands she'd sworn were the second coming of Linkin Park. And as she looked across the table at Tim, she felt a pang of guilt. She wasn't giving him the experience he deserved. She held out her hand to him as she spoke. "Come on."

He immediately took her hand but eyed her curiously. "Where are we going?"

Quinn jerked her head toward the crowd. "You're not getting the full college-date experience back here."

Tim smiled and followed her as she led him to the stage. "Now what?" he yelled over the crowd.

"Now we act like fools," Quinn replied as she began jumping up and down with the rest of the crowd.

Tim looked unsure at first, but he quickly joined in. Pretty soon the two of them were headbanging with the best of them. With every passing song, they became less and less reserved in their movements, until they were twirling around each other, voguing and roboting like idiots. Their dancing didn't match the timbre of the music, and it didn't blend in with the rest of the crowd, but that didn't matter. Tim and Quinn were acting like stupid, drunk college kids, and the best part was that, since they were sober, they wouldn't have to deal with a hangover in the morning.

Despite the evening being something that was completely foreign to both of them, it was actually a great time. Letting loose, not caring what the world thought of her, gave Quinn a freedom that she felt most often when she was with Tim. Even with her list completed, Tim still had a way of bringing out a side of her she hadn't known she had.

The band played for about two hours or so, and Quinn managed to survive, though not without a few battle wounds. Her pale yellow tank top was splattered with something sticky, which she could only hope was some sort of drink. And she was pretty sure she had sweat on her that wasn't hers or Tim's.

A little past one a.m., after chatting with the band for a bit, they finally exited the bar. Quinn was thankful for the fresh air. Well, as fresh as it could be with the smokers outside. They walked around the corner toward

Quinn's Jeep, the humid summer air a welcome visitor in her lungs.

Quinn could still hear a ringing in her ears when she spoke. "I think I'm old."

Tim laughed loudly, his whole body shaking. It was the kind of laugh that Quinn wished she could bottle up and keep so it would be with her forever.

"I'm serious," she said. "I feel like I just got into a fight with a zebra and lost."

Tim raised his eyebrows, obviously confused. "A zebra?"

"Yeah. They can kick harder than any other species. I saw it on Animal Planet," she said as she unlocked her car.

Tim shook his head and put his hands on Quinn's shoulders, massaging gently. "Come on, old lady. Let's get you to bed."

"I think I need a shower first."

"Mmm," he said, pulling her into a soft kiss. "I think that can be arranged."

Tim didn't expect Quinn's response—a heady combination of assertiveness and desire—to manifest itself as soon as they got to her car. She grabbed hold of Tim's T-shirt neckline and pulled him hard against her, causing his lips to collide with hers once more. He smiled internally. This was the Quinn he knew lived somewhere inside her. And he was glad he could be there every time she made an appearance.

"I think we have one more item to check off before we head home."

"Yeah?" Tim asked, a playful gleam in his eye as he hoped Quinn meant what he thought she meant. "What's that?"

Quinn answered his question with a click of her key fob. "Get in," she said, opening the back door.

Tim smirked. "You're serious?"

"Of course I'm serious. Now, don't ruin the moment with stupid questions."

"Won't happen again," Tim said through a laugh, although part of him was tempted to say something dumb again intentionally just so he could hear Quinn boss him around a little bit more. Tim climbed in the back passenger-side door and turned to pull Quinn in on top of him, leaning up to close the door behind her. He let his fingers tangle in her red hair, which looked darker than usual in the soft overhead light that was fading above them.

Quinn moved against him, her body seeming to already respond as Tim's hands massaged her back and then her firm ass with rough pressure. Quinn let out a low moan.

"Feel good?"

She exhaled. "*Everything* you do feels good."

If Tim's cock hadn't already been pressing hard against his jeans, that comment would have made sure of it. Now he felt like he could fucking burst. Especially with Quinn rubbing herself faster against him. He gripped her hips, helping her move over his length.

Then suddenly, almost as if Tim didn't expect it either, he flipped her over so she was underneath him. His hands pulled her shirt up roughly so he had access to her soft skin underneath. He licked and kissed her hungrily on her ribs and up to her breasts, giving them the attention they deserved. Then he hovered above her for a moment that was just long enough to hike her skirt up above her hips.

"You know," Quinn said, seeming surprised, "that actually *is* as hot as it looks in the movies."

Tim laughed. "It really is." Then he reached into his back pocket to retrieve a condom from his wallet. He slid the wrapper back into his pocket as he pulled his pants down and slipped the latex over himself.

He kept his hand between them, rubbing her clit as Quinn moaned with pleasure. Once he could tell she was close, he plunged two fingers inside her, moving them in a calculated motion until she begged him not to stop. But he pulled them out slowly, knowing their absence would drive Quinn wild. "No way I'm letting you come like that. I want to feel you let go around me."

"Then fuck me already."

Tim nearly choked on a laugh at Quinn's boldness. "I think I like you when you're feisty," he said with a nip to her ear as his cock found its way deep inside her.

"I think I like you all the time," she replied.

Tim's hips moved slowly at first, and then more rapidly, as if to match their increased breathing. He thrust himself into her over and over again, never tiring of her body writhing beneath him. Quinn's nails dug into his back through the fabric of his shirt, and he loved it.

The two moved rhythmically together, sweat beading between them as their warm breath filled the small space. Finally, when Tim didn't think either of them could wait a moment longer, he reached between them to stroke his thumb against her clit.

"Holy shit, Tim!" she yelled.

Tim followed her over the edge, coming hard into the condom until he was sure he'd filled it. He withdrew from her slowly, pinching the condom and balling it up into a tissue that was in Quinn's console and slipping it into his pocket. When both of them had fixed their clothing, Tim chuckled, gesturing to the window that was streaked with Quinn's handprint. "Couldn't resist, huh?"

"Well, I'm not one to turn down an opportunity when one presents itself." She smiled at him, letting him know he had something to do with that. "At least not anymore."

The past week had been better than Tim had imagined. Sure, the sex was fantastic. But more than that, he and Quinn had *fun* together. He'd never experienced that with a woman before. And as he stared into Quinn's bright blue eyes across from him and thought about how gorgeous she looked in a dress of nearly the same color, he wondered how he'd resisted her for as long as he had. For the first time in his life he felt truly happy. It was a foreign feeling, one he still felt undeserving of, but he wanted to ride it out for as long as he could.

Quinn's lips tightened a bit before she spoke, as if considering something. "Why do you look so . . . pensive?"

Tim's mouth turned up into a small smile as he took a sip of his water. She knew him so well. "I was just thinking."

"Well, yeah. That's what pensive *means*." She laughed softly and dipped a piece of calamari into the marinara sauce. "I meant what are you thinking *about*?"

Tim shook his head, trying to get all of the stupid comments out of it before they slipped from his mouth. Quinn already had such a hold on him. Sometimes he found himself saying dumb things to her, like an inexperienced teenager. But he didn't *feel* like one. In fact, he felt the opposite. Like the past weeks had given him time that he once felt he'd lost and wouldn't ever get back, given him the "adult relationship" he'd never let himself have until now. "You," he said simply, finally answering her question.

Quinn's playful expression seemed to transform into one that was more serious. "And just what exactly are you thinking about me?"

Though Tim hoped—and thought—that Quinn had similar feelings to his, neither one had expressed them through the words that lingered on the tip of his tongue. He'd never told any woman he loved her before. Well, any woman except his mother. And he hadn't even told *her* that in probably ten years. Though he was sure that's what he felt about Quinn, he just couldn't bring himself to say it. At least not before she did. There was too much of a chance that those words wouldn't be reciprocated. Too much of a chance that he would feel rejected. He'd had enough rejection in his life, and he wouldn't risk that again. "Just wondering why you only eat the rings and not the whole squid."

Quinn's face seemed to fall a bit at Tim's lighthearted

comment. "Because," she said, seeming to realize she needed to elaborate, "those are just gross, that's why."

"This coming from someone who eats bacon and jelly together."

"That's different. I don't like to see the whole animal when I eat it. I'd rather pretend it didn't have a life before it entered my mouth. It's easier that way. And don't act like you're too good for bacon and jelly. Even *you* said it was good."

They both laughed as the waiter returned with their entrees: eggplant caramelle for Quinn and Tim's cowboy ribeye. "If you don't mind cutting into your steak, sir, to make sure it's cooked properly." He gestured toward Tim's plate.

Tim sliced through the center carefully and looked at the deep pink color. "Perfect. Thank you."

The waiter nodded in acceptance. "Is there anything else I can get for the two of you at the moment?"

Tim looked to Quinn, who smiled at the waiter and let him know they were fine for now. When he left, Quinn took a bite of her pasta and let out a sound that he'd heard come out of her only during sex. It made his dick jump in response.

"How's your pasta?" Tim asked, a smirk on his face that he didn't even try to hide.

"So good," she answered, drawing out the words and closing her eyes as she chewed and continued to make little moans of enjoyment. "You have to try this," she said, finally putting an end to the noises he'd been enjoying so much.

"Don't stop," he said as he rubbed a hand over his

jaw. "I bet you could give Meg Ryan a run for her money." He finally took a bite off the fork Quinn had been holding out for him and looked to the elderly couple a few tables away. "It's probably the most action those two have seen in a few decades," he said after swallowing the bite.

Quinn's cheeks flushed with embarrassment. "Oh, stop. I don't even think I could fake an orgasm if I tried."

"Well," he replied, raising his eyebrows, "lucky for you, you don't have to. What do you say we take dessert to go and find out how *not* fake those orgasms can be?"

Tim wondered if Quinn was conscious of the fact that she ran her tongue along her bottom lip. It made him want her tongue somewhere else.

"I say that sounds like a good plan."

Quinn wouldn't have been surprised if she'd left a wet spot on the seat of Tim's truck. Well, that may have been an exaggeration, but not much of one. Just sitting across from Tim at dinner had been a turn-on. Combine that with the mention of leaving the restaurant early and Tim's fingers circling her inner thigh as he drove, and she'd been nearly ready to explode.

Finally they made it to Quinn's apartment. Quinn unlocked the door and stepped inside, enjoying the feel of Tim's hand on the small of her back. She walked slowly toward the kitchen, not wanting to break the contact. Pulling open the refrigerator, she placed the crème brûlée inside.

"Now, how am I supposed to lick that off of you if it's in there?" Tim's low voice asked from behind her.

Quinn wasn't sure if Tim was serious, though she hoped he was. The idea of getting all sticky from sugar and Tim's tongue made another rush of warm wetness seep out of her.

Tim reached into the fridge and removed the foil container she'd just placed inside. "No one takes crème brûlée to go." He paused, turning to face her. "Unless, of course, they plan to eat it immediately."

Oh, he is serious.

Then his hand drifted to her hip to press her against the edge of the granite countertop. When he released her, she didn't move a muscle. She watched him as he made a show of lifting every metal ridge of the round container slowly, spinning it in his hands as his stare seemed to set fire to her body. Finally he popped the lid off and tossed it aside. Then he dipped a finger into the smooth dessert and put it to Quinn's lips, waiting for her to open. When she slid her mouth around his finger, he let out a low groan, and she could only imagine he was wishing another part of his anatomy was inside her mouth instead.

He repeated the action, this time bringing his finger to his own mouth. "Tastes so sweet," he said, his voice raspy with desire. "Though not as sweet as you."

Quinn swallowed hard and released the large breath she'd just taken. Tim seemed to catch it when his mouth enveloped hers in a deep kiss, the barbell and his tongue working expertly against hers. And as his kiss moved from passive to demanding, she realized Tim kissed like he lived his life: with practiced balance. Sometimes

Quinn felt him become more aggressive—biting her lips, gripping the back of her neck to pull her so close that her skin became red against his stubble. But other times he was gentle, moving slowly, allowing the kiss to develop at its own pace, or even letting Quinn take the lead. And she loved that about him—how he could be so assertive, so bold, and then give over control so easily.

Quinn hadn't even noticed Tim had put the dessert down on the counter until one of his hands skated under her dress and the other slid down the zipper. With his help, she shimmied out of it, letting it drop to the tile. She could feel his erection pressing against her lower abdomen, and she wanted nothing more than to wrap her hand around him. But when she made a move toward the button of his dark gray pants, Tim gripped her wrist firmly and placed her hand gently on the edge of the counter. "Uh-uh. This is about you."

Thankfully though, Tim did remove his shirt, letting Quinn's eyes devour every muscle and every color on his skin. Again he reached into the crème brûlée and then traced a cool, sugary trail down her neck and between her breasts, ending at the top of her thong.

Quinn didn't even have to guess what Tim had planned next. His tongue followed the path he'd just made for himself, deviating from it only to give her breasts adequate attention. He sucked hard on her nipples, pressing them between his fingers, licking every inch of sensitive flesh until he returned to his original route.

By the time his tongue had cleaned every bit of dessert from her, Tim had dropped to his knees—his mouth just above the area she wanted it most. If Quinn thought that sight was arousing, it had nothing on when Tim finally looked up at her, locking his gaze with hers as he slid her panties down her legs, brushing her skin softly with his fingertips. Everything about the man was sexy—the way the dim light accented the hints of copper in his unruly hair, how his strong hands wrapped around her calves one by one as he removed her heels and underwear.

But nothing—Quinn thought for an instant before her mind was incapable thinking altogether—was sexier than seeing Tim's face settle between her legs as he kissed, licked, and stroked her toward what she was sure would be nothing short of a mind-blowing orgasm, especially with the barbell working just as magically as his tongue was.

He knew exactly what she loved without having to ask. He knew she loved his fingers plunging deep, hitting that spot inside her that made her knees feel like they could give out at any moment. And he knew she loved it when he swirled his piercing around her clit, flicking it every so often until she felt like she couldn't wait any longer. But Tim also knew her body, knew that no matter how badly she desperately chased the release, she loved the journey toward it almost as much.

Then, just like every other time she'd been with Tim, the moment she felt it couldn't possibly feel any better, it did. She felt herself tense uncontrollably, every muscle in her body clenching as the waves of her climax pulsed through her. Tim's hands and tongue slowed gradually until they ceased their movements completely and all that was left between them were the sticky remnants of their encounter.

Tim stood, bringing his face up to meet hers. And Quinn kissed him, needing to taste the combination of the two of them on his tongue, a salty sweetness she could never get enough of. But finally she pulled away. "I think it's your turn," she said as she palmed his straining cock through his pants and gripped hard.

"Mmm," he growled against her throat. "I think I'd like that."

Tim inhaled a shaky breath as Quinn's soft tongue gently moved over his ear and traced his jawline on the way to his lips. She'd already been palming his dick through his pants for long enough. He was certain it had been only a few minutes, but the feel of her stroking him through the fabric was nearly unbearable. Tim massaged the back of her neck, pulling her to him for an aggressive kiss. "I need this mouth on me now," he rasped.

He felt her smile against his lips. "Bossy tonight, aren't we?"

Tim wasn't sure whether to respond or to let it go, but when he felt Quinn tug on his pants, he decided to let his hands do the talking. His fingers pulled on Quinn's nipples, which were still hard against his skin. He fucking loved them. How they were just the right shade of pink when she was turned on, how they jutted out perfectly in his hands, how she moaned every time he swirled a tongue or a finger around them.

And when Quinn's warm palm slid over his cock, it

was fucking sensory overload. His head lolled back for a moment as she rubbed her hand over his hard length. But his gaze returned quickly to her as she kept her eyes trained on his.

Then she did the sexiest thing he'd ever seen any woman do. She slipped her finger over the precome that was already pooling heavily on his tip, brought her finger up to her mouth slowly, and fucking licked it. She let her teeth drag gently over her nail on the way out of her mouth. He'd never wanted to be a finger so badly in his entire life. "You keep doing shit that hot and I may never let you leave this apartment."

"Well, in that case," Quinn said, lowering her voice to just above a whisper as she slid down his body like it was a damn stripper pole. *Holy fuck.* Quinn still had her fingers wrapped tightly around him, but she loosened her grip and slid her hand further toward his base to make room for her mouth. And the feeling made Tim groan. Her movements began as slow licks and gentle pulls of her lips against his tip as he entered her mouth over and over again.

Quinn's hand worked up and down his shaft, which was soaked from her mouth. He'd been doing his best to hold off the climax he knew was only moments away, but he didn't know how much longer he could wait. "Jesus, Quinn," he rasped as he tried to resist plunging deep into her throat. "I can't wait much longer." He began to push gently on her shoulder, a sign he hoped would let her know how close he was. Though she'd done it once, he didn't want to assume he could come in her mouth anytime he wanted to.

But his gesture was met with Quinn's greedy mouth taking as much of him as she could handle. And when he felt the head of his cock touch the back of her throat, he nearly lost it. The feeling of his orgasm barreling down his spine felt almost as good as the orgasm itself would, and he wanted the sensation to last. He held off for as long as he could, groaning hard as Quinn's nails dug into the meat of his ass as she pulled him further inside her mouth.

Finally the wet warmth of her tongue swirling around his cock brought him to the edge, and he couldn't help but fall over it. Gripping Quinn's head, his fingers tangling in her hair, he came with a low exhalation of relief. He felt himself empty into Quinn's mouth, and the feeling of her swallowing against his shaft only prolonged his pleasure. "Come here, you," he said softly, bringing her up to meet his gaze. "I'm not done with you yet."

Quinn licked her lips and locked her arms around his waist. "Who said anything about being done?"

The corners of Tim's mouth crept into a slow smile before he quickly swept Quinn up and threw her over his shoulder. She let out a playful squeal when he smacked her ass on the way to the bedroom. He was one lucky son of a bitch. And he planned to show her just how lucky he felt.

Chapter 18

Scald

"My parents want to meet you."

Quinn's statement made Tim's hand cease its light caress of her shoulder. They were lying on the couch, Quinn's head resting on his chest as he gently stroked her arm. Her words instantly made him tense, though he tried to mask it. He began to leisurely drift his hands over her exposed skin again in an effort to deflect his initial reaction.

"You have any thoughts on that?" Quinn needled.

Shit. In his attempt to regain control of his physical reaction, he'd forgotten that words were also required. "Umm, okay, I guess?" *Jesus, why am I so awkward?*

He felt Quinn smile against his bare chest. "Aww, is my big, strong Tim nervous?"

"Quiet, you," he replied, skating his hand down to poke her in the ribs. He laughed at her squeal, but that didn't stop the truth from burdening his mind. He *was* nervous. Tim didn't think he was meet-the-parents material. Sure, her friends had accepted his new place in Quinn's life, and Scott had been fucking thrilled. But her *parents*? What would they think of him? The past few weeks with Quinn made him want to forget about his inadequacy. How unlikely it was that he would ever be good enough for her. He'd never been in a relationship that had reached this point before. So he hadn't the slightest idea how to impress a girl's parents. *My own parents didn't even want anything to do with me. How am I going to win over someone else's?*

The thought made his entire body begin to overheat. His mind was quickly spiraling, and he was helpless to stop it. Even if things went well, Tim would never have to introduce Quinn to his mother. She'd never experience even a fraction of the nerves he was feeling because she'd never have to prove to anyone that she deserved him. Tim tapped Quinn's shoulder. "Let me up, babe. I need some water."

Quinn wordlessly sat up, never taking her eyes off the silly chick flick she'd conned him into watching. Retreating to the kitchen where he could try to get ahold of himself, he pulled open the refrigerator and grabbed a bottle of water, twisting off the cap and downing nearly the entire thing. As he braced his hands on the counter, he bent slightly at the waist, letting his hands support his weight. He focused on his breathing, willing himself to calm down. He had just begun to feel settled when slender arms slid around his waist, a sexy body pushing against his back.

"You okay?" Quinn rested her cheek against him.

He stood straighter, reaching down and entwining his fingers with hers. "Yeah, I'm good."

"Is it too soon to meet my parents? Did I freak you out?"

Tim turned and drew Quinn into his arms, placing a chaste kiss on her forehead as he silently cursed himself for making her feel insecure. "No. I mean, I'm a little freaked-out, but not because it's too soon."

"Then why?"

Tim blew out a breath. "I guess it's just latent insecurity. Something I probably would have gotten over in high school had I not spent the duration of it high off my ass. I never had to deal with a girlfriend's parents. And I have absolutely no idea how to convince them that I'm good enough for you. Especially since I'm pretty sure I'm not."

Quinn pulled back a little so she could look up into his eyes. When she narrowed them at him, he knew he was fucked. "You're about as intelligent as a high school boy too."

Tim couldn't help smirking at her gibe. "And what exactly does that mean?"

"It means you're a moron."

Tim barked out a laugh. "Well, no one will ever accuse you of mincing words."

"I'm a writer. I know the importance of saying what I mean."

They stared at each other for a beat, getting lost in each other like they so often did. Quinn tightened her arms around his waist. "Do you think I'm stupid?" she asked quietly.

Tim felt his eyes widen. "What? No. Why would you ask that?"

"Do you trust my judgment?"

"Of course."

"Then why the hell would you think that you're not good enough for me? Do you really think I would waste my time on a man who wasn't worth it?"

Tim rolled his neck. "Quinn—"

"Don't give me that. I want you to listen. Really hear me, Tim. Every time you say stuff like that, which you do more often than you probably realize, you're questioning my judgment. You're basically telling me that I'm not smart enough to know what's best for me. I'm not a child. I know what I want . . . what I need. And that's you. So stop doubting me." She paused, biting her lower lip, as if she clearly had more to add but was still deciding if she was actually going to voice it. Taking a deep breath, she seemed to make up her mind. "Stop doubting *yourself*," she added quietly.

Tim didn't know what to say to that. He'd never thought about his self-deprecating feelings in those terms before. If someone as intelligent as Quinn wanted him, maybe he *did* have something to offer. Suddenly a thought occurred to him, and it set his entire body at ease. "I'll go and meet your parents. But there's something I want you to do for me first."

"Anything."

"I want you to meet someone important to me too."

Quinn hugged him tightly, burying her face in his chest. "I'd love to."

*   *   *

Tim ushered Quinn into the Iron Rose and made his way to the hostess desk. "Hi. Jacobs, party of three."

"Yes. The other member of your party is already here. Right this way."

She led them through the trendy restaurant toward a booth against the far wall. Roger stood when he noticed them approaching. Tim put his hand in Roger's extended one and allowed himself to be pulled into a one-armed hug.

"How ya doing?" Roger asked as he released Tim.

"Pretty good. How about you? You look like you lost some weight, old man," Tim joked as he pretended to land a soft jab to Roger's ribs. Tim didn't wait for Roger to respond before wrapping an arm around Quinn and tucking her to him. "Roger, I'd like you to meet my girlfriend, Quinn. Quinn, this is my sponsor and good friend, Roger."

"It's a pleasure." Roger smiled and held his hand out to Quinn, who immediately took it.

"Great to meet you, Roger. I've heard a lot about you."

Tim tried to shake the sudden wave of guilt that hit him. The truth was that he'd barely told Quinn anything about Roger other than the basic information. Despite how big a role Roger had in his life, Tim had been hesitant to divulge all of that to Quinn. Granted, she already knew about his sordid past, but he didn't want to remind her of it by blabbing on about his sponsor and how dire Tim's life had been before he'd met him.

"Uh-oh." Roger laughed as he motioned for them to sit.

Tim looked at Roger, tilting his head slightly. He'd been teasing when he'd said Roger had lost weight, but it was true. He also looked . . . odd. His coloring looked off somehow. Tim shook his head, chalking it up to the dim lighting. "You been here before?"

"Does this look like the type of place I'd frequent?" Roger taunted as he took a sip of his water.

Tim watched the movement, noticing the slight tremble in Roger's hand. *Something is definitely up with him. Is he nervous about meeting Quinn?* "You chose the place. I figured you'd choose somewhere you liked."

"I was more interested in choosing somewhere Quinn would like." Roger smiled kindly at Quinn, who returned the smile.

They fell into easy conversation from there, speaking of families, work, and trying to find common interests, which there were more of than Tim would have expected.

"Siena, Italy, is one of the most beautiful places I've ever seen in my life. The Piazza del Campo is one of my favorite places on earth," Quinn gushed. "I've always been a sucker for a place with history. Its Gothic architecture and medieval city made me feel like I'd been transported back in time to the twelfth century. Breathtaking. I can't wait to go back one day."

"I don't blame you. Ever been there for the Palio?" Roger asked as he bit into his dessert.

"Yes! It was incredible."

"Okay, what the hell are you two talking about?"

"It's a medieval horse race held twice a year in the town center. You can stand right along the track. It's amazing."

Tim looked wide-eyed over at Roger. "Who knew you were so cultured?"

Roger waved a hand at him. "Trust me, boy. I've been a lot of places in this world. Not all of 'em good, but most of 'em memorable."

Tim let his eyes linger on Roger, knowing his words spoke of things beyond tourist destinations.

"If you guys will excuse me a second, I'm going to run to the restroom," Quinn said, bringing Tim's attention back to the table.

Both men half stood as she rose from the table. "Such gentlemen," she joked as she walked away.

They were barely reseated before Roger spoke. "I like her."

"I do too."

"And more importantly, I like who you are when you're with her."

Tim rested his forearms on the table and leaned on them. "And who am I?"

"Someone comfortable in his own skin." Roger's reply was immediate, but his words made Tim focus on another issue that had been bothering him all night.

"Speaking of that, are you okay?"

Roger cleared his throat and reached for his water. "Yeah. Why?"

"Don't take this the wrong way, Rog, but you don't look so good."

Roger set his water down and glanced quickly at

Tim, then just as quickly diverted his eyes. "I had a nasty virus that turned into a small bout of pneumonia. I'm on the mend now. It just ran me down a little."

Tim narrowed his eyes. "Why didn't you call me?"

"What are you, my mother?" Roger was smiling, but it was tight. Uncomfortable.

"Don't be an ass," Tim replied with a laugh.

"You deserve it, you know?"

Roger's words startled Tim out of his reverie. "Deserve what?"

"To be happy." Roger leaned forward and fixed a gaze on Tim that wasn't only serious but was also swirling with emotion Tim had never before seen from the stoic man. Things seemed to pass between them that neither of them had ever expressed. All the gratitude Tim had for Roger. All the pride Roger had for Tim. It all came out in that one silent moment across the table. Then Roger glanced over Tim's head and straightened his posture. But not before whispering a low "Don't blow it" at him.

"What'd I miss?" Quinn asked as she sat back down between them.

Tim looked briefly at Roger, nodding his head slightly, letting Roger know that he'd gotten the message. Then he slid his arm around the back of Quinn's chair. "Not much. Just bullshitting."

They wrapped up dessert and, for once, didn't fight over the check. Roger grabbed it, and though Tim offered to pay, he didn't argue with Roger when he insisted. Walking out of the restaurant and into the thick night air, they stopped to say their good-byes.

"It was great to meet you," Quinn said as she gave Roger a friendly hug.

He hesitated briefly before putting his arms around her and returning the embrace. Tim stepped up to him next, hugging him just as Quinn had. "Take care of yourself," he whispered into Roger's ear.

"Don't worry about me. You just keep working on you."

Tim went to pull back, but Roger's arms remained around him, halting his movement. "You're a good man, Tim. One of the best I've ever known. Don't ever doubt it." As soon as his words were spoken, Roger dropped his arms and pulled away. He looked at Quinn, a smile rising to his face, then back to Tim. "I'll be seein' ya." And with that, Roger turned and walked down the street, hands in his pockets, whistling happily.

Quinn slid an arm around Tim's waist. "I like him."

Tim smiled in reply as he continued to watch Roger walk away, the weight of the moment heavy for reasons Tim couldn't identify.

"Thank you. For introducing me to him. I know how important he is to you."

Tim finally turned his head to look down at the most beautiful face he'd ever seen. "And now that two of the most important people in my life have met, it's time for me to meet some of your important people."

Chapter 19

Stew

Pulling off the quiet tree-lined street onto the circular driveway, Tim scanned the expansive property. The three-story brick Colonial sat upon no less than two acres of land, and the open doors to the separate three-car garage off to the side gave Tim a perfect view of what was inside. He'd recognize that car anywhere. It was one every guy dreamed of driving: a 1969 Camaro. "Jesus," Tim whispered as he pulled in front of the Sawyer home and took the keys out of the ignition.

Quinn looked over the hood of Tim's truck as she shut her door. "What?"

"Huh?"

"You just said 'Jesus,' and I know you aren't religious." Quinn tossed her hair in front of one of her shoulders and gave him a sweet smile.

"Oh yeah, sorry." Tim glanced over his shoulder at the garage one last time as he made his way up the stone walkway. "I think I'm in love."

"Isn't that sweet?" said a voice that was much too deep to be Quinn's.

With a quick whip of his head, Tim locked eyes with Mr. Sawyer. Tim wasn't sure just how much of a sense of humor Mr. Sawyer had, but from the looks of him, it wasn't much of one. The man stood at the front door, his arms crossed in front of his chest as he seemed to appraise Tim. Quinn's father was about the same height as Tim, with dark hair that had clearly been turning gray for some time. Tim suddenly felt the need to hurry up the path, his hand outstretched as his long legs covered the distance between them. "Tim Jacobs, sir. It's a pleasure to finally meet you. And I was talking about the Camaro. Not your daughter." *Real smooth, asshole.* He hesitated, unsure of what to say, as he took a cursory glance at Quinn out of the corner of his eye. Her expression confirmed everything he already knew. He hadn't even formally met Quinn's parents and already he was blowing it. He *did* love Quinn, and he hoped she knew that. He just hadn't said it in so many words yet. And confessing his true feelings for her was better done anywhere else than on this man's front lawn.

"Well, that's *one* way to introduce yourself. Glad to hear you love the car," Mr. Sawyer said before hesitating just as Tim had. "And *not* my daughter." The thin line of Mr. Sawyer's expression revealed nothing of his thoughts. "Please call me Peter," he added, calming Tim's nerves a bit. "And this is Quinn's mother, Julia."

Tim saw the resemblance between the two women immediately. Julia had the same red hair he'd always loved on Quinn, but her mother's was cut much shorter, just above her shoulders, and styled to perfection. He had no doubt that Julia had looked nearly identical to her daughter when she was her age. "Nice to meet you," Tim said, taking Julia's hand in his and giving it a gentle shake. "Now I see where Quinn gets her good looks."

Quinn quirked an eyebrow up at Tim. "Hitting on my dad's car *and* my mom. Should I be jealous?"

Tim opened his mouth to speak but shut it just as fast. He'd already done enough talking. Quinn had clearly been joking, but it only added to Tim's rising insecurities.

Julia's mouth turned up into a warm smile—one Tim was sure she'd formed intentionally to make him feel more at ease. "We're happy you could come for dinner," Julia said before turning toward Quinn to wrap her daughter in a warm embrace.

The Sawyers led Tim and Quinn inside, thankfully ending the awkward greeting. As he made his way through their foyer and back to the kitchen, Tim let Quinn's parents carry the majority of the conversation. Other than commenting on what a lovely home they had and asking what he hoped were a few innocuous questions about some of the photos they had displayed from various family vacations, Tim stayed relatively quiet.

"What would you like to drink, Tim?" Julia asked as she set the shrimp cocktail down on the breakfast bar where Tim and Quinn were seated. "I know Quinn will have some Moscato," she said as she got a wineglass down and began to pour. "We have beer, wine, iced tea, soda . . ."

"Just water'd be great. Thanks."

Mrs. Sawyer handed Quinn the glass of wine and gave Tim a bottle of water out of the fridge. "Is sparkling okay?"

"Perfect. Thank you." Tim opened the bottle and took a long drink, feeling the need to do something with his mouth other than talk. Instead, he was content to listen to the family discuss Quinn's job and the vacation her parents had just taken to their home in the Keys. He managed to make it through the next twenty minutes or so without saying much of anything until Quinn's parents finally ushered them into the formal dining room for the main course: mahimahi with a spicy mango salsa.

"Why don't you sit here, Tim?" Julia said, gesturing to the seat opposite her husband at the other head of the table.

Tim sat, putting his drink down in front of him and scooting in his chair gently, almost as if he were afraid that his presence alone would disrupt the perfection surrounding him. The long cherry table sat beneath a crystal chandelier, and the high-backed chairs made Tim feel smaller than he would have liked. Julia sat on his right side and Quinn on the left. Peter sat at one end of the table, with Tim at the other. Tim couldn't ignore the irony of feeling vulnerable while sitting in a place of power.

The last time he'd sat opposite the man of the house in such a formal setting had been more than twenty-five years ago. He had just turned ten, earning him a seat at the head of the table for Christmas dinner. He was "second in command," as his father had put it, since he was in the double digits. His mother had sat on one of the sides, opposite Scott, as she watched with pride as her older son began to grow up. And Tim had taken the knife his father had and helped carve the turkey as well as any child could. Because that's what he was: a child.

But that was the last time he'd felt like one. The last time his mother would give up her place so Tim could take it. The following year he'd unknowingly thrown a wrench into the proverbial spokes of his parents' marriage. And nothing had felt the same since.

"So, Tim," Peter said, pulling Tim from his memories, "Quinn tells us you're a chef."

Tim swallowed the sip of water he'd just taken and threw his gaze to Quinn for a moment before speaking. "That's right."

Quinn reached a hand over to squeeze his forearm. "I told you he was the *executive* chef. At The Black Lantern."

Tim nodded as he put a Red Bliss potato in his mouth and chewed it slowly. He knew the reason for Quinn's correction. She didn't want her parents thinking he was just some short-order cook at a local diner. They would know how expensive The Black Lantern was even if they had never eaten there. And the place had already been recognized in a few local newspapers and magazines. "Right. *Executive* chef."

"I was nervous to cook for you once Quinn told us

what you did for a living," Julia said. "I hope my meal stacks up." Julia's smile was warm and kind.

"You have no reason to be worried," Tim replied, giving Julia a sincere smile. "It's delicious. Really."

Peter raised his eyebrows from across the table. "An executive chef at one of D.C.'s new restaurants. That's no small feat. You must have had some impressive experience prior to your current position." He dabbed his cloth napkin on his short mustache before returning it gently to his lap. "Did you go to college for hotel and restaurant management first, or did you go to culinary school right out of high school and then study abroad? Our friends' son is in Italy right now doing that exact thing."

Tim cleared his throat, unsure of exactly how to answer. So he took another bite of his fish to give himself a moment to choose his words carefully. "No. I took some time off. I didn't go to culinary school until about six years ago, actually." He put his fork down on his plate, feeling as though he needed to release all of the extra weight he could. "I wasn't really sure what I wanted to do with my life after high school." He could feel Quinn's eyes on him, swore he could hear the beating of her heart increase as she worried whether he would tell her father exactly *why* he'd taken so much time off. "The owner of The Black Lantern is a friend of a friend." He gave Quinn a small smile. "It's all who you know, right?"

Quinn's father gave a slight smile and then took a drink of his red wine. "It's nice when things work out in our favor like that, isn't it?"

Tim locked eyes with Quinn only briefly, but it was long enough to read her. Over the past month and a half he'd gotten so good at recognizing her tells. She was letting him know it was okay. "Yes, it is. I'm pretty lucky," he replied. "So Quinn tells me the two of you own a few businesses yourselves," he added, eager to move the topic of conversation away from himself.

Julia swallowed the food in her mouth and then straightened in her seat, clearly preparing to elaborate. It was exactly what Tim had hoped would happen. She told him about how her own mother had been a florist and she had worked with her as a teenager. "When I met Peter, he was just finishing his business degree and was looking for a solid investment."

"Julia knew the business, and I had some money saved, so I could provide the financial backing. As far as investments go, opening up a flower shop seemed like a safe bet."

Tim didn't have to look at Quinn to know she was probably smirking at the mention of playing things safe.

"Now we have a few shops in the D.C. area and provide arrangements for a lot of corporate events and political affairs. The business has really expanded."

Julia's eyes widened. "We even got to meet the president last year."

"That's incredible," Tim said. "It must be a great feeling to start something from scratch like that and have it grow to be such a success."

"It is," Mr. Sawyer replied. "Nothing quite like it really. But I have no interest in hanging around a flower shop all day. So I find hobbies to keep me busy." He put his fork down and then took a drink. "I think you saw one of those hobbies in the garage. Maybe after dinner I can take you out there and you can see her up close."

Tim could feel his eyes light up with excitement. "Absolutely!" Despite his initial fears, things seemed to be going well with Quinn's parents.

Over the course of the next fifteen minutes, Tim did his best not to appear as though his only thought was getting out to the garage. But as he shoveled food into his mouth at a speed that would rival the car itself, he was fairly certain his efforts were futile.

Finally Mrs. Sawyer spoke. "Why don't you boys go out to the garage while Quinn and I get dessert ready?"

"Are you sure you don't need some help with the dishes?" both men asked nearly in unison. Tim hoped the answer would be no, but his offer was sincere. These people had cooked a delicious meal for him. The least he could do was help clean up.

Julia stood up, stacking a few plates on to one another silently while Tim waited for her response. She took a few steps toward the kitchen before turning around and smiling in a way that told Tim the suspense she'd caused was intentional. "Nope. We got it. I'll come get you when dessert's ready."

"You heard the woman, Tim. Let's get out of here before she changes her mind."

Tim ducked under the hood again as if he hadn't spent the last fifteen minutes examining the Camaro inside and out. He'd walked around the exterior, admiring the sparkling bloodred paint before Peter had popped the hood to show him the modifications he'd made to the car's performance. "This thing's even better up close. I'd love to work on something like this eventually."

"Yeah, this garage is my hideout. Anytime I want a little fresh air or just to relax for a while, I come out here to work on her." He strolled over to where a brown leather couch—which looked much too clean to be in someone's garage—sat against the wall and reached into the fridge next to it. "Plus," he said as he extended a bottle toward Tim with a small laugh, "there's beer out here."

"I'm fine. Thanks," Tim said as casually as he could.

Mr. Sawyer put the beer back without a word, and the next few minutes followed much the same way.

Tim tried to busy himself with the car, finally sitting in the driver's seat and running his hand softly over the dash.

"So I gotta know," Peter said, finally breaking the silence that had hung in the air like a thick fog between them, "what's your story?"

Well, that didn't take long. Tim had been wondering how long it would take for Peter to make up his mind about him. Turns out, it took about two hours. "My story?"

"Yeah, I mean you aren't exactly who I pictured when my daughter said she was bringing her new boyfriend to meet us."

Tim exited the car slowly, carefully, as if any sudden

movement might disrupt the fragility of their conversation. "Who *did* you picture?"

Mr. Sawyer let out a sharp laugh. "You know, I'm not sure really. I guess I just expected someone more like . . . Quinn."

Tim's first instinct was to defend himself, to defend what he had with Quinn and tell Mr. Sawyer that if he thought Tim was nothing like Quinn, then he clearly didn't know his own daughter. But he kept his mouth closed, knowing that his own insecurities would start to show, making him afraid of what might escape if he spoke.

"But she shows up here with this tattooed . . . *man*," he said as if the word left a bitter taste on his tongue. "And I'm guessing you had something to do with the new jewelry on my daughter's nose?"

"It was something she wanted to—"

"It wasn't something she wanted to do before she met *you*." Mr. Sawyer let out a long sigh. "I know my daughter's an adult. But she's still my daughter." Quinn's father set his beer down on a metal shelf and crossed his arms, his stare meeting Tim's with an unmistakable intensity. "I don't know just how serious you are about this relationship. But I do know Quinn. And she clearly likes you." Mr. Sawyer dropped his eyes to the ground and rubbed his shoe on a stained patch of concrete before returning his gaze to Tim. "Look, you seem like a nice enough guy. You're charming, well-spoken, but I don't *know* you."

"Do you usually know people you're meeting for the first time?" Tim's retort was quick and firm. He felt the muscles in his body stiffen with Peter's words, the anger and hurt rising within him. It certainly wasn't the first time a person had made assumptions about Tim based on the way he looked. But he'd hoped that the people who'd raised a beautiful girl like Quinn would be different. Being judged by these people—*Quinn's* people—stung more than he'd expected. And what sucked even more was that his past didn't prove their assumptions incorrect. Tim had barely graduated high school and had a history of drug use that would've made GlaxoSmithKline blush. And while he didn't openly talk about his addiction with strangers, he refused to hide it either. It was as much a part of him as the ink on his skin, and there was no use hiding what they were bound to find out anyway. Finally realizing that Peter was looking at him, clearly choosing to ignore Tim's initial rebuttal and still expecting a more suitable response to his question, Tim replied. "What is it you want to know?" The words sounded cold and dry. But he couldn't bring himself to care.

Mr. Sawyer shrugged casually as he picked his beer back up and took a sip. "How about we start with why you don't drink?"

Tim knew his request to have water with dinner hadn't raised any red flags. But rejecting a beer your girlfriend's dad offered you doesn't go unnoticed. It went against every rule of male bonding. Tim exhaled a long breath and folded his arms across his chest. Though he was about to open up about his past to a person he'd just met, he felt the need to stay physically closed, as though his arms might serve as some sort of a barrier. Finally, he brought his gaze up to meet Peter's, knowing that his stare probably revealed the strange cocktail of emotions he'd been feeling since he'd pulled up to the Sawyers' home. "That choice is a pretty standard one for people in recovery."

Quinn's father gave a short nod and twisted his lips as if he were biting back a comment he knew he should keep in. "Fair enough," he said. "So you're an alcoholic, then."

Tim swallowed hard. He hadn't anticipated that Peter would assume that, though he didn't know why. "Addict would be a more accurate description."

"Hmm," Mr. Sawyer said quietly, and Tim stayed silent, knowing that Peter wasn't finished. "You mind if I ask what you were addicted to?"

Tim let out a disgusted laugh and shook his head. "Does it matter?"

Mr. Sawyer thought for a moment, his eyes narrowing. "You know, it probably doesn't."

"Look, I don't mean to be disrespectful. Any father has the right to know the man who's dating his daughter. I get that." Tim ran a hand roughly through his hair. He felt himself wavering, felt his uncertainty about everything he was sharing. "What I mean is, the only thing that should matter is that I'm clean *now*. After wasting more than ten years of my life, I finally got it back on track. And I'm happy. I haven't taken a drink, picked up so much as a joint, or swallowed a pill—not even an Advil for a damn headache—in almost eight years."

Peter's silence made it difficult for Tim to read his

reaction. Eventually he spoke. "What finally made you stop all of that self-destructive behavior? You made poor choices for more than a decade and then you're just able to quit? What changed?" he asked, his brows furrowing as if he wasn't sure whether to believe that Tim was really clean. Or maybe it was more that he wasn't sure he'd stay that way.

Tim inhaled deeply, letting the oxygen settle into his blood and work its way through his body. "I almost lost someone I love, someone who loves *me*. My brother." Finally Tim relaxed his arms, allowing one to hang at his side while he slid his other hand into his pocket. "Scott could've died in the passenger seat of *my* car because I was too damn high to even give a second thought to driving. My stupidity and selfishness nearly took the life of my own brother." Tim's head hurt with the tears that were forming behind his eyes, but he held them back. He always did. "I was done destroying people's lives. And that included my own."

Mr. Sawyer raised an eyebrow. "That's quite a story."

"What is?" Quinn's voice floated through the garage before she actually appeared.

Her father glanced at Tim and then back at his daughter. "Your boyfriend here was just telling me about something that happened at the restaurant the other day."

"Oh. Well, speaking of food, Mom told me to come get you guys. Dessert's ready."

"What are we waiting for, then?" Peter threw an arm around his daughter, squeezing her tightly as he led her out of the garage and away from Tim.

*   *   *

The ride home was exactly as Tim had expected it to be . . . *needed* it to be: relatively quiet. Quinn had tried to make conversation about the night—how he liked her parents, what he honestly thought of the food. She even joked about how not heading up to her old bedroom had been a missed opportunity. "Maybe next time, then," she said.

"Yeah," he replied. Much like the rest of his responses, that one was clipped and devoid of any inflection. Eventually, after he was sure Quinn could sense something was wrong, her attempt at conversation slowed until it stopped completely.

"You want to come up?" Quinn asked when he pulled up in front of her apartment building.

"Not tonight." *God, I really* am *a dick.*

"You okay?" she asked, concern in her eyes as she rubbed a hand on his shoulder.

"Just tired."

Quinn cocked her head to the side for a moment, as if she were deciding whether or not to press him for more. Thankfully, she didn't. "Okay. Call you tomorrow, then," she said, more like a question than a statement. Then she leaned in to him, placing a soft kiss against his lips.

He couldn't help but want more. Not because he was some horny bastard who couldn't kiss his girlfriend without wanting to rip her clothes off. But because no amount of Quinn ever felt like enough.

But if there was one thing he'd gotten exceptionally good at over the past seven years, it was resisting temptation. He pulled away slowly without a word, returned his eyes to the windshield in front of him, and said good-night as Quinn exited the car.

Once she was safely inside, the quiet he'd enjoyed dissipated rapidly. Now he was alone with a voice much louder than Quinn's: his own. And that voice told him the same thing Mr. Sawyer was trying to tell him without using the exact words. Tim wasn't good enough.

And the more Tim thought about it, the more he felt Quinn's father had a right to judge him. Tim tried to imagine what it would be like to have a child—a daughter—and to see her come home with someone like Tim. He couldn't deny that he'd have a reaction similar to Mr. Sawyer's. It wasn't enough that he had a successful career, or that he was polite and intelligent. What father in his right mind would knowingly allow a recovering drug addict to date his daughter?

No matter how much Tim tried to cast a shadow upon the person he used to be with the person he wanted to become, there was no hiding who he was. You can gift wrap a present any way you want to. But all the pretty wrapping paper doesn't change what's inside the box.

And it was that thought that caused a physical pain to shoot through his chest, caused his heart to *actually* hurt inside his body. It didn't matter how many times Quinn tried to convince him otherwise. It wouldn't change the truth Tim had fought so hard to ignore.

He wanted what was best for her. And Tim wasn't it.

Chapter 20

Withdrawal Letter

Nothing.

Quinn stared at the text, not sure how to reply, or even if she should. Her mind was scattered, trying desperately to come up with a reason for Tim's distance. But like his text said, there was nothing.

Ever since having dinner with her parents, he'd been weird. And in the five days that followed, Quinn hadn't seen him. They'd had only two stilted conversations and had exchanged some texts that were clipped and awkward. It was such a departure from the warm, compassionate conversations they normally had, she didn't know what to think. Finally, she'd reached her breaking point and asked him what was wrong. That's when she got the Nothing.

Her fingers warred with her brain, the former desperate to reply that something sure as fuck was wrong and the latter not wanting to risk making things even worse. Quinn quickly retreated to the safe side, and she was instantly disappointed in the choice. She thought she'd kicked the safe, innocent Quinn to the curb weeks ago. But with Tim pulling away, she felt her courage retreat with him. It concerned her: was she only strong when Tim was there to back her up? Had she not *really* made the changes she'd convinced herself of, instead wrapping herself in Tim's self-assuredness and passing it off as her own?

Can I see you tonight? she typed, praying to get a response that wouldn't make her feel so . . . sad.

Sorry. I'm working tonight.

It was the same thing he'd written every time she'd asked that week. He was either lying or his job had decided to employ slave-labor tactics. Opening her desk drawer on a huff, she threw her phone inside and slammed it closed. If he wouldn't willingly talk to her, then she'd just have to barge in there and leave him with no other choice.

Quinn had been staring at Tim's door for a while. She wasn't sure just how long, but the ache that was developing in her high-heel-clad feet indicated that she'd been standing still for a while. She heard sounds from inside. *Clearly not working.*

She'd wanted to be mad that he'd lied. Wanted to be furious, actually. But she couldn't quite muster it. At least not as the dominant emotion racking her body. She was too busy fluctuating between panic and all-out fear. She had no idea what awaited her on the other side of the door, and she was almost too afraid to find out. Almost. But the journalist inside of her eventually won out, her curiosity getting the better of her. So she knocked.

She heard muffled footsteps approach the door, but it didn't open right away. Quinn knew he'd looked through the peephole. Knew he'd seen her. And he didn't open to let her in. *God, this is brutal.*

Finally the door opened, and there he was. The object of her fantasies for almost a year, the man who knew her in ways no one else did, the man who had irrevocably changed her forever. But he didn't look happy to see her.

"Hey," he said.

"Really? 'Hey' is the best you got?" *Okay, so maybe I can muster some anger after all.*

He shrugged in reply.

Quinn took a moment to look at him. He looked . . . young. Timid. Resigned. Of course she couldn't be sure, but she had a sinking suspicion that the Tim standing in front of her looked even worse than the addict he'd once been. He hadn't shaved recently, his posture was slumped, and his emerald eyes lacked the vibrancy they normally held.

"You going to let me in, or are we just going to stare each other down across the threshold?"

Tim wiped a hand over his face before backing away from the door and gesturing her inside. She heard him softly push the door shut behind her. "You want a drink or something?" he asked.

She walked a little farther down the hall and turned

in to the kitchen, with Tim following. "Oh, I want something, all right. For you to tell me what the hell is going on here."

Tim shoved his hands into the pockets of his sweatpants, looking down at the floor. "Nothing. I've just been—"

"I swear to God, Tim, if you tell me nothing or that you were working one more time, I'm seriously going to do you bodily harm." Quinn gestured to the kitchen with her arm, pointing out the pan sizzling on the stove. "You're obviously not working. So stop lying, and level with me." She closed her eyes and took a breath. Her voice was calmer when she pleaded, "Please. I can't do this. Not knowing what's going on. We've never had secrets between us. But you're keeping them now, and I need to know why."

He continued to stare at the floor, his jaw ticking like the seconds that passed them by. Finally he released a breath that sounded as though it weighed a thousand pounds and spoke. "I don't want the same things you do, Quinn. I thought I did, or that I could. But I don't and I can't."

Quinn shook her head in disbelief. "What does that even mean?"

"Exactly what it sounds like. We started . . . all this," he said as he swirled his hand between them, "to help you write an article. But in the process of all that, it made me revisit some dark places. And maybe I clung to you because I was afraid that I couldn't face those demons alone. But now I realize that that's not true. I'm actually better off facing them on my own."

"Dark places? We've had nothing but good times since we started hanging out. I don't understand any of this."

He did look at her then, his eyes detached. Hollow. "How could you understand?" His words were devoid of any emotion, as though he were reading them off a page. "You haven't had to walk in my shoes, Quinn. And believe me, I'm glad for that. The things we did for your article, for you they were about stepping outside of yourself, walking on the wild side for a little while. But that used to be my *life*. Shoplifting? I used to do that shit multiple times a day, both to survive and to feed my habit. Hitchhiking? Nothing new there either. I signed up to help you because I liked what you were trying to do for yourself and I thought I could handle it. But I can't. I can't be your knight in shining armor, or your hero, or whatever skewed image you've morphed me into. I'm barely holding myself together. I can't hold you too. And it's not fair of you to ask that of me."

Quinn felt like she was standing in front of a stranger. He'd never even hinted at any of that before. He was basically calling her selfish, and there was no way she was going to stand there and let him make her out to be the problem between them. Especially when there hadn't even been a problem a week ago. "First of all, I haven't morphed you into anything. I see exactly who you are. It's *you* who sees a lie when you look in the mirror. *Your* perception that's skewed. Second, I won't let you act like I'm some selfish prima donna. I'm a good person, Tim. And I will *not* let you twist that into something ugly. Just like I won't let you twist what's between us that way. Because you and me? We're fucking beautiful."

"You only see what you want to, not the truth."

"Then show me the truth."

He stretched his arms out. "I am. It's right here. This scarred, tattooed criminal is the truth. I don't fit in your world, Quinn. You were fooling yourself to ever think I would. And I let you fool me too. But not anymore."

Quinn winced at his words. "I didn't fit in my world either. Not until you. Together we fit. Together we're perfect."

Tim let out a humorless laugh. "Look at me. Do I really look perfect to you?"

"No. Right now you look like an asshole."

"Well, you asked to see the truth."

"I know. And I'm still asking. Stop bullshitting me. That night at that restaurant, when you told me about your tattoo and how it represented the Kipling poem, you said it reminded you to never give up. But that's what you're doing. Something spooked you, and you're quitting instead of telling me what happened. Was it my parents? Did they make you uncomfortable somehow? I can't fix it if I don't know what happened."

"Nothing happened. Your parents are nice people. But I don't belong in some big house that sits on two acres of land. That life kicked me to the curb a long time ago. It isn't me anymore, and I don't want it to be."

"I'm not asking you to be anyone other than who you are."

"Maybe not, but I feel the pressure to be all the same."

Quinn sputtered. How had they gotten this far off track? "Those feelings are all self-imposed. You can't blame me for them."

"I don't want to argue about this anymore," Tim said with obvious agitation. "It doesn't matter what we say. Nothing will change how I feel."

"Tim, you can't just walk away without trying to fix things. We're so good to—"

"Being with you makes me unbalanced. It makes me want to use, Quinn."

It was a dirty thing to use against her, but he couldn't help it. Because the longer she stood there, fighting for him, the weaker his resolve became. He couldn't lose this battle. For her sake, he had to push her away. And when he saw the fight instantly drain out of her, he knew it had worked.

He watched her brace a hand to her chest as if she were manually trying to prevent her heart from breaking. The sight made him want to fall to the floor and curl into himself. Instead, he stood there, resolute. He needed her to believe the words he'd been spouting, needed her to see him as the piece of trash he felt like.

Ever since dinner with her parents, Tim had tried to figure out what the right thing to do was. The last thing he ever wanted to do was hurt Quinn, but he hadn't been able to see any other way. It was either hurt her now, while things were new and she'd be able to recover quickly, or let them get even more enmeshed only for her to discover what he had known all along, what he was sure her parents knew: that Quinn deserved more than some tatted-up chef with a rap sheet.

It didn't matter that she made him feel worth something, because ultimately he made her worth depreciate. She was like a beautifully ornate kite, and he was the string that would tether her to the ground when she should be up in the air flying. No matter how hard she bucked into the wind, desperate to see where it would lead her, a guy like him would always force her back down. Because Tim had realized as a teenager, no matter how well he did in school or how accomplished he was in sports, he would never truly fly. No one as afraid of falling as he was could ever make a life up in the clouds.

She blinked rapidly, her eyes bright with moisture. Her chin jutted before she reset it and hardened her features.

She is so fucking strong. Stronger than I could ever even hope to be.

"I, umm, I don't . . ." She cleared her throat. "I'm not sure what to say."

Tim looked down at the floor again like the coward he was. "Then let's just say good-bye."

He glanced up to see her nodding sadly. She walked toward him, putting her arms around his neck when she reached him. He didn't return the hug. "I never wanted to make things harder for you. I thought . . ." She pulled away from him and averted her eyes. "It doesn't matter what I thought. Take care of yourself, Tim."

With that, she walked down the hall, through the door, and out of his life.

He couldn't understand how something could be the right thing to do and still hurt so fucking bad. Tim walked over to the counter where he had been prepping his dinner. With a yell that sounded like an animal in excruciating pain, he hurled everything to the floor. He then pushed his hands through his hair, gripping tightly on the ends and pulling, needing physical pain to match the emotional devastation he was feeling. He turned, leaning back on the counter as his legs gave out. He slid to the floor, knees bent with his elbows propped on them so he could maintain the pressure on his scalp. It wasn't calming him like he'd hoped it would. Finally letting go, he fished in his pocket for his phone. He didn't even let himself think as he scrolled until he found the name he needed and called.

The phone rang a few times before going to voice mail. "Hi. This is Roger. You know what to do."

Once Tim heard the beep, he unleashed on the only man he thought would understand. "Roger, it's me. I— I . . ." Tim banged the back of his head against the cabinet door. "I'm so lost, Rog. I'm just so fucking lost."

Chapter 21

Sear

Only one word appropriately described the middle of July: oppressive. Not only did the unbearable humidity cause Quinn's hair to stick to the back of her neck as she made her daily trek from her car to the doors of her office building every morning, but her mind had been experiencing severe discomfort as well.

She hadn't talked to Tim in the eight days since their breakup—if it could have even been called that. The whole thing made her wonder if they'd really been as close as she'd thought they were to begin with. And the more she let their conversation weigh on her mind, the less sense it made. He'd called her selfish, claimed that being with her made him feel "unbalanced." Something just didn't add up.

But as much as she wanted to ask him about it, to further question his motives, she knew better than to do it. Because as much as Tim *seemed* to be the poster boy for getting your life back on track, clearly he wasn't. That car had left the race long before Quinn even realized it had a flat tire. And now it was so completely broken, no pit crew in the world would be able to fix it.

She had to accept it. Tim was gone. Gone from her life, and for all intents and purposes, gone from his own. The man who had spoken to her in Tim's apartment wasn't him. He'd gotten that much right at least. Quinn had seen the emptiness behind his eyes, heard the coldness in his voice. And nothing she could have said or done would have changed that.

And she didn't want to try. She was scared to flip a switch in him that he wouldn't be able to turn off. And the last thing she wanted to do was be the cause of his relapse.

But she'd never even gotten to tell Tim how she really felt about him. The thought ate at her like a parasite. And now here she was, staring at a blank computer screen, trying to think of how the hell she was supposed to write an article that had just as much to do with him as it had to do with her.

"What's wrong?" The question came from Lauren, who was sitting beside Quinn in the backseat of Cass' car.

"Huh?"

"You've been staring out your window since we picked you up," Lauren replied.

Quinn turned away from the glass just in time to catch Cass' eyes in the rearview mirror.

"Nothing's *wrong*. Just trying to think of what to write for that article. The deadline's soon and I don't have a clue where to start. I usually don't get writer's block like this." The fact that all of that was true made Quinn feel slightly better about not mentioning the breakup. She hadn't said anything about it to the girls yet. Partly because she hadn't seen them since it happened and partly because, well, she just didn't feel like talking about it. She'd figured agreeing to see a movie would be a safe night out with her friends—one that would allow her to sit passively and get her mind off of Tim while still enjoying the company of her three closest girlfriends.

"Did Tim give you any suggestions?"

Damn it. It was an innocent question and one that was probably meant to make Quinn feel at ease. But it triggered the opposite effect. She noticed herself shift toward the window reflexively as if the physical space between her and her best friend would conceal how uncomfortable the mention of Tim's name made her feel. "I haven't talked to him about it."

Quinn felt Lauren's hand on her forearm before Lauren even spoke. "What is it? Something's definitely wrong. Did you and Tim get into a fight or something?"

"Yeah. Something," Quinn answered.

"Come on, Quinn. It's just us," Simone prompted. "If you guys are fighting, we can help. God knows Laur's kicked enough men in the balls to be able—"

"That was *one* time," Lauren shot back. "And I actually used my knee."

"Well, I meant it mostly metaphorically," Simone added with a short laugh. "Sometimes you just need to put a guy in his place."

Quinn let her skull fall back hard against the headrest, causing her brain to rattle inside it as she let out a long huff. She didn't feel like getting into all the details. At least not right now. But she needed to let them know what happened, if for no other reason than so that they would drop it. "I'm pretty sure he knows his place," Quinn finally responded. "And it's not with me."

The girls exchanged brief looks of confusion—the narrowing of eyes, the biting of lips—before the full meaning of Quinn's statement sank in. It didn't come as a surprise that Simone was the first one to speak. She was definitely the most emotionally mature of the three. "I'm sorry, Quinn" was all she said.

Quinn knew her girls well enough to know they wouldn't press her for information. They'd accept whatever little bit she'd tell them without pushing her for more.

"Yeah, I feel awful," Lauren added. "I would've been there for you. Scott didn't tell me." Then she paused for a moment as if she'd just realized something. "I don't even think Tim told him. I'm sure if he did, Scott would try to talk some sense into him, ya know? It took Scott a while to come to his senses and realize that I'm the best thing for him," she said with a small smile. It was a poor attempt to lighten the mood. "I'm sure Tim will do the same. Maybe he just needs time."

"Yeah, I'm sure he'll come around. I agree with Laur. Give him some time," Cass said, more sweetly than Quinn was used to. "And if that doesn't work, give him a good knee to the balls."

Quinn could see the crinkle of Cass' eyes in the mirror. And for what felt like the first time since her breakup with Tim, Quinn couldn't help but smile.

The dark living room offered Tim comfort he knew he had no right to. With the curtains drawn and only the faint light from an illuminated lamp across the room, he had sheathed himself in near blackness.

He sat forward on the couch, his elbows resting on his knees, his head angled toward the floor. Tim felt like he'd spent the past two weeks in this position, though of course he hadn't. He'd forced himself upright long enough to go to work, where he'd been a surly prick. Or at least that's what he'd overheard someone on the waitstaff call him.

His cell phone rang beside him, and he was instantly annoyed at it for casting any more light into his vicinity. But when he glanced down at it, the fact that it was Roger's daughter's name on the display caught his attention, so he decided to do something he'd done only seldomly over the past week: answer it. "Hello?"

"Tim?" a familiar, yet throatier than normal, voice said.

"Bridget? What's wrong?"

"It's Dad. He's gone."

And that's when the earth fell away completely. Tim hadn't heard back from Roger since his desperate call to him after his breakup with Quinn. He'd tried calling again, but the phone hadn't even rung that time, going straight to voice mail instead. It was so unlike Roger not to call him right back, but Tim had lapsed so deep into his own depression he'd chalked it up to just one more person who was sick of his shit. Even though logically he knew that would *never* be the case with Roger, Tim just hadn't had it in him to search for a better reason. It was something he knew he'd never forgive himself for. "What—" Tim took a deep, steadying breath. "What do you mean he's gone?" His voice cracked on the last word no matter how much he'd tried to steel himself against it.

"The cancer. God, Tim. Even though I knew it was coming, I'm still in shock. We lost him Sunday." Bridget was crying quietly even though her sniffles told Tim that she was trying to hold it back. "What am I going to do without my dad?" she whispered.

Tim didn't know what the hell to say. When he'd lost his dad, at least he'd been an adult. As well as high as the fucking stars. But Bridget was only nineteen, still in college, still so much life ahead of her. Now here she was tasked with calling people and telling them her father had died. Though Tim's mind wouldn't let him dwell on any of that long. "Cancer?"

Bridget was quiet for a second. "You mean . . . Shit, Tim, did he not tell you?"

Tim was reeling. *Roger was dead? Of cancer? Cancer the bastard had known about?* He tried to keep his voice even, not wanting Bridget to have to deal with his breakdown too. He knew, despite all she was dealing with, that she'd worry about him if he sounded as distraught as he felt. Tim had met her about six years ago, when his relationship with Roger moved beyond addict-sponsor and more toward father-son territory. Since then, Tim had been present for birthdays, graduations, some holidays, and random special occasions. Bridget knew Tim's story, and could understand it in ways most others couldn't since she'd lived with a recovering addict her entire life. He cleared his throat and replied. "No, he never said anything about it."

"That asshole," Bridget said with a small laugh. She used it as a term of endearment, the fondness for her father evident in her voice.

Tim almost laughed too. It was the same candor she'd always had with Roger. She never let him get away with anything, which Tim suspected was a huge contributor to his lasting sobriety. That and the fact that Roger loved his daughter with every fiber of his being, and when she'd gotten old enough to start noticing that something was wrong with him, Roger had quit drugs cold turkey and he'd never looked back.

"He told me that he was going to talk to you. Tell you about his cancer. It started in his liver. It came on fast. By the time he went to the doctor, he was already in stage three. Within a month, it had spread to his lymph nodes, moved into stage four, and the doctors gave him six months. He only lasted three." She sucked in a shuddering breath. "I'm so sorry, Tim. He should have told you. You know he never wanted to look weak in front of anybody, the stubborn ass."

Tim wasn't sure what to say. He'd lost Quinn for a greater good, but there was nothing good in this. Losing Roger was a blow he just wasn't sure how to handle. He sank his head into his hand, wondering what the hell he'd ever done to deserve any of this. Tim was a champ when it came to taking responsibility for his actions, but this was bordering on cruel. He hadn't done anything to warrant losing Roger. Tim fucking *needed* him. "I just . . . Fuck, Bridge, I got nothing." Tim ran his hand over his face. "Is there going to be a service? Do you need anything?"

"Mom and I are organizing everything." Bridget's mom had divorced Roger right after Bridget was born, but they'd become friends after he'd gotten clean. "We're just having a memorial service at Gracci Funeral Home. Dad didn't want anything big. It's Thursday at ten."

"I'll be there."

"I know." Bridget's voice was warm, and Tim let himself bask in it. "Tim?"

"Yeah?"

"He loved you. We owe it to him to keep it together. Both of us."

Her words both fractured him and made him feel whole. Hearing her say that Roger loved him was something he'd needed. Because if ever Tim needed to know he was loved, it was then. But the fact that the source of that love was gone, that he'd lost someone else who gave a shit about him, broke him. Hearing the concern in Bridget's voice didn't help. She was afraid he was going to relapse. This nineteen-year-old kid had just lost her father, and as she grieved her loss, she had to check in on her dad's junkie friend to make sure he didn't raid the nearest pharmacy. "I'm good, Bridge. Promise. I'll see you Thursday. Sooner if you need me."

"Thanks, Tim."

Tim wanted to scoff at her words. There was nothing to be thankful for. Especially not to him.

Quinn wasn't sure that she was doing the right thing. In fact, she was pretty sure she wasn't. When Lauren had called her yesterday to tell her about Roger, Quinn had gone completely numb. She had met him only the one time, but it was clear what he had meant to Tim. Despite how they'd ended things, Quinn had no desire for Tim to be hurting. She loved him too much.

That had actually been one of the hardest parts of the previous weeks. Sure, Quinn knew she was falling for Tim, but having nothing but time to process just how far she'd actually fallen had not been a fun experience. Coming to the realization that she was in love with someone who wanted nothing to do with her was the most painful thing Quinn had ever endured. And it was still nothing compared to what Tim was probably feeling in the wake of losing Roger.

So that's why she was standing outside Tim's apartment forty-five minutes before Roger's service was due to start. She didn't want to show up at the memorial for fear that she'd make things more difficult for Tim. But she also wanted him know that she was there if he needed her. But as she stared at his door, she began to wonder if that was selfish of her. If he wanted her around, he'd let her know. *Right?* Was her desire to be there for him more about her needs than his? Quinn was growing tired of the near-constant internal struggles she waged against herself. She wanted to be the person she'd set out to find two months ago when she'd pitched her article. The article she now clutched in her hand. Writing it had been a purge. She'd gotten out of it what she'd needed to, but she had also lost more than she'd probably ever fully recover from. Vowing that the strength she'd found would be enough for her to see this through, she raised her hand and knocked on Tim's door. It was pulled open quickly, and a harried, profoundly sad man stood before her.

"Tim," she gasped as she took him in.

Emotions rolled over his face, but they shifted too quickly for her to identify any of them. Except the last one: annoyance. "Now's not a good time, Quinn."

Quinn straightened her spine. "I know. I heard about Roger. I just wanted to stop by and check on you." She thought she saw his eyes glisten before he cleared his throat and diverted his gaze.

"Thanks. But I'm fine. And late. I've got to get to the memorial."

Quinn knew it was probably just an excuse, but she didn't call him out on it. "I won't keep you long."

Tim seemed to be having an internal struggle all his own as he stood there looking at her. Finally he took a step back into his apartment and motioned her inside. He dug his hands into his pockets as she walked past, and she couldn't help but wonder where her strong, confident Tim had gone.

"What did you need?" he asked.

"To know you're okay."

He rolled his eyes. It made her want to slap the shit out of him. "I said I was fine."

"I know what you said."

"Then why are we having this conversation?"

"Because I'd like to hear the truth."

Tim stood up a little straighter, narrowing his eyes at her. "What reason would I have to lie to you?"

"Only you'd know."

"Quinn, I really don't need this shit right now."

He started to move toward the door, but she stepped to him quickly, grabbing his arm. "I'm not trying to fight with you."

He looked down at her hand on his arm. "Could've fooled me."

"Don't do that."

"Do what?" he spat.

"Act like it bothers you when I touch you. Act like you don't need anybody. Act like you're fine when we both know you're not."

"Who said I was acting?"

"I did."

"And you're who exactly?" He waited a beat before continuing. "Oh, I get it. This is the new and improved Quinn. The one who gets her nose pierced, hustles a bunch of degenerates at pool, and slums it with a junkie so she can get ahead at her job. Nice to meet you, but I really have somewhere more important to be."

He went to move away from her, but she tightened her grip and he didn't pull his arm free. Quinn took a deep breath, keeping her anger in check. "I get that you're hurting. And I'm more than happy to be your punching bag if it helps. But I will not *ever* let you say that what we had was simply me 'slumming it.' You don't want to be with me anymore? Fine. But we were friends before all of that. Whether you want to admit it or not, I know you better than almost anybody. So stop bullshitting me and let me be there for you."

Tim let out a humorless laugh that Quinn hoped she never heard again. "You can't just insert yourself into someone's life, Quinn."

Quinn looked at Tim for a second, analyzing the face she had gotten so familiar with over the past two months. She barely recognized it. Giving his arm a final squeeze, she let go, offered him a small smile, and began to walk around him toward the door.

"I'm not trying to hurt your feelings." His voice caused her to turn back toward him. "I just . . ."

"You don't have to explain. I get it. See ya around."

He nodded at her, and she made her way to the door. She hesitated next to the table that sat near the door and held up the envelope she'd been carrying in her hand. Without looking back, she said, "This is my article. When you're ready, maybe it can set a few things straight." She set it down on the table. "Bye, Tim." And then, for the second time, she left Tim's apartment heartbroken.

Chapter 22

Correspondent

Tim let his gaze drift over the coffee shop patrons before taking a long gulp from his cup. "So what was so important that you had to drag me out of bed on a Sunday to come *here*?" he asked, expressing his innate aversion to the place.

Scott let out a sharp laugh and rolled his eyes. "You know, I'll never get used to making plans with someone who doesn't have to be at work until the afternoon." He glanced at his watch. "It's eleven in the morning. Most people are up by now. And it's coffee, not the Boston Marathon."

The comparison had clearly been meant as a joke, but Tim couldn't help but think that the Boston Marathon actually seemed preferable to the coffeehouse. There was something to be said for the struggle of running more than twenty-six miles, something to be said for the toll it takes on your body and mind. He would have embraced the sore muscles, the sweat. But this place was just too cheerful for him. Some of the customers picked leisurely at pastries as they clicked around on their laptops or iPads without a care in the world. He could hear the elderly couple at the small table beside them discussing their upcoming trip to the beach with their young grandchildren. It was all too . . . happy. Too lighthearted for how heavy his heart felt.

When Scott had called the night before and asked Tim to meet for coffee the next day, he'd known there was a reason behind it. He could hear the urgency in Scott's voice. And even if Tim was dealing with his own shit, he still needed to be there to help his only brother deal with his. Tim pulled his sunglasses out of his pocket and slid them over his eyes in an attempt to block out the sunlight that was streaming in through the window next to them.

"Don't do that," Scott said.

"Do what?"

"Be one of those douches who wears sunglasses inside."

Tim shrugged—an attempt to seem more casual than he felt. "It's sunny. They're sunglasses," he said. "Now, tell me why we're here before I start singing the Corey Hart song and embarrass you completely."

Scott cocked a brow, obviously confused.

"'Sunglasses at Night'?"

Scott's face gave no indication that he recognized the song. Finally, after a moment or two of staring at his brother, he responded. "God, you really *are* old."

Tim was sure his own stoic expression mirrored

Scott's exactly. "Out with it," he finally said, gesturing with his hand for Scott to start talking.

Scott sighed dramatically. "Fine. But you should know you suck the fun out of *everything*." Then he reached into his pocket and pulled out a black box. It took Tim only a second to realize what was inside.

Scott didn't have to even bother opening it. But he did anyway, revealing a diamond ring that nearly blinded Tim as the sun hit it. *Thank God I'm wearing sunglasses*. He also worried about what Scott might see in Tim's eyes if he showed them: all the hurt, the pain he felt over letting Quinn go. And it was only magnified by Scott's news. Tim was actually surprised Scott hadn't proposed to Lauren sooner. He loved her like he'd never seen another person love anyone.

"I've had this for a while," Scott said. "I just haven't had the courage until now to—"

"I think the two fellas next to us are homos, Sally."

Scott stopped midsentence to turn his attention to the old man next to them, but Tim was already speaking. "Oh . . . no . . . we're not—"

But Scott's voice interrupted him. "We're not going to sit here and let you ruin such a special moment is what we're not going to do." Scott caught Tim's line of vision briefly, letting him know to keep his mouth shut. Apparently, the elderly gentleman got the same message, because he remained silent as Scott continued. "I love this man. And I'll do anything to make him happy. And if you think that that's going to change because there are people in the world who are too closed-minded to accept that others aren't exactly like them, then you should probably find another place to eat your breakfast."

But Scott's last comment was unnecessary. The couple had already started to stand and was headed toward the door.

"What the fuck was that about?" Tim asked, eyes wide.

Scott tossed a piece of his cherry turnover into his mouth as if he hadn't done anything out of the ordinary. "I'm just tired of people expecting others to be someone they're not and acting like people can change who they love like you change your fucking underwear. You can't. You know what I mean?"

"Yeah," Tim said quietly before taking off his glasses and rubbing his fingers hard across his eyes. "I do."

Chapter 23

The Column

Why did I come here? As Tim sat on his stool looking at the pool table, that thought was on constant repeat in his head. Normally he jumped at the chance to hang out with his friends, especially since it was rare that they all were able to hang out together. But Tim wasn't feeling normal. He was just feeling numb.

It didn't help that the guys had been up his ass since he'd told them about Roger. Tim appreciated the support system, but he ultimately wanted to be alone. And it wasn't only because he was still reeling from the loss of Roger, though that fact made him feel like a total prick. His sponsor, his good friend, was dead, and all Tim could think about was how much he missed Quinn. How much he regretted how callous he'd been. And sometimes, when he was feeling particularly down, he regretted even pursuing a relationship with her in the first place. Life was better when he hadn't known what he was missing.

"You doin' okay, man?"

Tim startled at the intrusion to his thoughts. Looking up, he saw Rudy's concerned face. "Huh? Oh yeah. Yeah, I'm okay."

Rudy took the stool next to Tim. "You know, you can stop bullshitting me anytime now."

Tim rolled his eyes. "I'm not bullshitting you. Losing Roger sucks. I miss him, and it hit me hard. But I *am* okay. I'm not looking to run to the nearest alleyway and score, so you guys can stop hovering."

"Well, I'm glad to hear all of that, but that's not what I was referring to."

"Then what the hell are you referring to?"

Rudy eyed him curiously for a second. "Where's the redhead?"

Shifting in his stool, Tim felt his jaw flex. "Her name is Quinn. And I don't know where she is."

"And *why* don't you know?"

"Because it's none of my business."

"Are you going to be a dense asshole all night?"

Tim felt his mouth lift into an involuntary smirk. "Probably."

"Fine. You don't want to talk, then you can listen. I've known you for a long time, Tim. Known you through drugs, rehabs, bad times, and good times. I've seen you at your worst, and I've seen you at your best. Do you want to know when you were at your best?"

"I thought I just had to listen."

Rudy continued as if Tim hadn't spoken. "When you brought that spitfire down here to hustle our asses in pool. That night, when you stared at her like she belonged to you, and she looked back at you like that was the only thing she'd ever wanted, *that* was when you were at your best. And I wouldn't be surprised if it was when she was at *her* best too."

Where the hell does he get off? Like I need this shit right now. "You don't know what the fuck you're talking about." Tim's voice was calm, but there was anger building behind it.

"No? Then set me straight."

"She's not at her best with me. How could she be? Quinn is . . . special. She deserves so much more."

"More than a guy who looks at her like she's the best thing next to OxyContin?"

Tim glared at him.

"Sorry. Bad joke. But seriously, it's obvious to anyone with eyes and half a brain that you're totally into this girl. What else could she want?"

"Oh, I don't know. Maybe someone she can go out and have a drink with after a long day at work. Someone she doesn't have to worry will pass down addictive tendencies to her offspring. Someone who doesn't have a criminal record. Someone her parents won't give the third degree to. Someone—"

"You met her parents?" Rudy had a horrified look on his face.

Tim agreed with the sentiment. "Yeah, and it was fucking brutal. But I'm thankful for it because it confirmed what I already knew. I don't fit in her life."

"Don't fit in *her* life or in her parents' lives?"

"What's the difference?"

"Said the guy with an ice queen for a mother. There's

a huge fucking difference. You're dating her, not her folks. Who cares what they think?"

Tim stood abruptly. "I do." Tim pointed a finger at himself for emphasis. "I fucking care. Her family is important to her. What am I supposed to do? Go over there for Sunday dinners and pretend I don't know they wish she'd brought home a lawyer or a stockbroker, or anyone other than a guy with a drug history that could rival Al Capone's? I can't do that, Rudy. I won't win at that game. I don't even know any of the fucking rules."

"So make your own rules."

"What are you talking about?" Tim threw his hands into the air. He was over this conversation. Rudy was just like him. So why couldn't he understand where Tim was coming from?

"I'm talking about love, Tim. Not the bullshit Hallmark type, but the real, gritty, painful kind that makes you say 'fuck everything else,' because if you don't your heart will drop right out of your goddamn chest. The kind that would make you do anything for the other person because their happiness is all that matters. The kind that makes even the worst days okay, just because they're in it with you. The kind you have with Quinn."

Tim was shocked. For a player, Rudy sure seemed to know a lot about an emotion he had never given the slightest indication he'd ever experienced. But no matter how wise the words were, that's all they were. Real life was so much more complicated. "Don't you see? It's *because* I wanted to ensure her happiness that I walked away. I wouldn't have been able to give that to her. Not long-term. So just . . . let it go." Tim stood and started moving across the pool hall.

"You really are a dumb motherfucker—you know that?"

Tim stopped and turned his head toward his friend. "Yeah, I know. But we both have very different reasons for thinking it." And then he snatched a stick from the wall, walked over to the table where the rest of the guys were bullshitting, and put the three ball into the corner pocket.

Tim hadn't stayed at the pool hall late the previous night, his talk with Rudy souring his already poor mood. Since it was Monday, he didn't need to go into the restaurant until later in the afternoon, but he was crawling out of his skin sitting around. Deciding that even a walk down the hall to his mailbox would be better than continuing to pace inside his apartment, Tim grabbed his keys and headed out the door.

It was too bad that it took all of thirty seconds to walk to get his mail. *Not quite the distraction I was hoping for.* As he walked back to his apartment, he thumbed through the letters. Bills, junk, a letter that was meant for the apartment next door, more bills, and then—*what the hell is this?*

Tim looked at the envelope in his hand as he unlocked his door and threw the rest of the mail on the table. The return address bore the name of a man he thought he'd never hear from again: Roger Whitaker.

Walking into the living room and sitting down heavily on the couch, Tim continued to stare at the envelope in his hand. He was both elated and terrified. This letter, whatever was written in it, would be the last words Roger would ever have to offer him. Opening it would be like experiencing his loss all over again. Tim wasn't sure how long he sat and held the envelope, but he finally decided that he needed to open it. After carefully sliding his finger under the flap and removing the paper inside, Tim began to read the last words from a man he considered a second father.

Dear Tim,

I know, I know, I'm an asshole. I tried to tell you so many times about the cancer, but I just couldn't. It was a selfish decision. I didn't want you to remember me as a sick old man. It was bad enough that my daughter had to see me that way. There was no way I could handle you seeing it too. But hiding it from you has had its own dilemmas. I haven't been able to tell you all the things I've wanted to. Being mushy has never really been our thing. But with death on the horizon, there are some things you simply need to know, no matter how much it may emasculate me to actually write them.

You've been the son I never got the chance to have. And even though you are a muleheaded SOB sometimes, I couldn't be more proud of the man you've become. I hope you don't take that as condescending, but as the simple truth that it is. You're a good man, Tim. The best kind of man. Life

wasn't always good to you, and you went through
things that would've tested a saint. But you never
placed blame, made excuses, or gave up. It's actually
part of what kept you down for so long: the fact that
you took sole responsibility for the state of your life.
It's easy to keep letting ourselves down after we've
done it once. It takes a special kind of man to decide
that he deserves better for himself. From himself.
And that's the attitude that got you clean and kept
you that way.

There's just one problem, Tim. You never gave
yourself enough credit for being what someone else
deserved too. And until you brought that pretty girl
to dinner, I thought you never would. You two
deserve each other. You deserve a woman who can see
the truth of who you are beneath your hardened
exterior. And she deserves a man who's already been
to hell and back but would gladly make the trip again
if it saved her even a second of misery. Stand beside
her, walk through life with her, let her lean on you,
and don't be afraid to let her support you from time to
time either. But most importantly, know that
happiness isn't guaranteed to us. It's a gift we give to
each other. It was clear to me that you are her
happiness, Tim. Don't ever take that away from her.
It's a regret no man should have to shoulder. Trust
me. I know.

I let a lot of people down in my life. But with you,
I finally got it right. You let me make up for the
damage I caused. I'll always love you for that. Just as
with every life you are a part of, mine was better for

*having you in it. Never doubt that. See you on the
other side, old friend. I'll miss you.*

> Sincerely,
> Roger

Tim didn't even realize he'd been crying until he read Roger's name, let the letter drop from his hands so he could bury his face in them, and felt the wetness streaming down his cheeks. So he gave himself over to it, let the sobs rack his body, purging it of all the hurt he felt. Once his tears ran dry, he picked up the letter from the ground and laughed. "I'm not sure how you managed it, but even in death you're still calling me out on my bullshit." Tim's smile faded. "What the hell am I going to do without you?"

Quinn wanted to go to her parents' for dinner about as much as she wanted to undergo a lobotomy, but her mother's persistence wore Quinn down until she agreed. She hadn't seen her parents since she'd been there with Tim; nor had she told them that she and Tim were no longer together. *Tonight's going to be a real blast.*

Quinn drove up the driveway and put the car in park. She didn't get out right away, choosing to sit there and mentally prepare a little more. They were definitely going to ask about Tim. And what the hell was she supposed to say? Did she really want to explain to her parents that the guy she'd been so excited for them to meet had dropped her like a bad habit less than a week later? *Hell no.* But she couldn't lie to them either. "Okay," she whispered to herself. "Let's get this nightmare over with." Quinn pushed open the car door and got out. She hated how much she dreaded being there. It was the first time she didn't feel comfortable in her childhood home.

As she traipsed up the path to her parents' front door, she again wondered what had happened here to push Tim away. She wasn't stupid. *Something* had caused a shift in Tim that night. Was Tim feeling awkward because Quinn was so close to her parents? Could one of them have said something to him? Quinn didn't know. Maybe it was about time she found out.

She pushed open the front door and immediately heard her mother. "Quinn? That you?"

Who else would it be? "Yeah, it's me."

Her mother came out of the kitchen, drying her hands on a towel before hugging Quinn briefly. Looking around, she asked, "Oh, I assumed you'd be bringing Tim."

"Nope. Just me."

Julia looked like she wanted to say something, but didn't, instead wrapping an arm around Quinn's shoulders, leading her into the kitchen, and beginning to talk rapidly about country-club gossip as Quinn slid onto one of the barstools.

It was times like those that Quinn was thankful her mother knew her well enough not to force her to have a conversation Quinn wasn't ready for.

Peter joined them soon after, walking over to his daughter and pressing a quick kiss to her forehead. "Where's Tim?"

"Um, he couldn't come." Quinn sighed. "Didn't

want to come actually. He, uh, he and I . . . We aren't seeing each other anymore."

Julia's face fell, but her dad just nodded his head. "Can't say I'm surprised."

"Peter," her mother warned.

"What do you mean?" Quinn asked as she rose off the stool she'd been sitting on.

Despite the glare Julia was directing at him, Peter spoke anyway. "Just didn't think it was a good fit, is all."

"Good fit? What are you talking about? What wasn't?" Quinn forced herself to keep her voice calm.

"The two of you." Peter shrugged like he was talking about something as inconsequential as the weather.

"Why weren't we?" Quinn was having trouble wrapping her brain around her father's words.

"Come on, Quinn. The man is clearly not in your league. He looks like total riffraff."

"And what do you think you look like? You're judging a person you barely know."

"I know enough. I've seen a lot of guys like him in my fifty-seven years, and I don't want one around my daughter."

"His father was a prominent doctor in Falls Church. Tim belonged to country clubs and went to private school."

"And now he's a cook with a drug problem."

Quinn couldn't help the retreating step she took. It was as if her father had physically pushed her. She didn't even know this callous man in front of her. She took a calming breath before speaking, hoping that her words might bring back the man she knew. "First of all, he's an executive chef at an up-and-coming restaurant. He's not manning the fryer at Arby's. Second, he doesn't *have* a drug problem. Yes, he struggled with addiction, but he's been clean for more than seven years."

"Quinn—"

Quinn reached across the countertop, taking her father's hand in hers. "Dad, please. I know you love me, and I know your sole purpose is to protect me. And I love you for that. But I'm an adult who's capable of protecting myself and deciding who deserves a place in my life and who doesn't."

The corners of her father's mouth turned up just enough to let Quinn know he understood what she was saying and agreed with her.

"I also know that whatever you said to him, however you made him feel, that your intention wasn't to hurt anyone. But you did. You hurt him. And you hurt me too. He broke up with me after we came here." Quinn's eyes moved between her parents. "I love him. He was good for me. Made me feel special. I'm sorry that you didn't see how great he was. That you didn't give him more of a chance. We all lost out because of that."

"Sweetheart, your father told me about his conversation in the garage with Tim after you two left that night. And while you can trust that your father wasn't exactly warm and inviting," her mom said as she cut a glance at Quinn's father, who had the good sense to look sheepish, "I think there was some overreaction on Tim's part. What your dad said, it shouldn't have been enough to run a man away who really wanted to stay."

Quinn let out a sigh as she let go of her dad's hand. "I don't doubt that. But there are things neither of you could possibly understand. Things even *I* can't even understand. What I *do* know is that Tim's been told he wasn't good enough for most of his life. And having it confirmed by his girlfriend's father was the last thing he needed."

"But you never told us. How was your father supposed to know?"

"I didn't expect him to know. I just expected him to trust my judgment." Quinn pushed in the chair quietly. "I think I need a little time to process all this. I'll call you guys later." And she would. Quinn knew she couldn't fully blame her parents for what happened. Tim was the one who'd left. In a way, her mom was right—if he'd wanted her, he would've fought for her. Even if the one he had to fight was himself. In that moment, the realization that he couldn't do that told her all she needed to know. Tim was gone—and maybe she needed it to stay that way.

Even with Roger's words echoing in Tim's head, it still took him a couple days to get himself together enough to take the next step. He had something else he still needed to read. As he withdrew it from the drawer, he felt nerves prickle along his spine. Banishing all other thoughts from his mind, he opened the envelope and began to read its contents.

Will the Real Quinn Sawyer Please Stand Up: The Story of a Woman's Journey to Find Herself

I've never been a rebel or an adventurer. I've never ex-plored the unknown or pushed boundaries. I've never been fought for; nor have I ever fought for anything. Not really, not truly. And until this past May, I never thought I would. But then an idea happened, an article happened, he happened. Now I'll never be the same.

In May I volunteered to write an article that would take me on a journey, though I didn't realize how pro-found it would be at the time. Initially it was merely an excuse to let my hair down, release my inner badass, and have a little fun. But it became so much more. I constructed a list of tasks—things my respectful, timid, good-girl personality would never have let me experience before. I quickly found that these excuses to be "bad" were ultimately leading me on a quest to un-cover the real me, the me who had lurked beneath the polished veneer I projected to the world. I enlisted the help of a friend who, now that I truly reflect on it, was always more than that, and we began tackling my list. Together.

First up, lying to my boss to get out of work (sorry, Rita; please don't fire me) so that I could go to a local convenience store and steal a pack of gum. What I learned: while I was a successful thief, I'm still pretty bad at it. I ended up returning to the store and paying for the gum.

Next, I got up in front of a roomful of strangers and sang karaoke. What I learned: I can't sing. At all. I also have horrible stage fright and am rendered nearly mute when confronted with uncomfortable situations. Until someone reminded me that I'm not all alone. Until someone, my more-than-a-friend someone, made an ass out of himself by singing a song he knew none of the words to just so I could know that I wasn't alone anymore. And since we're being honest here, I may as well admit that I fell a little bit in love with him that night even though I ignored it at the time.

After that came a nose piercing, which was really a failed mission because I was supposed to get a tattoo. What I learned: only guys who love you back will get a tongue piercing in order to make you less nervous to drill a hole in your body. I wish I'd understood that sooner.

The following task on my list was by far the dumbest, yet it was the most worthwhile. While I don't recommend hitchhiking as a means to finding yourself, it certainly speeds up the process. What I learned: trusting someone enough to keep you from being murdered by a drunk clown wielding a box of condoms is the highest compliment you can pay someone.

Asking a stranger on a date is something I never would have done before my "rebel" mentor made me. What I learned: you shouldn't go looking for things when everything you ever wanted is sitting across from you.

Lastly, I posed nude with the one person I wanted to see naked more than any other. What I learned: I have impressive self-control.

So what did all of this mean for me? Did it change

me? Am I a whole new Quinn after undertaking my list of boundary-pushing endeavors? Have I been redefined by these experiences?

No.

It wasn't the experiences that changed me. It wasn't the quest beyond my comfort zone that made me a better person. It was him. He made me look at the world differently. He made me realize that people aren't always what they appear to be. He taught me that the best things in life are only the best because you share them with someone else.

And then he left. But he didn't take the girl he helped create with him. She'll always be here, she'll always be grateful, and she'll always be whole. Because he helped build her that way. Together we built a woman who is not a rebel but does not shirk from adventure, a woman who not only explores but discovers, who not only pushes boundaries but breaks them down. A woman who fought and will never give up until she finds someone willing to fight for her in return.

I may not be new, but I am forever improved. Have finally outgrown my Sherpa. And it's a good feeling to know that, even alone, I'm okay. More than okay. I am the real Quinn Sawyer, and I'm finally ready to stand up.

Tim hadn't known he could be rocked by words on paper before the last few days. Quinn had accomplished exactly what she'd set out to. He was so proud of her he felt he would burst. But there was also a sinking feeling in the pit of his stomach. Quinn—just like he always knew—was fine without him. Her strength was intrinsic. A fundamental part of who she was.

That wasn't the case for Tim. At least not anymore. He *needed* Quinn. For the first time, he could fully admit that he couldn't live without another person. It was both freeing and terrifying.

Chapter 24

Retraction

Tim had been staring at her door for at least five minutes. He thought he'd come up with something to say on the drive over, but he'd been wrong. His brain was a muddled mess of Quinn. The desperation he felt was preventing him from putting logical thoughts together. All he could envision was the gamut of her facial expressions over the past months: happiness, curiosity, surprise, nervousness, mischief, and sadness. The last gutted him every time he imagined it.

I'm such an asshole. But he'd still like to be *Quinn's* asshole if there was any way she'd be able to get on board with that idea. And he needed her to get on board. He needed her in every way. Which was why his speech had to be perfect.

Putting his hands on the doorjamb, he bent over slightly at the waist, let his head hang toward the floor, and took some calming breaths. *Come on, Tim. Get it together. You're too old to act like such a pansy.* He'd finally gotten his breathing under control when the door unexpectedly opened. As he lifted his head to see a startled Quinn standing with her purse draped over her shoulder, his brain completely short-circuited.

"I love you." *Fuck. Way to jump into the deep end without a life jacket, dickhead.* That was *not* the way Tim had wanted to start out. Not because it wasn't true or because he had anything better to say, but because he had a lot of explaining to do. His actions over the past weeks hadn't exactly been demonstrative of his love for Quinn, and she deserved to hear why before he threw around words his actions hadn't proven.

Other than a slight widening of her eyes, her face was impassive. Clearly she was as unimpressed with his tact as he was.

"Shit. Wait. I didn't mean . . . I mean, I did mean, but . . . Fuuuuck, I'm so bad at this."

He saw Quinn take a deep breath and cross her arms over her chest. This was not going well.

Pushing off the doorjamb with his hands, he straightened and looked into Quinn's beautiful blue eyes. "I'm an idiot."

She didn't contradict him.

"Three months ago, you asked me to help you change your life."

"I didn't ask. You offered."

He felt his lip twitch at her correction. She had spoken to him. *That's a good sign, right?* "You're right. I did offer. And it was the best offer I've ever made. See, you thought you needed me. You thought that you weren't strong enough to accomplish the change on your own.

And since it's what you wrote in your article—which was amazing by the way—you evidently thought that I would be strong enough for you to lean on, to get you through the transformation. But I wasn't. I let you down when it mattered most, and I'm sorry for that."

Quinn released an annoyed sigh. She clearly didn't want to hear apologies. He was fucking this up.

"I'm not putting myself down again. I promise. I just . . . I need you to understand a few things." *Here goes nothing. Or everything.* "Did you know that Scott didn't want to take over my dad's practice?"

Quinn's furrowed brow told him she didn't.

"He wanted to be a surgeon. Neurosurgeon actually." He hesitated, giving himself a second to rein in his emotions. "I cost him that."

Quinn dropped her hands but didn't speak.

"The accident I caused, when Scott was injured, he suffered more than a broken bone. There was damage to the nerves in his arm. His dream of operating on people was over before he ever got a chance to pursue it. I cost him everything because getting high was more important than taking care of a person I love. And that has been the heaviest guilt I've had to carry. Until the things I said to you."

Quinn's entire body softened. It was like watching a lightbulb go on, like some of the things she hadn't quite been able to place finally started to click together.

Tim let himself hope for the first time in weeks. Maybe, just maybe, he hadn't lost her after all. "I didn't mean those things, but I said them anyway, for a variety of reasons that don't even make any sense. You could never make me feel unbalanced or like using, Quinn. You're the best reason to stay clean I've ever had." He let the quiet admission wash over them both, letting their truth seep into them. "I've had nothing but time to think about the hows and whys, and I realized I can't keep blaming myself for things that can't be undone. Accept the things you cannot change and all that," he added with a smirk. "I want to focus on the things I *can* change. The things I can make right. And this," he said as he gestured between them with his hand, "hopefully this is one of those things."

Her face gave nothing away, and Tim was almost thankful for that. He was going to have to work for her forgiveness. He didn't want it any other way.

"I've carried my past like a fucking scarlet letter. But the truth is, I've known for a long time that I'm not that guy anymore. Tim the drug addict is gone. He died in that crash seven years ago. And while addiction is something that will always be part of me, it isn't *who* I am. I don't need to keep holding myself accountable for debts I've never been asked to repay. Scott doesn't blame me; only *I* blame me. And I'm finally ready to let that shit go. Because if I don't, it'll fucking drown me. I don't want to drown, Quinn."

A tear slid down her cheek before she lifted her hand to wipe it away. The only sound that came out of her was a subtle sniff.

"I meant what I said. I love you. So much. My life, it means something when you're in it. It's like all the bull- shit was worth it because it led me here. To you. And while I'll probably never feel good enough for you, never feel like I quite deserve you, I still want the chance to try. Because you and me, we could be something extraordinary. And I'm not willing to walk away from that. Not anymore."

They stared at each other as if the remaining answers wouldn't be found in words, but rather in the depths of the eyes looking back at them. When Quinn looked away first, Tim wasn't sure if it was because she had found answers she didn't like, or if she hadn't found any answers at all.

Either way, he wasn't having it.

"Look at me. Please."

Quinn closed her eyes tightly before lifting her head. She opened them slowly, expectantly.

That's when he knew. He still had a chance. He just had to take it, even if it completely stole Scott's thunder. "Marry me."

Her head jerked back as if she'd been jolted by a zap of electricity. "Marry you? Are you . . . ? Have you lost your mind?"

"Marry me, Quinn. I know this seems crazy, and abrupt, and all kinds of fucked up, but I know what I want. This is the most logical decision I've ever made. You see me as the man I've always wanted to be. And you make me believe that I can actually *be* him. Because for you, I'd be anything."

"I've only ever wanted you to be yourself."

"I know. But I never really knew who that was until I met you." Tim hadn't come here intending to propose, but goddamn did he want her to answer. It wasn't ideal, but he wanted it to be as right as it could be. So he dropped to one knee and looked up at her with every ounce of love he had. "When I was reading your article, all I could think was that you had it backward." Quinn's mouth parted a bit as if to speak, but Tim continued before she had the chance. "It wasn't *you* who had to find yourself, make yourself a more complete version of who you really are inside. It was me. I know I've come here completely unprepared, and you deserve a perfect moment, but as we both know, I'm not perfect. Not by a long shot. So I hope you'll remember this not as the time when I totally botched one of the most important events of your life, but when I finally got it right. Because this is the most honest I've ever been. You wanted me to be myself. Here I am. Down on one knee—though very noticeably without a ring—hoping like hell you like what you see." His eyes blazed into hers. "When we started this experiment, I told you to say yes. So do it again, Quinn. Just say yes."

Quinn's jaw jutted out as her eyes filled with tears. She tried to blink them away, but a few errant ones fell anyway. "For the record, I always liked what I saw. It's what *you* saw that was the problem."

"Yeah, I'm kind of a dick that way."

She laughed, just as he'd hoped she would. Looking down at him, she grew serious. "I can't give you an answer right now. There's somewhere I have to be."

Tim couldn't help the way his stomach dropped, though he tried to school his features. He slowly rose to his feet. "Sorry. I guess my timing wasn't too great. I didn't mean to keep you from anything. I'll go, and then maybe you can call, if you want, and we can talk more. Or—"

"Tim?"

"Yeah?"

"Be quiet, okay?"

Tim exhaled deeply. "Okay."

Quinn stepped out of her apartment, forcing Tim to move back. She locked the door and then turned away from him and started down the hall.

"Can I ask you one more thing?"

Quinn stopped, but she didn't turn around.

Tim took it as a yes. "I just . . . I know I don't deserve to know, but I need to ask anyway. Do you still love me, Quinn?"

She was silent so long, he almost didn't think she'd answer him at all. But finally words came. "I don't think I can answer that right now either, Tim."

Yes, the words came, but he suddenly wished they hadn't And as he watched her walk away, all he could think about was how that had not gone *at all* how he'd thought it would. Not that he'd convinced himself she'd take him back, but he hadn't expected her to leave him standing in the hallway either. Though after he'd completely overplayed his hand and practically begged her to love him, he probably shouldn't have been surprised that she'd run away from him. *Pathetic.* But he wasn't going to give up. No, it was time for plan B, which he would think up as soon as he was able to pick his heart up off the floor.

Chapter 25

The Kicker

Quinn had been waiting weeks for Tim to come to his senses, to deal with whatever shit he'd needed to work through. But all the times she'd imagined how Tim's apology would go, she'd never pictured it ending with a proposal.

She also hadn't expected the anger she'd felt when she saw him on the other side of her door. She'd tried to talk to him twice, tried to work things out, tried to understand where he was coming from. And then he decided he was ready to speak to her and she was supposed to drop everything to hear him out? Not to mention respond to a marriage proposal. *Screw that.*

So she'd taken a few days to get her head back on straight. He'd taken his time; surely she was entitled to some as well. Tim hadn't contacted her since she'd walked away from him, and Quinn wasn't sure how that made her feel. On the one hand, she appreciated the time to think about what he had said, to think about where she stood. On the other, she didn't like the idea of Tim disappearing again either. It was all so . . . infuriatingly confusing.

Quinn knew she wasn't going to find any answers on her own. And she desperately needed some enlightenment. So she found herself at the only place she could get it: Tim's.

Not wanting to be as indecisive as he had clearly been, she stepped up to his door and knocked. Minutes passed, but he didn't open the door. She knocked again, but was again met with silence. For some reason, she hadn't considered that he might not be home. She'd talked herself up for this visit, infused confidence into every fiber of her being. It all began to seep out of her as she stood there, her shoulders slumping slightly.

"Quinn?" a voice, *his* voice, said from behind her.

She turned and there he was, looking at her as if she were an apparition. He was standing completely still in front of the elevator he had just exited, looking as though he was scared she'd disappear if he moved toward her.

She suddenly realized that it was her turn to speak. "Hi." He began walking down the hall, and she let herself look him over. He looked casual, relaxed, and sexy as hell. His plaid button-up was rolled up at the sleeves and fit perfectly across his chest as he slid one hand into the pocket of his fitted khakis. "You look . . . Why do you look so . . . fancy?"

Tim laughed and cocked a brow at her. "This is fancy?"

Quinn shrugged. "No, I guess not. Just . . . good. You look good."

Tim smiled slightly, and Quinn nearly passed out. It had been weeks since she'd seen that smile. And she'd missed the hell out of it. "You want to come in?" he asked as he slid his key in the lock and pushed open his door.

"Yeah."

He looked over his shoulder at her before he stepped inside, moving against the door so she could enter and he could shut it behind her.

She walked into the apartment and stopped, unsure of where to go or what to do now that she was in there. Quinn had loved this space, loved spending time there. But that felt like a lifetime ago.

Tim put his keys down and began walking toward the kitchen. "You want something to drink? Eat?"

Quinn followed. "No, thanks."

Tim opened the refrigerator and pulled out a bottle of water, twisting off the cap and taking a drink.

The action threatened to weaken her resolve as she watched his neck pulse with each swallow. She had to keep her mind on the task at hand. "You really hurt me."

He looked momentarily stunned as he lowered the bottle. Then he just looked sad. "I know I did."

"I didn't deserve it."

"No, you didn't."

"And that proposal was bullshit."

Tim placed the water on the counter and braced his hands on the smooth granite. "With that, I have to disagree."

Quinn hadn't known it when she'd arrived, but that

was *exactly* the response she had been hoping for. "You do?" Her voice was quiet, unsure.

"I know I can be"—Tim waved his hand in a circular motion as he seemed to be trying to come up with the right word—"impulsive. But that doesn't mean I wasn't sincere. Maybe I just shouldn't have done it right then."

Quinn shot him a "no shit" look.

"Okay, I *definitely* shouldn't have done it right then. But it is what it is. I can't take it back. And I don't want to." He stood and walked to stand in front of her. "The way I treated you . . . I know I don't deserve you to say yes, or to get an answer at all, but—"

"Enough. You've already said your piece. I don't need to hear it again. I also don't need to hear about what you don't deserve anymore. We deserve what we get, Tim. Our lives are in *our* hands. There's no list that says this person gets to be happier than that person. Our stories are what we craft them to be, what we put into them. Nothing more and nothing less."

Tim widened his stance and pushed his hands into his pockets. He looked at her like he was waiting for her to continue, waiting to give her the chance to say everything she needed to say. She damn sure planned to take advantage of the opportunity.

"The last few weeks"—she blew out a breath—"have really sucked. I thought I'd found the person I was going to spend forever with. And then you had one less-than-stellar interaction with my dad and you bolted. I thought I meant more than that. I didn't think I'd be so easy to walk away from."

"Quinn—"

"It's not your turn yet," she reprimanded. "I shouldn't have even come here. I shouldn't be talking to someone who didn't fight for me—for us—the way he should have."

Tim looked briefly down at the floor, and she saw his neck swallow a lump that must have formed there.

"But what would that really prove?"

His head jerked up, his eyes boring into hers. The hope she saw in them. The love. The regret. It was enough.

"If I walk away now, then I'm doing the same thing you did. Repeating the same mistake. I know you have regrets, Tim. But I refuse to be one of them. And I won't let you be one of mine either."

He sucked in a steadying breath. "Are you fucking with me?"

"Anyone ever tell you that you really know how to ruin a moment?" Quinn couldn't help the smile that spread over her face.

"No. I haven't had moments with anyone else." He moved so quickly, she didn't even have time to brace herself for it. His hands wrapped around her, his lips pressed to hers, and the world fell away. She was back where she belonged. With this beautiful, brave—and sometimes incredibly stupid—man.

"I've missed you so much," he murmured against her mouth. "I promise, I won't mess up again. This— you, me—I won't lose it a second time."

Quinn returned his kiss with everything she had,

allowing her body to say what she didn't have words for.

She hadn't realized how much she'd missed the feel of Tim's body enveloping hers, how safe she still felt in his strong arms, despite what he'd put her through. Immediately her body responded to his as she willingly let him guide her toward the counter, which he lifted her onto. Her legs opened immediately, hugging his waist as she relaxed into him.

They stayed that way for longer than she'd anticipated, Quinn rubbing against Tim's hard length as much as she could manage with the layers of fabric between them. Tim's hands slid inside her shirt, pulling her bra down to play with her nipples. She'd forgotten how good it felt to have the perfect amount of pressure—a feeling, no matter how hard she'd tried, she was never be able to give herself. "Mmm," she moaned into Tim's neck. "I like that."

Tim's mouth moved to her jawline, the scruff on his face tickling her skin as he breathed against her. "Yeah? What is it you like?"

Everything. "This," Quinn answered honestly. "Us. The way I feel when we're together."

"And how is it you feel?" Tim's voice was brusque, raspy with desire.

"Whole." She'd said it before she realized how it sounded. It wasn't that she hadn't felt complete before Tim. She'd never need a man to feel that way. It just felt like a piece of herself had disappeared when Tim had. "It's not like—"

"Shh," he said as he brought two fingers up to her lips. "You don't have to explain it."

So she didn't.

He lifted her off the counter and carried her to his bedroom, placing her down gently on his bed. "I'm going to spend hours loving this body. Loving you."

Quinn sat up just enough to pull her shirt off. Her bra followed. "Better get started then."

Tim pulled back slightly, leaving one leg on the bed, his knee between her thighs, while the other was planted on the ground as he slowly unbuttoned his shirt. He let it drift open, revealing a white tank top that was perfectly molded to his chest. He flexed his shoulders back, shrugging off his shirt and dropping it to the floor. Then his hands moved to his belt, working it open with ease before popping the button on his pants and dragging the zipper down. Tim left his khakis hanging open as he pushed his hand into his tight black briefs and gripped himself.

"You're being a real tease," Quinn complained.

That sexy smirk she loved so much spread over his face. "I told you . . . hours."

As Tim continued to stroke himself, Quinn realized that two could play that game. She quickly undid her shorts, pushing them harshly down her legs so that she was left only in her red lace thong. She made a show of toying with her nipples before sliding her hands slowly down her body, circling her belly button and then gliding over her thong and down to her clit.

Tim's eyes widened and his breathing became audible.

Quinn's moans filled the room as she worked her fingers over the sensitive bundle of nerves. "I hate to tell you this. But lying here, watching you touch yourself, I'm not going to last hours."

Quinn's words had the desired effect. Tim pushed his pants and boxers off and crawled over Quinn, propping himself on his elbows placed on either side of her head. "You don't play fair."

"I know. Now stop talking and take this off," she said as she pushed his undershirt off. "I want to feel all of you against me."

Tim complied, made a quick detour to his bedside table to withdraw a condom, and then lowered his body onto hers. He began to kiss her everywhere he could reach.

"You forgot to take my panties off." Quinn sighed as Tim sucked on her earlobe and rocked his cock against her.

"No, I didn't." Tim rolled slightly to the side so that he could tear open the condom and roll it down his length. Then he resettled himself above her, moved her panties to one side, and thrust into her. "Jesus Christ," he ground out. "You looked so hot touching yourself in these that I didn't want to take them off of you."

Quinn couldn't explain why, mostly because she was incapable of coherent thought in that moment, but Tim's words were insanely hot. They kissed like they were trying to consume each other. Tim's hand pinched her nipples, and Quinn threaded her fingers through his hair and held him close to her. Their breathing was harsh and frantic—a perfect harmony for the raw and needy way Tim was fucking her. She had never been so aroused, so desperate for release, so loved.

Tim ran his hand over her skin. "This is mine. All of this . . . it's mine."

"Yes, God yes, it's yours." Her thong was creating a delicious friction against her clit, rubbing her every time Tim thrust into her. She felt her orgasm building. "Close. So close."

Tim lowered his lips to her and kissed her passionately before letting his lips graze over her cheek and to her ear. "Come for me, Quinn."

Quinn had always thought coming on command was bullshit. It wasn't. There was something about the words themselves that seemed to push her over the edge. Her entire body seized at his words, her clit throbbing with spectacular sensation as Tim thrust one final time, and she felt his cock pulsing deep inside of her, releasing his own orgasm.

They didn't move for a few minutes. Or maybe it was a few hours. Quinn didn't know; nor did she care. Eventually Tim rolled to the side, removed the condom, tied it off, and tossed it in a nearby trash can. Then he leaned close and nuzzled into her. As they both drifted off, she relished the soft breaths coming from the contented man beside her.

It was a song she knew she'd never tire of hearing no matter how many times it was played.

"Get dressed," Quinn said suddenly. "We're going out."

"Um . . . okay?" Tim followed Quinn's lead, standing to put his pants back on. "I was kind of counting on staying naked for a while longer," he said, walking around the bed toward her so he could run his hand up her bare arm. "Should I even ask where we're going?"

"Three months ago I asked you to start something with me that we didn't finish. It's time we saw it through."

Tim had no idea what she was talking about, but it didn't matter. He'd follow her anywhere.

And in this case, "anywhere" meant around the corner to her car. "You sure you don't want me to drive?" Tim asked.

"Yes. You don't even know where we're going."

Tim raised his eyebrows at her. "That's the point. Then you'd have to tell me."

"Just shut up and get in."

"You're cute when you're bossy," he said before walking around the car and opening the passenger door so he could slide into the seat beside her. He glanced at Quinn, who had already turned the car on and was staring ahead as she clutched the wheel.

Tim could have thought about where they might be going during the car ride, but he was content to let his mind focus on the beautiful redhead next to him as he ran his fingers through her hair.

Once she pulled into a space and Tim took note of his surroundings, he knew exactly why she'd brought him here. The pieces of Quinn's puzzle suddenly fit together. She'd said they'd started something months ago that they'd never finished. And that "something" came in the form of a needle and ink. "Seriously?" Tim said, drawing out the word in disbelief. "You're really going to get a tattoo?"

"That's the plan."

"Wasn't that the plan last time too?"

Quinn shot him a scolding look as she hit the button on her key fob to lock her car doors. "No. The plan was for me to get a piercing. Which I did," she said, pointing to her nose.

"Oh, that's right. Because it wasn't permanent," Tim said, rolling his eyes playfully before opening the door to the tattoo shop so Quinn could step inside.

"Exactly."

"So what tattoo are you going to get?"

Quinn shrugged, a sly smile appearing on her face. Then she marched right up to the counter. "I'm here to get a tattoo," she proclaimed so loudly that a few of the other customers who were waiting on a nearby couch looked up from their phones.

Tim bit back a laugh and shook his head.

A burly man who had been sitting with his back to them as he drew up a design spun in his seat to face them. "That's why most people come here, darlin'." His sarcastic words didn't match his pleasant tone. "What'd you have in mind?"

"Uh . . . I have an idea. Sort of." Her eyes darted to the floor and then around the room. "Is there a long wait?" she asked as she noticed the three other customers.

"Not if you don't care who does it. They're all waiting for specific artists," the man said, pointing to the other people. "Depending on how long it would take, I could do it for you now. My next appointment's not for another two hours. I'm Gary, by the way."

"Thanks, Gary," Quinn said. "It's only going to be like this big." She held up her thumb and index finger to show about two inches in length.

"Color?"

"Just black."

The man nodded. "Why don't you come on back and we'll talk about the design."

Gary began to walk down the narrow hallway, and Quinn and Tim followed behind him. But suddenly Quinn's head whipped around to face Tim. "You have to wait in the lobby."

Tim gave her a confused look.

"I'm going to be a huge baby," she said. "And I don't want to be tempted to back out when you tell me I don't have to do this."

"You don't."

Quinn's head tilted, and she gave her lips that pouty look he loved. "I know. I *want* to." Then she grabbed his hand. "Just wait out there," she said sweetly before releasing his hand and giving him a playful shove.

Tim hesitated. The thought of being rooms away when Quinn was in pain didn't sit well with him, but something told him he needed to let her do this. "Okay," he finally said before giving her a small peck on the lips and returning to the lobby to wait.

Tim busied himself flipping through *Inked* magazine and reading an article about the Nationals on his phone. He looked up when Gary returned to make a copy of the design to put on Quinn's skin. But he couldn't see what it was from where he was sitting.

The next twenty minutes or so passed excruciatingly slowly. Tim shifted in his seat, paced the room, looked out the window at least three times. All he could think about was Quinn. Especially when a few minutes later he heard her call his name.

He turned to face her. "You okay? Did you do it?" he asked, his voice holding as much excitement as relief.

"Yeah," she replied. "I did it." She strolled toward the door casually, as if she hadn't just done something she'd never thought she could. Tim followed her out the door and around the corner of the building, where she stopped to lean against the brick. She paused, exhaling slowly. Then she turned over her right wrist to reveal the word "yes" tattooed in her own handwriting.

Tim furrowed his brows for a moment in confusion. He'd never pegged her as a person to get a word tattooed on her. Maybe a butterfly or a flower. "What does it—"

He didn't get time to finish his question before Quinn spoke again. "A few days ago you asked me if I still loved you. And I never answered you. I should have told you I loved you, Tim. Because I do. I'm not even sure when I *started* loving you. The only thing I'm sure of is that I'll never stop."

It was at that moment that he realized the meaning of her tattoo. Tim's eyes widened as a wave of emotions washed over him. He'd waited forever to hear Quinn say those words.

"But this tattoo is more than that to me," she continued. "For so long, I never wanted to do anything I couldn't take back. But when you asked me to marry you—for us to be with each other for the rest of our lives—at the time, I didn't know how to respond. It scared me that you might change your mind."

"I won't."

"I know," she said quietly. "And neither will I. This . . . us," she said, gesturing between them, "it's permanent."

Tim felt the wide smile move up his face as he blinked back tears.

"So, yes, Tim. Yes, I'll marry you." Then she hesitated a moment. "I mean, if the offer's still on the table. Tim Jacobs," she said, inhaling a long breath, "will you still marry me?"

There was no way she couldn't know his answer to that, but he responded anyway. "You're goddamn right I will." Then he pulled her in to him, his hands holding the sides of her face as he kissed her, tasted her lips, felt her soft skin on his thumbs as they stroked her cheeks.

Finally he pulled away, holding on to only her hands, and he turned one over to admire the script on her wrist once more. "Looks unbalanced with nothing on the other side," he said.

Quinn cocked her head in that cute way he knew he'd never get enough of. "Are you insane? This hurt like hell. There's no way I'm getting another one."

Tim let out a loud laugh as he turned her hand over. "I was thinking more like a diamond ring," he said, rubbing her left ring finger. "Let's go pick one out." Tim slipped his hands down to her waist and pulled

Quinn against him. "Unless, of course, you just want to get one tattooed on your finger instead."

"Not a chance."

He wanted to disagree. To tell her that he was living proof that anything could happen. You just had to have the balls to go after it. But rather than spoil the moment, he wrapped his arms around her, leaned down, and whispered, "There's always a chance," against her lips. Then he kissed her deeply, the way he planned to do every day for the rest of his life.

Acknowledgments

We want to start with Sarah Younger, who is always quick to support us in every way possible. Your ability to calm us down, focus us on what's important, and invigorate us to keep at it shows that you're the perfect agent for us. Thank you to everyone at the Nancy Yost Literary Agency for supporting us. And to Mama Younger, thank you for helping us kill our first character. You're the best.

To our editor, Laura Fazio, we never thought we'd have anyone tell us to add more sex scenes. But we think you got it right. Your ability to tactfully tell us we need to redo parts of our book without hurting our feelings is truly a unique talent. Thank you for your continued belief in us. Your guidance and input have made us better writers, and we are eternally grateful for that.

Thank you to everyone at Penguin Random House who had a part in *Just Say Yes*. We are happy to have you on our team.

Alison Bliss, you're a terrific critique partner. You always find the little things (and sometimes big) that we need to work on. Your insight always helps us improve our work, which we appreciate greatly.

Amanda—words can't even capture it—Petal. You've

been there for us from the start, and we love you for it. This journey wouldn't be nearly as fun if you weren't a part of it. Thank you for being a reader, a critique partner, an assistant, and a great friend.

We want to thank our Padded Room Street Team for being the battiest mix of broads to grace the romance scene. The excitement and support you offer us is mind-blowing. You make us want to be the best writers we can be because you ladies deserve it. We also want to thank our expert pimpers who spend time every day making sure people know who we are. Becky Anderson, Megan Cooke, Dawn Stanton, and Kris Umile: Thank you so so much for all that you do for us. A special thanks to Megan for creating the band name Waiting for Someday. It's absolutely perfect.

Erik, thank you for being a terrific husband and father. Without your support, both in my writing and in my everyday life, I wouldn't be pursuing this dream. You, Mya, and soon-to-be Baby #2 are who drive me to do better, be better, and strive for better. I love you guys. ~Elizabeth

Hayley, this hasn't been a long journey, but it's been deep with memories, good times, rough patches, opportunities, and hindrances. But we've endured, and we've done that because we have each other. Thank you for doing all the tedious crap I suck at, thank you for making me dream a little bigger, and thank you for allowing me to be the Elizabeth to your Hayley. Love you. ~Elizabeth

Nick, I'm going to keep this short and hopefully sweet (two things I'm not really known for). I wouldn't be where I am today without you. Thank you for helping me live the life I've always wanted. Nolan, maybe one day you'll read the acknowledgments of Mommy's books (though hopefully not the books themselves). Always know that I believe you can do anything, and always know how much I love you. ~Hayley/Mommy

Elizabeth, there isn't really anyone who can put up with me like you do. I'm married to the only other person who can. Thank you for always motivating me when I need someone to give me a kick in the ass. Without you by my side, I would have given up a long time ago. I know I can get carried away, so thanks for bringing me down to earth when I'm up in the stars somewhere. And thanks for joining me up there every once in a while. Love you. #Lemons4lyf ~Hayley

Curious as to whether a career woman
can ever settle down?
Read on for a sneak peek at Cass' story
in Elizabeth Hayley's

THE WEDDING AGREEMENT

Available from Signet Eclipse in May 2016.

Cass grabbed hold of the bowling ball and strutted confidently up to the line, unfazed by the fact she was sliding a bit as she pulled her arm back and threw it forward, releasing the twelve-pound burden from her hand. Then she spun around quickly toward her group of friends, who were craning their necks to peer around her.

"I thought you said you bowled a couple of months ago?" Lauren asked as Cass heard the ball land in the gutter with a loud thud. Quinn's eyebrows rose, and Simone bit her bottom lip.

"I did," Cass shot back quickly, surprised by the question even though she'd only knocked down a total of six pins in the last three frames. "I just forgot to mention it was on a Wii." She let her eyes dart quickly to where Alex was seated toward the end of the group. His eyes twinkled with amusement, but he didn't open his mouth. "Fine, the Wii game wasn't my best performance either."

This time Alex clearly couldn't resist. "'Best performance'? My seven-year-old daughter's got more game than you."

"First of all, I'm pretty sure Nina's got more game than *you* too," Cass snapped back with a smirk. "You couldn't pick up a chick in a henhouse." Her comment elicited a roar of laughter from Scott, Xavier, and Tim and a soft chuckle from Alex, who'd become used to Cass teasing him. "And speaking of games," Cass said, her eyes darting to Lauren and Scott, "when are you two going to stop playing musical wedding dates? You two have been engaged for months. Have you guys decided on a day yet or what?"

Lauren shrugged her shoulders. "We're between a couple places. Both venues have Saturdays in April open, so it'll probably be then."

"April? That's like over a year away," Cass protested. "You guys drag your feet doing everything. Scott had the ring for like five months before he even proposed, and you didn't have the engagement party until two months later."

"Whoa, wait a second," Scott cut in. "I was all set to ask Lauren to marry me, but then my impulsive older brother had to go and propose to someone he wasn't even dating at the time."

"Well, when you say it like that—" Tim started.

"How else can I say it?" Scott joked. "See what I get for being the polite sibling and not stealing your thunder?" Scott settled back into his seat and slid his arm around Lauren. "Not everyone can make life decisions as easily as picking what to order at a drive-through," he added on a laugh.

"You act like I proposed and we rushed off to have Elvis marry us in some Vegas chapel or something. I knew what I wanted," Tim said, giving Quinn a seductive glance that he didn't try to hide. "Besides, we put a lot of thought into the actual wedding. So much thought that we even managed to convince Mom to come. And we all know she couldn't stand the sight of me for the better part of the last decade." Tim's smile had a way of adding a bit of humor to an otherwise sensitive subject. His struggles with addiction had caused a rift between Tim and his mother that no one thought could be fixed. Not even him.

"Tim's right, Laur," Cass insisted. "Quinn somehow managed to help repair a severely damaged relationship, *and* they planned an entire wedding . . . all in like seven months. It can't be that difficult."

Tim rose to take his turn, pushing up the sleeves of his shirt first. He released the ball with ease and turned back toward the group as the ball sped toward its targets. "In all fairness, *I* didn't plan much of anything." Cass rolled her eyes as every pin fell. Tim trotted over to take a seat between Quinn and Scott, who shifted slightly to make room for his brother on the row of beige plastic seats. "Quinn took care of all the logistics and I just gave my two cents when it came to all of the fun stuff like food tasting and picking the band."

Cass had a feeling that Tim had had more of a hand in the wedding planning than he'd let on, but she didn't question him. "Well, as a bridesmaid, I think I should have a say in some things, Laur."

Xavier stood, holding two empty pitchers. "Enough wedding talk for me. I'm going up to get us a refill."

"Well, as the bride, I think you shouldn't," Lauren said, ignoring Xavier's departure completely. She kept her expression even, but Cass could tell she was holding back a laugh. "We're just taking our time to make sure we're both okay with everything. Planning a wedding's a big undertaking. You'll find out if you ever get married."

Cass stuck her tongue out at her friend. Though Lauren's comment would have offended most twenty-eight-year-old women, Cass understood Lauren's intended meaning. She wasn't saying that Cass couldn't find anyone to marry her. It was *Cass* who had chosen the bachelorette life years ago, opting to put her career in public relations above having a family. And she didn't keep her intentions a secret. She'd had boyfriends in the past, and every one of them was more than comfortable with her choice. After all, how hard is it to convince a twenty-something-year-old guy that you're not looking for anything serious? "Fine, fine," Cass finally said. "But just for the record, I haven't seen this much thought go into planning a wedding since Kim and Kanye tied the knot."

Scott shook his head. "Would it make you feel better if we promise not to name any of our future children after one of the cardinal directions?"

"Yes," Cass said simply.

"That's a shame," Simone chimed in, "because I always thought South Jacobs had a nice ring to it."

Alex sat up a little straighter. "If you ask me, marriage isn't worth the hassle. I've done it once, and I don't plan to do it again."

Cass had been wondering when, if ever, Alex would give his opinion. The tense relationship between him and his ex-wife, Tessa, was no secret to anyone in the group. For that reason alone, she couldn't blame him for never wanting to walk down that road again . . . or in this case, that aisle. That's why, even though Alex was thirty-three, Cass had no reservations about the casual sex the two of them would have every so often. She knew it would remain just that.

"Too many people focus on the trivial details like dresses and flowers and cake," Alex continued. "None of that shit matters—"

"Cake always matters," Cass interrupted as an attempt to bring more lightness back to the conversation.

Alex leaned forward, resting his forearms on his thighs

as he averted his gaze from the group and focused his attention on the beer he held between his hands. "None of it matters in the long run," he repeated, this time more to himself than to everyone else listening. "The marriage is what matters and when you don't give a shit about *that*, who cares if you have roses or"—he gestured with his hand wildly as he looked to everyone for help— "or . . . What's another type of flower?"

Scott answered immediately. "Tulip, gardenia, calla lily, peony, lily of the—"

Tim shook his head and grabbed Scott's arm. "You're not helping."

"Right, sorry," Scott said.

The rest of the group had already erupted in laughter, including Alex, who needed it more than anyone. He wasn't sure why he'd gotten onto his soapbox, but he knew he needed to get the fuck off it. "It's fine," Alex assured Scott before draining the last of his beer. "Now let's just focus on the game. For Christ's sake, the girls are only seventy-four points behind us and there are only three frames left. I'm worried we might not cover the hundred point spread." That earned him a hard punch to the arm, courtesy of Cass. "Ouch. That actually hurt a little," he said, surprised. "You know, you'd make a much better professional boxer than you would a bowler."

"Clearly," Cass replied, tossing her blond hair over her shoulder with a smirk. "Someone better tell Laila Ali I'm coming for her."

"She's retired," everyone said almost in unison.

Cass glanced around at the group in disbelief. "How did you *all* know that?"

There were some shrugs and some "I don't know"s in reply.

"Well, okay then. I guess Laila's safe from the wrath of Cassidy Mullen."

"I bet she's thankful for that," Alex joked as he stood to take his turn.

The guys ended up covering the spread, which caused the girls to demand a rematch. And that was how most of the night continued, with the group of friends doing what they did best: joking, drinking, and talking about nonsense until they were laughing so hard Alex could feel tears forming in the corners of his eyes. Finally, after one more game, the night started to wrap up.

"We should probably get going," Scott said. "I have some patients I need to check on at the hospital tomorrow morning before I head over to the satellite office, and Lauren has an early appointment coming in too."

"God, you guys are so old," Tim joked. He was actually six years Scott's senior, but as a chef, Tim rarely had to get up early, so he seemed to take every opportunity to poke fun at his little brother when he'd skip out before the rest of the group. "Anyone want to go to that place up the street that lets you cook s'mores at your table? They're open until midnight," Tim asked the rest of the crew after Scott and Lauren had left.

Quinn didn't give anyone a chance to respond before she grabbed Tim by the arm. "We're going to take off too. And don't worry," she added. "Someday I'll fill you in on what it's like to be married to a fourteen-year-old."

Alex chuckled. "You might not want to say that too loudly in a public place."

"Oh, right," she said, her face reddening.

After a few minutes, the rest of the group headed out to the parking lot.

"So how about you?" Cass asked Alex once Simone and Xavier were in their cars. "You have an early morning too?"

Alex didn't have to try hard to interpret Cass' meaning. They'd gone home together enough times over the last year or so for him to know exactly what she was asking. "Not early enough that I can't have a late night."

"Good answer," Cass said as she climbed in her car.

Alex grinned as he unlocked his door and hopped in to follow her. Cass' apartment was closer so that's where they headed. And within fifteen minutes of leaving the bowling alley, they were fumbling up the stairs to her apartment. Though her door was only steps away, Alex couldn't stop himself from backing her up against the wall when they reached the landing outside her apartment. He used his hips to pin her to the hard surface as his lips found hers, moving slowly but with a need he knew Cass would recognize immediately. His hands roamed her body, his fingertips lightly grazing her soft skin under her shirt. Already he ached for her, so he finally released her long enough to let her move toward the door. But Alex couldn't break contact for long. He nestled his cock against her denim-clad ass as she searched for her keys. Just as she found them and slid the correct one into the lock, Alex abruptly stopped trailing his lips up the back of her neck, and his body tensed.

"What's wrong?" she asked.

"Are your neighbors always that loud?"

Cass acted like she hadn't even registered the heavy metal music and raucous laughing rumbling from next door. "Sometimes."

"That's bullshit. Want me to say something?"

"Now? Are you kidding me? Right now I want to be making our own noise."

That was all Alex needed to hear. About a minute later, after removing his jacket and unstrapping his service weapon, he was rocking his hips against her as he tasted the cool mint of her gum that still lingered on her mouth. He stayed there, letting his tongue move softly over hers for a bit longer while he ground against her.

He allowed himself to enjoy the taste of her before his tongue left her mouth and worked its way down her neck with quick nibbles.

She laughed, the vibration of her throat humming against his lips.

"Suddenly ticklish?"

She squirmed below him. "A little."

Alex slid his hand under Cass' shirt and toward her back to undo her bra. She arched in response. "Mmm, sexy *and* helpful," he said, popping the clasp and moving his hand back toward her chest so his fingers could toy with her nipples.

Cass let out a breathy sigh. He stayed there for a few moments, letting her enjoy his touch. He loved how hard her nipples got between his fingers and how her soft moans increased in intensity as his hands moved over her skin. Cass gripped his back through his T-shirt, which she then pulled over his head in one quick jerk and tossed to the floor beside them. "Pants off. Now," Cass said, catching Alex by surprise.

He gave her an amused grin as he stood up, his cock noticeably tenting the fabric of his pants. "You're bossy when you're horny." She didn't answer, though he could tell she was biting back an insult. Slowly, he kicked off his shoes and socks before moving his hands to the button of his jeans and letting them hover there, unmoving. He was curious as to how Cass would respond.

She squirmed on the couch for a moment or two as Alex brushed a hand over himself to grip his cock through his jeans. "Let me show you how this works," she finally said, sitting up to pull her shirt over her head and let her bra fall down her arms to the floor. Then she leaned back onto the couch, popped the button of her jeans, and shimmied them down her legs until she could kick them off completely. "You show me yours, and I'll show you mine," she said, letting her hand skate down her torso until her fingers slid under the sheer fabric of her thong just far enough to give the elastic a sharp tug until it snapped back into place.

But Alex had gotten a glimpse of what was beneath. And what he saw made him grow even harder. It's not like he hadn't seen it before—her smooth skin just begging to be stroked—but it made him ache to be inside her, feel her stretch around him. This time when his finger touched the button of his jeans he didn't hesitate, removing them immediately and standing over Cass, his cock pushing out the fabric of his black boxer briefs. He knelt down to get a condom from his wallet and ripped the foil with his teeth. Then he reached down to remove his boxers and slide the latex over himself. He was so fucking ready. "Your turn," he said, gesturing to the small piece of material covering the area on Cass that Alex wanted most.

Once Cass was as naked as Alex, he settled himself between her legs once more, enjoying the sensation of them wrapping around him as he guided himself inside her. He started slowly, wanting to feel every inch of himself move in and out of her. He also knew how much it teased her—the gentle grind against her. Cass ceased the licking on his neck to whisper "Faster" in Alex's ear, a request he was always happy to comply with. He sped up and the two quickly found their rhythm, their heart rates and breaths increasing with every thrust. Alex could feel Cass tightening around him, bringing him closer to release.

"God, Alex," Cass let out as part of an exhalation.

He could tell she was getting closer, and brought his hand up to tangle in her hair, pulling gently as he increased the speed of his hips even more, working them both toward their much-needed release. At last he felt her clench around him, her body pulsating against his cock as she released a throaty moan and a few soft curse words. He let her ride out her orgasm before concentrating on his own, which came a few moments later as he pumped inside her, hard and fast.

He pulled out of her after a few seconds and headed to the bathroom. By the time he got back, Cass was already in a baggy T-shirt and flipping through the channels. "You going to hang out for a bit?" she asked. "I'm sure one of the eighteen *Fast and the Furious* movies is on somewhere."

Alex laughed, but it was the truth. He'd watch those movies anytime they were on, and everyone knew it. He thought about taking her up on her offer. There was nothing that appealed to him more at the moment than a movie and waking up curled around a half-naked— or fully naked—Cass. But before he could open his mouth to reply, Cass opened hers. Except it was to let out a slow yawn. Though it was hard for him to admit it, he knew it was in both of their best interests to get some rest. He gave her a small smile before he started collecting his clothes from the floor and dressing. "I actually have some work I should probably get done before I go in tomorrow morning."

"All right," Cass said, pulling her hair up into a loose ponytail as she walked Alex to the door so she could lock the dead bolt behind him. "Drive safely."

"Always," he replied with a smile. "And I'm going to stop by next door and say something about the music. You'll never be able to sleep with that going on."

Cass playfully rolled her eyes, but Alex didn't care. Protecting people close to him was something ingrained too deeply in his personality, and he couldn't shut it off.

"You want me to wait here in case they jump you?" she said teasingly, but he knew the offer was sincere.

"Nah, I'll be fine. If they start getting rowdy I'll flash

my badge and gun. That usually settles people down."
He shot her a mischievous smirk before she closed the
door behind him. Then he headed down the hall toward the noise. A loud bang of his fist on the door
caused the music to cut off and a shaggy-looking kid to
answer the door.

"Can I help you?"

Alex quickly appraised the person in front of him.
He was most likely a college kid. Alex wondered how
he could even afford to live in the building until Alex
saw the Tag Heuer watch on his wrist. *No doubt about it;
someone has Daddy paying the rent.* "Yeah, man, would
you mind turning the music down? Some of us have
early mornings."

The kid looked at Alex a second, probably trying to
assess whether he should do as he was asked or not.
"Sure, man. No problem."

Good answer. Alex was often thankful for his bulky
frame. It kept people from trying to fuck with him.
"Thanks. Have a good one." Alex didn't wait for a reply as he turned and started toward the elevator, wondering if there was any better sleep aid than bowling
and hot sex.

About the Author

Elizabeth Hayley is the pen name for "Elizabeth" and "Hayley," two friends who have been self-publishing romance novels since 2013. They are best known for their Strictly Business novels, including *The Best Medicine*, and their Pieces series, including *Perfectly Ever After*, *Picking Up the Pieces*, and *Pieces of Perfect*. They both live with their husbands and young children in Pennsylvania.

31901056849880